IN THE HEAT OF IT ALL

BROTHERS OF SOLEMN CREED BOOK #1

JODI JAMES

This book is dedicated to all the first responders who put their lives on the line and make a difference every day.

CHAPTER 1

*E*llie Richards inched her way down the mile-long gravel driveway, which ran adjacent to her property through robust pine and aspen trees. Water dripped from her toppled curtain of hair and soaked her once white T-shirt and fleece jacket from her previous nosedive into a puddle. What she could find of the contents of her purse were covered in mud and yuck and scooped into it. One of her polka-dotted boots was MIA, and her sock stuck to the floorboard. Water from the creek behind the farmhouse had filled the basement and breached the main level of her house. Before exiting onto Highway 13 South, she approached a truck parked near the trees, and a light blinked from the inside of the cab. If she hadn't known her ex-husband James was dead, she would have sworn it was him. An icy chill ran through her.

She had to get to work for the night shift. The domestic calls at the crisis center amplified when the weather was worse, and the electricity had been out for the past twenty-four hours. She would be safer there, and the phones would work, so she could call Jeffrey.

Hail shelled the windshield, and she could barely discern the reflective road sign. An erratic truck blasted its horn and nudged the bumper, forcing her to accelerate around the bend. The next jolt from behind, whipped her back against the head rest. Hi-beam headlights blinded her vision from ahead. A piercing horn shrieked, she swerved across the lane, and the front left tire rammed through the guardrail. An ache shot through her knuckles as she clutched the wheel. Her SUV careened down the embankment, her head snapped back against the seat. She sent a prayer to the heavens as globs of mud and rock ricocheted across the windshield. Pain exploded through the left side of her head when it hit the driver side window, shattering the glass.

Her heart thumped out of control and bile rushed up into her throat.

She locked her knees and pressed against the brakes with all her strength. Her jaw snapped open and shut as her teeth slammed together. The headlights illuminated the huge oak tree at the bottom of the ravine. *Oh my, God, I don't want to die.* The vehicle rolled end over end.

Darkness descended, and her world went black.

"That's enough," the captain barked. "Rookie, how much longer before dinner? We're not getting any younger, and I'm hungry."

A female voice muffled over the intercom system from dispatch, followed by a series of four different shrills and tones screaming as loud as the last. "Station 56, we need an immediate response to a single car crash on Highway 13, South, at mile marker 7A."

Lieutenant Connor Winslow ran down the hallway flanked by the sleeping quarters and hit the second-floor door that led to the top of the fire pole. Swinging forward, Connor looped his arm around the brass pole and gripped tightly as the rubber soles of his day boots guided him to the bottom.

No matter how many times the alarm went off and Connor ran to his position in the front passenger seat of the ladder truck, he was the little boy who got excited to ride in the big, red fire truck.

Silenced filled the cabin. An eerie calm contrasted the roar of the sirens. Intersections flew by, and bright lights of the city were replaced with jagged rocks of the foothills. As they turned the bend, flashing lights of police cruisers illuminated the roadway. The ravine was steep, so they would need to traverse down the dense slope.

Lieutenant Winslow peered into the rear passenger window of the SUV teetering on three wheels. The fourth wheel was nestled into the trunk of the tree. Easing in, he wiped the sludge away with the sleeve of his coat.

No child seats. He exhaled the breath he was holding. Children were always the worst calls. His boots crunched on remnants of broken glass from the front passenger window; there was no way to get to her from the driver's side.

A woman lay motionless behind the wheel. *Damn it. She can't be dead*. Connor knelt to secure the tension poles to keep the vehicle from tipping and hammered the chock blocks into place between the frame and wheels. He picked the remaining glass away as he eased through the narrow opening. His team was positioned behind him, holding the back of his turnout coat. The driver's head drooped forward. He pulled his gloves off and stretched through the narrow opening to check for a pulse. She hadn't moved since their arrival. Warmth flowed through his fingers as he touched her neck and waited for the rhythm of her pulse.

"She's alive. Can someone lift my legs and get me a little closer? I'm not sure where the blood's coming from, but it's everywhere." Unzipping his med bag containing the neck brace,

Connor stilled to hear over the noise of the cutters and spreaders and pressed the stethoscope against the woman's chest.

The woman stirred, and her head bobbed up and down slightly.

"Miss, you're going to be fine. I'm here to help you. Please don't move." No sooner did the words come out of his mouth, she was still again. He pulled the Velcro enclosure on the brace, positioned it around her neck, and placed the oxygen mask over her nose and mouth.

"Guys, back up, would you? I need a better angle. This Superman position isn't working." He had to get a line in and figure out where all this blood was coming from.

The team pulled him out of the vehicle, and Connor went back in feet first, kicking the glass away from the seat. The space was tight, so he repositioned and put the med-bag between the seats. A brown mass of waves covered her face. Most of the blood had dripped down her nose, which peeked through her sodden hair.

"Winslow, I need a report," the captain commanded.

He pushed the curtain of blood-soaked locks from her face. "Cap, there's a laceration, approximately two inches above the left eyebrow. There's swelling and a possible concussion. We have multiple contusions and cuts around the neck, chest, and limbs. Her pulse and breathing are shallow but stable." He grabbed an immobilizer and elastic bandage out of his med bag and examined her contorted arm. "The left arm is definitely broken. I'm making a splint."

Connor cut away the woman's blood splattered sweat jacket and cotton t-shirt, then stuck the adhesive heart monitor and electrodes along her chest and ribs. He pulled the plastic cap off the saline fluids and secured the tubing. Next, he hooked the bag on the rearview mirror and ripped open the alcohol swab to disinfect the top of her hand. She was small, frail, and so far, lucky to be alive.

Connor removed the needle from its wrap, tapped her skin to find a vein, and hooked up the IV line. Her pinky finger jumped, and all of her fingers clenched.

"I'm really sorry, Miss, but this needs to be done." He taped the line in place and eyed glass embedded throughout her skin. "The saline drip is in, Cap," Connor yelled over the noise.

"The frame was trashed, and the doors won't open. Let's rip this baby apart and get the car away from her," the Cap said.

Connor slipped under the tarp Garcia handed him. They had to remove the roof, which meant he had to hang tough in this shoe-box. His gut knotted as he clenched his teeth. A trail of sweat rolled down his back. He could feel his muscles tighten with every second.

The Jaws of Life engine revved, and the groan of the metal frame twisted as it was dismantled. The noise was deafening, the vibration disturbing, and the smell of oil and gas hung in the air. He did the only thing he could—console her. His teammates, Jax and Bill worked the weighted blades of the cutters and spreaders. They tore it away in one piece. He checked his watch. Another few minutes and the roof would be off.

The captain shot Connor eye darts before he hopped onto the bumper. "Winslow get your nugget under the tarp!" he shouted. "The back window's all mine."

The window collapsed from behind when the Cap pushed it in.

Connor's knee jackhammered, and he held his breath. He finally took another deep inhale and placed the stethoscope on her chest again. The woman was still breathing. A beam of light from his helmet illuminated the space under the cover. Slowly, he wiped the blood away from her face with a sanitized cloth. "Better." He exhaled. "Now I can see what you've got here." He tilted her head back. "This might hurt a bit." Connor positioned elastic strips to butterfly the laceration. His handy-work slowed the bleeding for a moment.

"I'm sure the head of the emergency room can stitch this wound right up for you, and it will barely leave a scar."

This kind of injury bruised badly with dark, black, and purple marks. Not to mention a wallop of a headache for weeks. She would need a lot of stitches, but facial cuts were the least of her worries. Her internal injuries were the priority.

She stirred again, gasping in a startled wheeze. She winced and leaned toward him. Her splinted arm worked over his bunker gear. Fear was familiar territory. Careful not to hurt or startle the patient, he reached over to unlatch her seatbelt.

Her pleading eyes locked onto his, and he paused. He was lost as he stared into her golden-flecked, coffee brown irises. Tiny freckles scattered across her pert nose. Her full lips pouted slightly at the corners. His heart raced as she leaned in against him. The woman whimpered with each subtle movement, her head resting against his shoulder.

She wasn't just another rescue––she was a woman.

Just inhale, dickhead. Through your nose and out your damn mouth. Breathe.

She struggled to pull off her oxygen mask and let out a primal scream.

"Be still." He rubbed her shoulder. Hail throttled down on the tarp and water soaked through the seams. "Why were you out here alone in this weather?" Connor looked around for a purse or wallet. Her eyes followed his every move.

Her arm locked tighter behind him as her face nuzzled into his neck, her breath warm on his skin. Connor swore she said something—or maybe in just a whisper—but it was hard to hear over the noise. He turned as she pulled away. The woman's big brown eyes dilated, and she licked her split bottom lip.

The hail softened to a hum, and in the hush of the moment

the engine calmed on the cutters and spreaders; quiet suddenly enveloped them.

They were nose to nose. "Someone ran me off the road." Her voice elevated, and she spoke faster. "They tried to kill me and wouldn't stop. Please help me... Don't leave me... I don't want to die... Promise me... I'm so scared." Her words faded away. Her eyes pooled with tears, and her teeth chattered.

"U-h, I...I promise." Bullets of sweat dripped down his face. "I'm not going anywhere, and we're going to get you out of here." Her hand slid down, her body limp in his arms. The monitor reacted. Her pulse slowed and then became faint.

Shit! Connor couldn't move. He was so powerless and could only hold her tight. "No..." He ran his hand through her blood-soaked hair. "Stay with me, please. I swear I'll get you out of here."

I'm not about to let her die. Not someone else. Not again.

"Guys!" He didn't recognize the shriek in his own voice. "We're losing her." He held her close. "Don't you dare give up. Hold on. I'm not going anywhere. I'll make sure you're safe."

CHAPTER 2

he ambulance screeched to a halt at the ER. Connor couldn't wait for the automatic doors to open, so he pushed them in. He almost knocked over his aunt Janet, head of the triage unit, and a hard cookie after years as a medic in the Gulf War. If anybody could save this girl, Aunt Janet could do it and she just clocked in for her shift.

"Simmer down now. Don't break the door in." Janet wore light blue scrubs, her highlighted hair tweaked out under her surgical cap. Bright multi-colored frames perched on the end of her nose. "I've been filled in through dispatch with all the vitals." She flipped the pages over her clipboard and slipped the pen behind her ear. "Are you okay, hon? That's not your blood is it?"

He shook his head. "I'm good." *I'm really not good at all.* He looked down at his bunker gear. Blood stained his uniform. *Her blood,* and a lot of it. The critical care team rolled the woman into an emergency bay and pulled the curtain closed behind them.

Janet walked backward, talking to Connor as he kept her pace. She grabbed her stethoscope off the counter. "Are you alone?" she asked. "Where are the rest of the guys?"

"Cleaning up the wreckage. There was no sign of her identification either. I didn't see a purse inside the SUV, and I looked everywhere," Connor said, scratching his head.

"For now, she's a Jane Doe, but she will get top notch care, name or not," Janet said with conviction. "We need to get her stable first, then we'll take it from there. Will you do me a big favor? Get out of here and sit down. You look awful." Janet disappeared behind the curtain where her team was working on the woman.

Unable to sit still, Connor paced the corridor. How much time had passed? An hour? Maybe two? Why did she make him promise he'd stay? He looked down the hallway toward Aunt Janet, Doctor Tallyn, the chief resident, and an aide pushing the woman on the gurney toward the elevators.

"Aunt Janet." He ran to catch up with them.

She turned to him. "Are you still here? I thought you would be back at the station by now."

"What's going on?" he asked.

"We're sending her up to CAT scan to make sure there is no swelling of the brain. Then an M.R.I. to check for internal bleeding and see if we've missed anything. It's too soon to tell." Janet shook her head. "She's critical, and we will get her stable. That's our job. Let the police find out who she is."

"Can you keep me posted? I need to know how she's doing." The doors of the elevator opened, and they pushed forward.

Concern etched Janet's face. "You did great out there. She just might have a chance. You know you saved her life." The elevator door closed, and Connor took one last glimpse. He hoped so. *I gave her my word.*

The rest of the squad picked Connor up from the hospital, returning to the station house and finally tasting Garcia's chili. The rookie was in charge of all the meals for the shift, but this shit was spicy as hell. Connor wouldn't give him the satisfaction of telling him his mama's recipe was too fiery or telling him his tongue was permanently whacked. Connor popped a few antacids into his mouth.

After clean-up, exhaustion hit him, and he headed to his bunk. Connor squeezed his pillow, knowing calls would come in all night and he needed to conserve his energy if he needed to stay until the storm cleared. But as he laid there, her face and those beautiful eyes haunted him. Her pleading expression reminded him of the look his mom had given him when he had watched her life slowly slip away. He shuddered at memories of the accident that changed his life came to the forefront. No matter how hard he tried, he couldn't save his mom. There was so much blood. He grabbed the latest edition of Sports Illustrated, but the words blurred on the page, out of reach.

Why was he so restless? He promised he wouldn't leave her. Why was she out there alone?

He reached for his phone on the desk beside his bunk and called Janet. She answered on the third ring.

"How's my favorite lady?"

"Why are you calling me in the middle of the night?"

He sat up on the bed. "I was curious if you would meet me for breakfast after your shift."

"Sure, I'd love to. But what's wrong?" she asked.

He could hear the speculation in her voice. "Nothing. What's wrong with asking you out for breakfast?"

"You can't con a con. I know my nephew better than you think." Janet laughed.

"So suspicious."

"I've got to run. They're paging me again," she said. "I'll meet you in the morning in the cafeteria."

He hung up the phone, tossed it on the desk, and laid his head on the pillow, finally able to doze off.

****

Janet was in the cafeteria doorway, talking with a few hospital employees. Connor waved to them when he snuck up behind his aunt. He hoisted her into the air.

She screeched and elbowed him in the ribs "Put me down, your big buffoon."

"Ouch." He winced and rubbed his rib. "I'm starving. Let's eat." He handed her a tray, and they filled up at the food line and sat in the nearest booth.

"Geez, Connor, you're going to have a coronary." She eyeballed his mountainous plate over her glasses. "I think the cheeseburger, French fries, eggs, bacon, and the chocolate shake are breakfast, lunch, and dinner." Janet stirred creamer into her coffee, shaking her head before spreading cream cheese slowly over her bagel.

"Don't forget the coffee and donut, too." He shoved the donut into his mouth. "It's fuel." He took a bite of his burger, followed by a handful of fries dipped in ranch dressing.

"Thank God you work out. I'm gaining weight just watching you," she said. "So, what gives with the visit?"

"Okay, here it is." Connor tapped his fingers on the tabletop. "I was curious how Jane Doe was doing?"

"Why?" Janet grinned. "You know I can't tell you anything." She tilted her bright colored glasses down her nose. "You are not her family." Janet bit into her bagel. "You know the HIPAA laws as well as I do. You are walking a slippery slope right now, and we can both lose our jobs."

"I don't want to break any rules. I just have to see her again." He folded his hands under his chin. "I'm heading up there to see for myself, as soon as we're finished eating."

"Connor Winslow, you will do no such thing!"

"I'm an employee here, too and I take care of patients. I may not spend as much time as you do, but I work enough shifts when I'm not working my rotation at the fire station". Besides she told me at the scene someone was trying to kill her. He swallowed the lump lodged in his throat. "And whoever wouldn't stop. I can't leave. You know I will march right up there. So, you can walk me up there if you like, but either way, I'm checking on the woman." Connor eased against the back of the booth and crossed his arms over his chest.

"You remind me so much of your father."

He clenched his jaw tight. "I know, I know. I'm a spitting image of him when he was younger."

"Well, yes…but not exactly what I meant. You have Thomas' dreaded stubborn gene of driving me crazy all my life. Well, his life." Tears welled in Janet's eyes before she stood. "I'll take you there, but I'm making sure you only look."

Connor stood up, towered over his Aunt, and wrapped his arms around her small frame. "I miss Dad, too."

Connor walked backward, pulling Janet by the hand toward the elevators. When the doors opened, he tugged her close and pushed the fifth floor for the intensive care unit. "You know I love you, don't you?"

They stood outside the ICU, and Janet broke, letting him inside. He ran his hand over his forehead and wiped off the beads of sweat.

Janet checked down the hall and touched his arm. "Only for a minute. I mean it. I need to get home because Dan's waiting for me." Her cheeks became rosy in color.

The idea of his captain and his aunt being a couple was an epic distraction. Her happiness was all he cared about but anything else was TMI.

Connor grasped the finger she pointed at him and kissed the

tip. He gave her a wink and disappeared into the Jane Doe's room. "Back in a flash."

"You're not going in alone," she tugged at his shirt. "I'll go in with you and then we will call security and let them know she was threatened."

"Come on then." He waved her on.

The room was bright, and the morning sun poured through the partially open blinds. Connor walked over to the bed. Purple hues from bruises painted the woman's skin. Her lashes fluttered when she opened her eyes. A bandage covered her forehead where the gash was hidden beneath. He didn't expect her to be awake. The pain she had endured had his gut wrung in knots, and a wave of nausea rolled through him.

"Thirsty," she whispered as she licked parched lips.

He poured water from the pitcher on the table positioned over the bed, secured the straw between his middle and forefinger, and steadied it between her lips. His heart pounded.

"Here, take only a little," he whispered.

"You kept your promise."

As she drew in the liquid, her head barely lifted off the pillow, wincing in pain. "Will you please come back to see me?"

"Sure. I'll be back and check on you again." Connor lightly touched the cuts on her arm.

"Promise?" she muttered.

She fought to keep her swollen eyes open, but the battle was soon lost. Her eyelids closed over her beautiful coffee colored eyes, and she faded into a slumber.

"You have my word," he said to her, then pivoted around to his aunt. "You heard her, right? She asked me to come back."

CHAPTER 3

*E*llie's head was going to burst. Tears trailed down her cheeks from the intensity of pain slicing through her body. Air whistled into her nose, making it easier to inhale, but her lungs burned. Her ribs ached with each rise and fall––it was pure torture. Something heavy weighted her throbbing left arm. A steady beeping sound echoed, and faint voices approached.

Where was she?

An ache shot up Ellie's back. How long had she been there? She looked down at her left hand and winced. She woke up in the fog of her stupor. Was she in the hospital? What day was it? Her vision was much better than before and now she could see the hands of the clock and the dry erase board.The date was plastered on the right upper corner.

She pinched her eyes shut, trying to find the memory of the last day she remembered.

"The eighth," she rasped. "I was going to work on the evening of eighth, and the electricity was out.It was raining—I remember I was on my way to work." She squeezed her temples with her thumb and middle finger of her only free hand.She reminisced about how much she loved her job and—headlights and being hit from behind. She heard a clatter in the÷ hall and snapped her head toward the sound. Her clammy skin started to shiver as she tried to move, but pain sliced through her. Squeezing her eyes tight and covering herself with the sheets she was almost paralyzed and concentrated on her breathing, lulling herself to sleep. She remembered even more of the accident and the man who helped her. She was safe

S tartled by the thump, tap, and squeak of rubber soles, Ellie opened her eyes wide.

"You're awake," he said. He was the poster boy of all of Ellie's fantasies. His deep baritone voice was like Grand Marnier—warm, fierce, and smooth. A smile tilted his stunning mouth. Ellie grabbed the sheet to control her shaking.

He was not a figment of her imagination. Nope, real as the moment she saw him. He was a jaw-dropping cover model of an epic romance novel. She placed a hand over her heart. Her toes curled, and she quivered. Warmth radiated throughout her body.

She stared down at scuffed well-worn boots. His swagger and strut appeared deliberate as he moved closer. Gold-and-yellow uniform pants hung low on his hips. His suspenders looped lazily down his sides. His drawn out steps lingered a few seconds. A matching uniform jacket was haphazardly over his shoulder and the navy blue, snugly fit t-shirt had an emblem on the left pocket. He was a superhero who saved kitties from trees. Yes! He was the firefighter who'd saved her in the accident.

Am I dreaming?

Abruptly, he stopped. Ellie blinked to clear her vision. She hoped the mirage was still there. She stared at his full chest and down the taught muscles of his arms. Ellie bit down on her tender lip to hold back her smile. He was in great physical shape. His light chest hairs sprouted over the top of his shirt. Her foot jittered. He was power in all senses of the word. The atmosphere in the room crackled in her ears.

Her throat grew thick. Her mouth was as dry as the Sahara. A scar feathered his upper lip near the cupids bow. His full sexy lips spoke volumes. She wanted to hear every syllable out of that perfect mouth.

His square face was balanced with a regal nose.The intensity of his obsidian slate gray eyes were an abyss of turbulence.

The drugs they were administering must be creating visions. She didn't care, she wanted a lifetime prescription. Ellie was in sensory overload. Her goosebumps had goosebumps.The man was the snap, crackle, and the pop in a box of awesome sauce.

The hottie turned and sprinted out of the room. Smoke lingered in his wake. Ellie closed her eyes and breathed in the memory of roasted marshmallows over a campfire.

"Ahem." She spoke, but again nothing came out. She wanted to call him back, but a thunder of commotion barreled toward her. A barrage of nurses and doctors clustered around the bed. Each one poked and prodded places that were hurting. A staff member checked the gauges of machines hooked to her, and an icy stethoscope skated across her chest. The glare of light blinded her. She winced and slammed into the horror of her reality. The hottie stood behind the staff at the doorway. His arms were over his head as he hung onto the doorframe.

Ellie blew puffs from her mouth at wavy tendrils of hair around her face. Perspiration beaded her forehead as she stretched her hand through the railing of the bed. Ellie waved him forward. He released his grip from overhead and shifted from one foot to the other. The man eyeballed one of the nurses from across the room and took his first step with trepidation, then pressed forward between the staff as he towered over them.

Connor couldn't believe she was finally alert and aware of her surroundings after eleven days. The woman's eyes sparkled and gleamed, and her complexion had a radiant glow. Her bruises and cuts nearly faded.

"You are going to be okay," he said. The woman's hand glided down his arm. Adrenaline rushed through him and tied his tongue. She carefully folded her battered hand into his, lacing their fingers.

Connor closed his eyes and tilted his head back. His chest heaved as he filled his lungs with air. He swirled his thumb gently into the palm of her hand, relaxed and unhurried. Connor eased forward almost light-headed, slowly lifting her hand as he kissed her wrist. He lingered there for a moment, trying to steady his pulse. Nothing mattered, no one else counted, and the noise muted around him. He was lost in the moment with this fragile woman he couldn't walk away from.

Connor dug a fist deep into his sternum to ease the ache, and his heart hummed from the emotionally charged connection. In the moment, his sadness…went away. The voices…were silenced. She was his promise of hope.

Mine. She is mine.

"Connor what are you doing? You need to get out of here. Can't you see she's in pain?"

He lifted his hands and stepped back. "I'm not doing anything."

Janet shooed him out the door. The woman in the bed slid down and sunk into her pillow.

He dodged and weaved around Janet, his gaze laser-focused at the woman. "What is your name?"

She smiled and peered through her fingers. She cleared her throat. "Ellie," she barely whispered.

"N urse?"

Janet turned. "Did you hear? Her name is Ellie. Now out you go." She grabbed Connor by the arm and walked him out. "I'll call security if I have to. Vamoose."

"Nurse." The woman cleared her throat again as her words amplified. "He doesn't have to go."

"Yes, he does, and please call me Janet." She closed the door and walked over to Ellie's bedside and filled the water glass from the matching dusty rose plastic pitcher.

Ellie relished at the cool slide of the liquid trickling down her parched throat. "Janet..." Ellie's voice grew clearer and stronger. "Has he been here the whole time? He's the firefighter who saved me in the accident, isn't he?" Ellie knew the answer in her core before the nurse replied.

"Yes, he is." Janet shook her head. "He's so darn stubborn. He's become a permanent fixture in here since he brought you in. He's been very adamant about staying."

"No. Please, don't get upset with him. I'm glad he's been here. I can't explain it, but I like his company. What's his name?" Ellie fiddled with the sheet on her lap and took a sip of water. "Every now and then when I woke, I'd hear him talking to me, or see him near, but everything was so surreal and fuzzy. I thought I was dreaming."

"Sweetie, you asked him to stay repeatedly, and you were as adamant as he was. Sometimes, when he wasn't here, you called out for him, or at least I think you were. Most of the time you had an iron grip on him. His name is Connor Winslow, and he's my nephew. I'll tell you something, he is a handful." Janet's chin rose as she laughed.

Ellie sensed Janet's pride in her knowing smile. She listened intently as she rolled his name over her tongue. "Connor," she said as her lips pulled into a smile.

"Watching over you is not in his job description, and he's walking a thin line with some of the hospital staff. But he's worked here for years, so he knows everyone and my boss's, boss's boss is a fan." Nurse Janet pulled the blanket up under Ellie's chin. "I have to admit, he's hard to deny.

"Now close your eyes. Your body has been through a lot of trauma, and rest is what you need. The last scan we did shows more improvement with your concussion. Once the remaining test results come in, you'll probably be transferred to another ward."

Ellie nodded. "Has my brother, Jeffrey been contacted?"

"Jeffrey?" Janet asked.

She cleared her throat. "Jeffrey Richard. He will be worried."

"We will find him."

She winced in pain. "I don't know where my phone is, I don't know the number to reach him without my phone and he's in Iowa on business. He's really hard to reach when he's on assignment." She looked around. "And I need to talk to the police, I was run off the road by a truck." She pinched the bridge of her nose.

"You were run off the road? Connor insisted and I called security to keep an eye on you and he called the police to take your statement as soon as you could. That's horrible." The nurse stroked Ellie's shoulder. "Don't worry, my dear. We have your name. The police have been looking for information since your accident, but you had no identification, so your brother's name will help and they will find him, I'll make sure of it and hopefully whoever is responsible for your accident. "

"No identification?" A flash of memory and falling outside of her house. Had she lost her wallet? Her thoughts were all scrambled, but... someone had rammed her from behind and run her off the road, without a doubt.

CHAPTER 4

The breeze floated over Connor's skin through the open window. He settled the thumping beat of his heart and jolted from another horrible dream. He swore he could feel the intense staccato thud through his veins. He rubbed his shoulder to ease the tightness. The damp air made his joint ache. The long road to rehabilitating his heart and soul was another story and going to take forever; he doubted if the pain would ever go away.

Dark clouds loomed in the sky, and heavy raindrops tapped on the rooftop. Another rainy day followed the past few months of the same dreary weather. He missed the sunshine. Colorado was never like this. He'd grown up in Solemn Creed, Colorado and the weather was usually so dry.

He eased in a calming breath. A sticky sweat covered his body as he threw the comforter aside. The nightmares were always there, even after all these years. This one reoccurred, as though he was living a bad version of the *Groundhog Day* movie.

He shook off the eerie chill he'd grown accustomed to. The smell of coffee filled his senses. Heavy footsteps pounded, cupboards closed, and dishes clattered from in the kitchen. It was weird getting used to someone being there again. The house had been so quiet the last few years.

His brother Cade was back from the Middle East and his army tour with the Green Berets. Severely banged up, a bum knee, and full of shrapnel, he was out of the service for good, and as loud as a bull in china shop. Home...and he was alive. The police force was fortunate to have him.

Relieved to have his bro back, he didn't know what he would have done if he'd lost him, too—a thought he couldn't fathom.

Connor cleared his head, wiping the sleep from his eyes. He just couldn't shake the nightmares, and they were getting worse instead of better. Thoughts went to the night before when he was at Johnny's Pub. The place was always fun but...

Who had he talked to the night before? A steamy looker who wanted more. Another beautiful face he used to hook up with. Always starting off hot and then leaving him cold, and Connor steered as far as he could from any complications. *Don't ever get close enough to get burned.* The happily ever after didn't exist regardless, not in his life. Not anymore. But other women didn't interest him. Ellie did.

The floor creaked and startled his thoughts. He focused on the figure lurking in the doorway.

"Damn it, cover yourself up, Connor. For Christ's sake. Not digging the peep show."

"Don't you know how to knock?" Connor reached for the sheet.

"Door's open, C. Can't knock on what's not closed." Cade shook his head. "I heard you yelling in your sleep, mumbling something. What gives? You woke me out of a dead sleep."

He shifted and swung a pillow aside. "Smells good. For me?"

"Do you have something in your ears? I know you heard me." Cade sat on the bed and handed Connor the mug.

He blew on it to cool and sipped at the dark brew. Even if the coffee was thick as oil and intense as hell he needed the caffeine. "Geez bro, you need to dilute this stuff a little. I swear it's coagulating on my tongue."

"Yeah, isn't it dandy? Food and drink in one. Come on. Talk to me."

Connor shook his head. He swore he still smelled the blood, gasoline, and smoke from the nightmare. His gaze went to the ceiling and then back to Cade. He cleared his throat. "Can't get the accident out of my head." Connor fisted the navy-blue comforter.

"I'll never forget it as long as I live." Cade sat on the edge of the bed and rested his elbows to his knees. His head shook from side to side. "You know what today is, don't you? Mom and Dad's anniversary." Cade turned and stared. "For them, I really wish you'd stop blaming yourself. Don't you think it's about time? You're killing yourself over this. Why didn't you tell me you were still having nightmares after all these years?" A haunted darkness filled his eyes. "It wasn't your fault. Don't forget... I was there, too. Mom and Dad have passed. They're never coming back, no matter how you overanalyze the should've, would've, and could've."

He sat up rod straight. "Don't you think it's a little too late for a psych session? I already have a shrink." Connor shifted to the edge of the bed. "All the motorcycles. There were three of them. The cops never found anything about who was driving them."

Cade stood and looked out the window. "Hmmm...You remembered there were three." He turned and raised brow. "I forgot about how many there were. You're remembering more?" Cade sat next to Connor on the bed. "All investigations on the accident led nowhere. I've looked over the files and didn't find anything. Jax said he recalled the Harleys, too, so did Aunt Janet. Cade pulled the soda cap out of his front pocket and rolled the Dr. Pepper insignia over his fingers. "Hey, aren't you going to be late for work?"

Connor jumped up and fumbled with the sheet around his waist. He shuffled toward Cade and almost face planted. "Get out of my way, bro. I need a shower."

"You're a klutz, please… do shower, I'd appreciate it. You stink something fierce."

"Shut up." Connor hauled off and punched him in the arm. "I should say the same to you. You're mighty ripe yourself." Walking away, Connor turned back to his brother mocking him as he winced, rubbing the brutal pop he gave him in the arm. Yep, like old times.

Connor regulated the water temperature and stepped under the warm spray. He could never wash away the sick feeling in the pit of his stomach. No matter how hard the memories were, the accident was always there, branding him deeply and etched into his soul. *What could I have done differently? Could I have done more?* He clutched his hair and pressed his forehead against the tile.

Toweling off after he finished his shower, he wiped away the steamy condensation from the mirror and noticed the purple shadows under his eyes, warning him the nightmares and lack of sleep were taking a toll. He was glad he rarely drank and never before his shift. The night terrors were enough. He shook off the chill and reached for his razor. Stretching his neck from side to side, Connor eased the tension from his shoulders.

After going to the bedroom, he put on his navy blue Solemn Creed Firefighter t-shirt and matching uniform pants. He latched his black belt into place and slipped into his black steel-toed shit kickers. Being a firefighter was his life. What would have become of him? He needed his career like air.

"Ready, Winslow?" he said out loud. "Put on your game face... Let's go save a life."

C onnor stalled in the hall when voices filtered out from Ellie's room. Maybe he should have called instead. He was about to leave when he recognized the officer coming out of her room. They waved each other on, and he knocked lightly at her door.

"Come in."

"Is everything okay? I saw the officer leaving." He placed his bunker jacket over the back of the chair next to her bed.

Ellie hesitated and said, "He took a statement." She trembled. "I remember I was forced off the road. Someone... tried to kill me." She sank lower into her pillow.

He remembered the vile act more than she knew, and it was part of the reason he'd never left her side. He hoped his brother Cade could find something out from the eyewitnesses on the scene of her accident and if anyone saw who caused the accident. "That's awful. You're sure?"

"I've never been more certain about something in my life."

Connor inched closer, the urge to comfort her taking over his body. "My brother is a detective on the force. He's excellent at his job; I could have him check into the cops' investigation if you like."

Biting her lip, she nodded. "Of course, I'd appreciate that."

She was more striking than he remembered. The swelling had gone down in her face, and the bruises were changing color. She watched his every move, those coffee eyes drifting over his hands, his shoulders, his face... What was she thinking, and why did she tell the staff he could stay?

"How do you feel?" A cold tremor ran through him.

She answered in a graveled whisper. "I've felt better, and I feel queasy. I need something to eat besides broth and Jell-O. I don't even remember the last time I actually had substance."

Her smile eased his rattled nerves. "Can I get something for you? I can go to the cafeteria."

"Cheeseburger. And ice cream." A blush spread across her cheeks and neck.

"I'm not sure it's a good idea, but I'll see what I can do. I'll check to see what you can eat and be right back."

She nodded, Connor looked back before he darted out of the room "By the way, you said your name is Ellie, right?"

"Yes. Ellie Richards." A shy smile formed on her lips. She attempted to tuck her hair behind her ear but was thwarted by the cast on her left wrist. She fought to keep her eyes open.

"Nice to finally put a name with the beautiful face. Ellie, it's a pleasure," he whispered.

Connor exited the room into the hallway and walked to the bank of elevators. He sprinted down the corridor to the cafeteria. He pulled his phone from his front pocket. He'd missed a call from Cade, so he dialed Cade's number on his cell phone, his voicemail picked up. "Sorry, I missed your call, but I'm at the hospital. I'll meet you at Johnny's later."

Hopefully, this infatuation or whatever it's called would have faded, but he needed to know more now than ever. Who was this woman and why did someone try to run her off the road? As long as she was in the hospital, he was there. She'd be safe and soon fed so she can get her strength back.

CHAPTER 5

onnor followed Jax and Cade into Johnny's Pub. Behind Cade he detected his limp from his injuries in Iraq was barely visible anymore. His brother was getting better every day. The rich mahogany wood showcased an old 1930's antique bar with original mirrors, etched glass, and copper pillars. Vintage lamps kept the bar dimly lit, giving off an air of romance. Overstuffed booths flanked the right side for privacy and were deep enough for intimacy. An eclectic menu was filled with flavors as authentic and unique as the people who frequented the establishment. Johnny's had a loungy, low-key vibe.

There were pool tables and a small corner stage with nicked up dance floor where local bands played on the weekends. A giant spotlight beamed down over an old jukebox. The relic was filled with songs from the past more than modern fair.

"Hi Nate." Connor walked toward the crooning star of the place. Those unfamiliar with the bar might assume he was just another old patron, but he was the entertainment nightly. Nate could draw in a crowd. Connor shook his hand and turned to the bartender. "Hey Johnny, can I get the usual for my friend?"

"Thanks, Connor. You know how it settles my stomach." Nate's shaky hand raised the glass to his mouth.

"I'm sure it does." Connor patted the burly man's back.

Jax, Cade, and Connor were wrapped in a huge Nate-bear hug. "I can't believe it. You guys get bigger every time I see you. Not like the runts you used to be." The old man had sat at the same velvet merlot-colored barstool every day since they were kids, sipping his blackberry brandy.

Nate's Coke-bottle-thick glasses, warm smile, and pot-belly made people feel welcome. He knew everyone. Crowds would come from all over Colorado just to hear Nate sing along with the old jukebox tunes. And could he ever sing tenor.

Connor waved a so-long to Nate as they found a table. Jax scoped out the terrain, looking for any potential suitors. The waitress was vying too hard for his attention as she leaned over with her top unbuttoned low and raked her nails across his back. Another ladies' night, and even though Connor loved this place, he'd rather be somewhere else. He needed to find out what Cade had dug up on Ellie Richards. He'd Googled her and only found out she'd done a lot of charity work for the family crisis center and had a food blog called Ellie Eating. Maybe he could contact someone at the crisis center and they could help?

"You know that crap will rot your teeth right out of your head." Connor pointed to Cade's glass of Dr. Pepper.

"Which is why I stay away from the hard stuff. My consumption of hard liquor in the service did more damage than a dentist appointment ever will." He chugged the sweet, bubbly drink down, wiped his lips, and belched. A sound worthy of Connor's respect and applause.

"Caveman."

"Smartass." Cade flipped him off.

"What did you dig up on the woman in the hospital? Did you find anything about her?"

"What's with the obsession, Winslow?" Jax interrupted.

"Shut up, Honeycutt."

"I will not, dude. The accident was pretty bad. It was a good save, and now you move on. I don't get it. You've been at the hospital every day you're not working, and when you're not, you're talking about her. Has someone finally penetrated your thick skin?"

"Maybe, but it's none-ya business." He white knuckled the table and his jaw muscle tightened.

"Slow your roll guys," Cade interjected, his demeanor calm but direct. "Connor, do me a favor and don't break the place. I'm a little partial to the atmosphere, and your vice grip on the table you might crumble it, so loosen your hold, please."

Without a doubt these guys were family and had his back, but Jax was barking up the wrong tree. Cousin or not, he was pushing his luck. Connor sat back down to hear what Cade had discovered. Maybe he needed a chill pill and not go all hulk on everyone.

"We found the owner of the mangled SUV," Cade said. "It's registered to a Jeffrey Richards and with Miss Richards help, he's been located somewhere in corn country, Iowa. The authorities should be talking to him soon." He looked down at his watch. "You need to accept this could be her husband." Cade squeezed Connor on the shoulder. "Have you talked to Aunt Janet?" He asked.

Connor shook his head no.

"She called me. One of the guys went to the hospital and took a statement from her. She said she was run off the road."

Husband? His gut twisted at the idea. "Why didn't she call me? We will soon find the answer. I know, Cade. I just want to locate her family, and then I'll back off." A sick feeling rose in his gut and his chest ached. *Now, what? Walk away. Sure, it's what I do best.*

"Earth calling, Winslow," Jax said. "She could be trouble."

He looked across the table at Honeycutt, and then to Cade. "What? Run off the road?"

Connor stood, took off to the bar, and ordered a shot. Cade and Jax raced to keep up, following close behind. Even if this woman was married, could he walk away? He ordered another shot at the bar. The cinnamon whiskey coated his throat. He motioned for another.

"She called me because you're not exactly yourself. What's got into you?" Cade asked him before lowering his voice. "You know if this woman is married, she's off limits."

"You can have your pick. Look around." Jax's arm swept the space like he was conducting a symphony. "There are a few eyeballing the goods right now."

Connor looked around the bar, but the same faces lost appeal now that he'd met Ellie. This was not like him. He wasn't obsessed with anyone but with her he wanted more. He chugged the amber liquid, then slammed the empty shot glass down on the bar. "I'm out of here. You guys have a ball."

"Are you sure you don't want to stay? It's going to be a full house," Jax yelled over the rising laughter and the band doing a sound check.

"I'm good." Connor threw a couple of the twenties down on the bar and walked out of Johnny's.

CHAPTER 6

*J*effrey pinched the skin at his throat and stared at his phone as he ended the call, still no response from Ellie. "Damn it." He jumped. Startled by the rap at the door, Jeffrey set his phone down. He walked to the door and peered out the peephole. Two uniformed officers knocked again, this time louder. He unlatched the chain, opening the door.

"Mr. Jeffrey Richards?" the shorter officer asked.

"Yeah, I'm Jeffrey Richards. What's this about, officers?"

"I'm Deputy Thompson." He pointed to his right. "This is Deputy Chief Larimer. We are with the Linn County, Sheriff's department. Are you from Solemn Creed, Colorado?"

"Yes, I am, just outside the city." Jeffrey shook their extended hands.

"Do you mind if we come in? We would like to talk to you for a minute."

"What's this about?" Stepping aside, Jeffrey opened the door farther. He waved the uniformed officers into his suite. "I'm sorry. Please come in."

"We are very sorry to come here unannounced, but we have

been searching for you for a few days now. It's came across the wire, and it has been difficult locating you with law enforcement agencies from here to Colorado."

"I travel more than I'm home lately and I've been on an assignment. I can't always take my personal phone with me. My sister had the aerospace direct line in her phone. I plugged it in before I left."

"We expect with your government clearance, you don't have a neon sign telling people where you're at 24/7? That explains why we haven't been able to reach you so easily." Deputy Larimer, the taller of the two, adjusted his hat before flipping through his notes.

"Why are you looking for me? "Jeffrey asked.

"Mr. Richards, are you the owner of a 2012 Mitsubishi Endeavor?"

"Yes, I just bought it about three weeks ago for a steal. Why?" He started to pace, pinching his bottom lip nervously.

The shorter officer asked, "Have you let anyone borrow said vehicle or is it a possibility it could be stolen?"

"Ellie has it. I bought it for her. When I get back to Colorado we were going to transfer it over to her name." He looked from one officer to another. "What's going on? Is she okay?"

Both officers narrowed their distance to him. "Sir, I'm sorry to inform you there was an accident in Solemn Creed involving your vehicle."

Jeffrey stomped to the rumpled clothes hung over the chair and pitched them into the luggage sitting on the stand. He tore across the room to the closet and swung the mirrored slider aside, heaving an armful of clothes along with their hangers.

He closed his eyes, leaned against the wall, breathing deeply, then wadded up the pile and slung it into the garment bag. He pounded to the bathroom to gather his ditty bag.

"Sir we need you to get on the next flight to Denver. There will be a car waiting to drive you and identify the woman in the accident. The last flight leaves in a couple of hours," the shorter officer said.

"Well, if you haven't figured it out—that's exactly what I plan on doing." He stood still. "Is Ellie dead? Am I going to the morgue?" The blood drained from his face, and he dry-heaved. "Is she... dead?" he stuttered. "Oh my god, she can't be."

"Calm down, take a deep breath. As we mentioned earlier, we have been trying to find you for days, and if this is your family, we need verification. So, we are counting on you to keep your wits sharp." The officers closed in to calm Jeffrey down. "She's not deceased." Deputy Larimer reached forward to console Jeffrey. "But you need to get to Solemn Creed Trauma Center as soon as possible. Our latest update we have is the woman is in critical condition, and the vehicle is totaled."

"I couldn't give a rat's ass about the damn thing. I only care about my Ellie." Jeffrey grabbed the keys off the table, zipped his luggage, set it upright, and threw the garment bag over his shoulder. Pulling his suitcase forward he placed his briefcase on the top. He turned. "Well, what are we waiting for?"

"Mr. Richards, I don't think you are in any condition to drive," Deputy Thompson said.

"I'm fine. I have a rental car I need to return at the airport. I'm ex-military. I can handle almost anything." He straightened.

The time was near midnight, Mountain Time. The officers assured Jeffrey no matter how late, he arrived back in Solemn Creed there would be an officer waiting at the Trauma Center to escort him to the woman's room for proper identification.

Jeffrey rushed to the front desk. "I need to find my—I mean, um... Ellie Richards." Jeffrey stood up straighter, closed his eyes and took a deep breath. "There is supposed to be an officer waiting for me to identify a woman brought in here several days ago." He leaned forward onto the admissions counter, nervously pinching his bottom lip. "I'm sorry. My heads not screwed on straight, and my nerves are toast."

"One moment, sir. Do you know when she was brought in?"

"I have no clue. They said she was a Jane Doe in critical care."

The receptionist motioned with her forefinger for him to wait. "I'll see if I can find someone to take you upstairs." She lifted the phone receiver. "Sir, I'll contact the officer assigned to the case, and he will be with you in a moment to escort you."

Jeffrey tapped his fingers on the counter. "Just show me where to go, and I'll head there."

"No, sir. He's on his way." She pointed.

A faint sound of footsteps drew nearer, and Jeffrey turned to see a portly-shaped, mustache-sporting man with a bulbous nose walking down the hall. No doubt, he was one of Solemn Creed's finest heading straight for him.

Jeff and the police officer approached the intensive care unit, where a nurse waited in a pair of blue scrubs with funky colored glasses perched on her nose.

She smiled tenderly and extended her hand. "Hello, my name is Janet Winslow, and I'm lead nurse in the care of the woman brought in ten days ago."

"*Ten days?* Are you kidding me? The officers said days, but *ten?*"

"She had no identification at the crash site or on her person," the officer stated.

"I understand she might be your relation? I hope so; if I'm not mistaken I can see the resemblance." The nurse's words became a distant echo. "Were you looking for her?"

"She always checked in, but when I finally was able to reach her I couldn't. I—I didn't know she was missing. Jeffrey wiped his forehead with the back of his arm. "I've been on a training exercise, so I couldn't. Personal phones aren't allowed at work."

"You're here now."

"I wasn't there for her when she needed me," he muttered.

"Nurse, this is Jeffrey Richards," the officer interjected.

"Follow me. She's in here." The nurse pointed in the direction to the room on her right.

The nurse escorted him forward, but the curtain was drawn.

"Whoa. Not so fast. I need to come in with you, sir." The officer yanked up his gun and holster that were sliding down with his loose pants. "It's protocol. I have to witness this for proper identification." He nodded and shooed Jeffrey ahead. "Go on…"

"Do what you need to, but I've waited long enough."

The nurse leaned to the officer and tapped him on the shoulder. "Don't you see the resemblance? They have to be related somehow, right?" she questioned.

Jeffrey twisted around to see beyond the drawn curtain to the bed. The room was dark, but when he pulled back the patterned off-white fabric, the ambient glow of an overhead light illuminated the silhouette of a woman, one familiar since birth—his twin.

She was battered, bruised, and frail. He gasped loud enough that the police and nurse moved closer. "You have a positive I.D, officer." Jeffrey's voice quivered as he cleared his throat. "This woman is Ellie. This is my sister." Jeffrey held back the tears burning his eyes. "She's hurt." Jeffrey winced in pain. "Now can I please get some damn privacy?"

"I'm sorry, sir. I know this is hard on you. My sympathies to you and your sister. I will follow up later and contact the proper authorities." The officer tipped his hat. "I hope your sister has a speedy recovery." The officer sympathetically nodded. "She said she was run off the road."

"Run off the road?"

"Yes, sir, so we will be back if we have any more details or questions. The officer hoisted up his gun belt and drew a finger under his nose. "Have a good day, Mr. Richards." He nodded.

"I know you are only doing your job, and I apologize for my behavior. I'm a little stressed out. She's my only family, and there is no one else but us. If I lost her…"

"I understand, Mr. Richards. I have a daughter about her age, and it's a shame, but she has a fight in her." The officer tilted his hat and exited.

The nurse followed the officer. "I'll give you some time alone," she told Jeffrey. "I'll be back later to fill you in on your sister's condition, if you like? Ellie's doing much better than she was, and that's a good sign."

"I'd like that. I can't thank you enough for taking care of my sister."

Jeffrey inched closer to the bed, pulled up a chair, and whispered. "Sis, it's me. I'm here now." He kissed the top of her hand. "God, Ellie, you're a mess. Everything is going to be okay." He looked at the cuts across her knuckles, then to the hard COLOR cast on her left arm. "You have the worst crap luck of anyone I know. You take a beating and persevere. Dammit, I wish I could take all your pain away; you deserve a break." Jeffrey pinched his lip and cried. "Whoever did this, I'll make sure they spend time in jail for what happened to you."

CHAPTER 7

*E*llie opened her eyes to a familiar face. "Baby bro," she croaked. Jeffrey lifted his head off the metal side rail. "They found you."

He smiled. "I've been worried sick, and I couldn't reach you. And then... the officers came to the hotel. I couldn't get here fast enough. I thought if I ever lost you, or if you died..." He stopped his words. "You're alive and that's all I care about."

Ellie raised herself and inched slowly to sit upright as she winced in pain. "I'm sorry I worried you."

"Sis, be careful. Don't move." Jeffrey stood and gave her assistance.

She coughed and wrapped her only free hand around her body to ward off the onslaught of knife wielding, fire scorching pain in her ribs.

Jeffrey reached for a pillow from the nearest chair. "Next time you cough, hold on tight to this. It might help a little. Can I call the nurse for more pain meds?"

"Oh no, please no more." She smoothed the pillow over her mid-section. "My gut is seriously *queasy moto* from all the pain killers. And I need to function better than a sloth."

"Okay. We'll leave you as-is for the moment, but if you're in any pain—any at all— I'm calling the nurse."

"Okay, bossy-britches." She breathed in slowly, clutching the pillow.

"Better?" he asked.

"A little."

Jeffrey moved over to the side of the bed and poured from the water pitcher. "El, what happened?" He leaned forward and handed her the cup.

She sipped at the cool liquid and cleared her throat. "The day after you left town, it started raining and storming worse than the weeks before. Rain poured down so hard the pond in the back overflowed and flooded the basemen. The sump pump stopped working when the electricity went out. I made it to work for the first few days and hunkered down for the week-end, but then my cell died. I thought I could get word out to you at work."

"I knew the weather was bad, but after the training ended…" Jeffrey paced the room. "I called you and nothing for days. I even phoned your bestie, Lina, but she was out of town training for her new job." He stopped and pinched his bottom lip. "Work could have waited, sis, and you shouldn't have risked your own life going out there."

"There was a truck in the woods. It scared me. I—I thought James came back to kill me."

"He's gone. Him and his unethical uniform he hid behind. What's this really about?"

"Jeffrey, I swear. I just have this weird feeling like I'm being watched. I was out of food, no more dry logs, and water neared the top of the main floor landing. I put bags around the house all weekend to stop the water from seeping through the windows. The third time down in the basement there was a snake, and I freaked." Ellie bit at her nail. "After my encounter with the squirmy thing, I just shoved towels under the door."

Ellie stuttered and mispronounced her words as her limbs shook. "Besides, I needed to get to work—I just had to. The women and children need me at the crisis center. The calls get so much worse with bad weather." Her lip quivered, and her eyes filled with tears. "I'd be safer there until you got home.

"Calm down, I get it. I'm sorry I had to go out of town for so long." He lifted her chin. "I know how important what you do is, and how much they mean to you." Jeffrey ran the back of his hand along her jawline. "They're lucky to have someone who cares so much for them. What happened when you were driving to work and before the accident?"

"I couldn't see, it was raining so hard, and… there were headlights from both directions, and the one behind me got closer." She dropped her head into her hands. "It was a huge truck and they kept blaring their horn and bumped the back of my SUV."

"Did you cut them off?" he asked as he pinched his lower lip.

"I tried to pull off to let them pass because I was going slow and I couldn't see, but they nudged me again. I got scared and kept going." Her lips and chin trembled. "I didn't know what to do, so I sped up and they kept pushing me. Jeffrey, they were trying to run me off the road."

Jeffrey caressed her shoulder. "You're absolutely positive?"

"On my life."

"You've been through enough. I'm sorry I needed to ask you these questions. I'll get to the bottom of it, and trust me, I'll find the demented idiot responsible. You rest now. I'm going to clean up."

Connor struggled with the terror of reliving every moment of the accident nine years ago. The car exploded, throwing him to the pavement. Dad was dead. His mother was in her blue paisley dress, covered in blood. Her body was lifeless in Cade's arms on the side of the road. His brother's eyes were glossy, and a waterfall of tears flowed down his face. His light green shirt and Jerry Garcia tie gleamed crimson. Connor grasped at the air to reach his Mom, his arms thrashing to touch her. He must save her if he could. No matter what he did or how hard he fought, he couldn't save her life. The gruesome scene faded away, leaving his eyes wide and haunted.

This time, Mom was replaced by a woman, and not in Cade's arms but in his. Unable to focus, he sought to decipher her features. Who was she? Then her face became clearer—*Ellie*. She was slipping away. He screamed out, wanting her to live. She had to live. He couldn't lose her, too.

Connor's own scream startled him awake. He lay in his bed, shivering from the perspiration covering his body. His chest heaved, and his heart fractured in two. Shards of grief sliced through his insides.

Clearing the murk from his brain, he shook the nightmare off. He untangled himself from the sheets and jumped to his feet. After his shower he geared up, tied on his shit-kickers, and grabbed his keys off the dinged-up, travesty of a dresser.

Connor made one stop to the flower shop before he went to the hospital. Connor was in remote terrain since he'd never bought flowers for anyone but his mom, but he found the perfect ones. The sunflowers didn't have a scent, but their bright yellow petals and sturdy constitution reminded him of Ellie—a will so strong and a yearning for life. A flower to be reckoned with, something so vivid it dazzled the darkest place.

He arrived at the hospital, and the elevator door opened to the corridor near her room. A man walked out of Ellie's room, going in the opposite direction. He was in street clothes, so he obviously didn't work here. Maybe he was her husband?

He rubbed at the gnawing pang in his chest, trying to ease the pressure, but nothing worked. Cade had told him a man was coming to identify the woman from the accident. The growing ache wouldn't go away, and he choked down the agony to get a grip. He was better off not feeling anything for Ellie. It was safer to not feel then to get hurt... or lose someone.

He hesitated before entering the room. With any luck, she would be sleeping. The card he bought with the flowers would explain why he would not be seeing her again. Connor needed to save what little pride he had left. He planned to drop them off, bolt, and stomp feet. Her husband was here, anyway.

He peered in. Dammit, she was awake. Those coffee brown eyes stared through him.

Delight spread across her animated freckled features. The ache deep in his chest throbbed like a snare drum. Normally, he'd be worried about all this response if he hadn't just gone for a physical. His body was betraying him, and his comfort zone was breached. He preferred not feeling a damn thing.

"Flowers? Are those for me?" She blushed and clapped with elation. "Sunflowers always brighten a room." She tucked a strand of her hair behind her ear. "Hey guess what, Connor?" she asked and paused. "I have some news."

He lifted them in her direction. Connor couldn't stand it anymore, and he didn't want to hear that her man was here. Ellie didn't need to tell him about the guy; he already knew. "Ellie, about... why I'm here." He steadied his pace to her bedside table and placed the vase of flowers down with the card. He was in no mood to discuss her husband. "I just wanted to let you know... now that your family's here... I have a lot to catch up on at work. I won't be coming around anymore. I'm here to say goodbye."

"So, you know? But I… uh… don't understand." She caught his steel gray eyes now stormy.

"I wanted to give you the flowers and wish you a fast recovery. You're getting much better. I was really worried about you, and I'm glad to have met you, but I'm a busy guy." The muscles in Connor's jaw clenched so tight he could crack a tooth.

"Why today? Why now? I want you to meet my—"

Connor cut her off. "I'm late for work. Gotta go." He couldn't drag this awkward moment out any longer. He turned to leave the room and nearly knocked over the same man who left her room a few minutes ago. "Sorry," he said and kept walking past him.

"Hey, wait a minute!" the man yelled. "Who are you and why are you in Ellie's room?" The voice behind Connor called out, again. "Hey!"

Damn it, he's following me. Heavy footsteps fell close behind him. Connor stopped and took a deep breath before turning around. So much for a quick exit.

He faced the guy. "I was just visiting your wife," Connor defended. "Now that family is here, and she's not alone, she won't be needing me." Connor dipped his head to the floor tiles. *Did she ever?*

"Hey, not so fast. Who are you, and what did you just say?" He drilled again. The man's suspicious eyes assessed Connor.

"I'm Lieutenant Winslow from the Solemn Creed Fire and Rescue." He scoped out the man who was the competition. He wasn't sure he could actually see her attraction to him. His mustache was so eighties. Maybe it was making a comeback? The man's burly arms were crossed over his pecs in defense. Was this a pissing contest? They were almost head-to-head and something in the dude's eyes appeared somewhat familiar.

He stepped back. "You must be the guy I've heard about.

You've been keeping Ellie company. Connor, right? Oh yeah, you're the firefighter who brought Ellie in." He rocked back and forth from toe to heel. His stance still protective. "I'm Jeff Richards. Glad to meet you. Thank you for saving her life. I heard the accident was pretty bad." Jeffrey cleared his throat. "I can't begin to express my gratitude."

Richards. He was her husband. *Dammit.*

Jeff released his arms from his chest and slowly slid his hands into his front pockets. "Ellie's not my wife." He snickered, still rocking toe to heal. Under his oh so ugly man-stache, his lips formed in a shitty smile.

"Girlfriend then?"

Jeffrey started to laugh and cough at the same time.

What was the big fuckin' joke? Irritation bit at the corners of his mouth not to say what he was thinking. This was no laughing matter. His nails dug in to his flesh.

"Sorry, Lieutenant Winslow. It's just your assumption is way off... So off, however, Ellie is the most important woman in my life, and she's all I have. She's my sister, older by a few minutes. We're twins, and before you say anything, don't even suggest a remake of an old movie with Danny DeVito and Arnold Schwarzenegger called Twins. I've heard it all before, my parents were the first. They loved the movie and I grew up watching it more than I cared to admit, my mom was a big Schwarzenegger fan." Jeffrey smirked. "So, not funny, not now and not then."

"What?" Connor shook his head. "Huh, what did you say? Ellie's brother? Excuse me. Say that again. I thought you were her husband." Connor rambled. "Brother, not husband. What movie? Brother." He definitely hadn't expected siblings.

Connor gave a throaty laugh, almost to the point of a giggle, and he couldn't undo the shit-eating grin plastered on his face. The weight in his chest dissolved immediately. The knot in his gut unraveled.

He glanced over the man's head to see Ellie struggling to push the I.V. stand into the hall. She leaned her head against the door. The oversize blue hospital gown hung off her. Ugly tan skid proof socks were on her feet.

"Ellie," Connor hushed. "Be careful, you're too weak."

He took off as fast as his feet would carry him. Her gaze clouded. He only had seconds before she fainted. Connor reached out to pull her up from her crouched position. He could feel her brother at his heels as he grabbed the pole carrying the fluids, keeping it upright before it fell over.

Ellie toppled into Connor's arms, her body nestling into his strong chest. She was lighter than he remembered. Her arms weakly draped over his shoulders, her nose nestled into his neck. Goosebumps prickled where her rapid breathing blew against his skin.

Connor tripped over the IV bag and stand, and Jeff stretched the tubing and moved it out of their path. Connor felt the deep drumming of his carotid artery, and his mouth went dry. What the hell is this battered up woman doing to him?

He carried her across the room to her bed to lay her down, but he'd admit he loved the feel of her. Just like she'd read his mind, she wrapped a tighter hold around his neck.

"Ellie, let go of me," he whispered into her ear. He should get her back in bed before she got cold.

"I can't." She turned to him. Their noses were tip to tip.

"I'm trying to put you down. You almost passed out."

"I did not almost pass out, and I don't want to let go. You'll leave." Her bold rebellion flared her nostrils, pinched her eyes, and arched her brows. The monitor beeped with her pulse, dancing to the beat of his own.

Her lips turned upright at the corners. Her lashes fluttered.

She was flirting with him. And damn, it was working.

"Don't even try to act tough, or I'll drop you right here," he told her.

"You wouldn't dare!" Her chin jutted forward, but her arms still draped around him as she snuggled in closer. She squeezed him tighter and deliberately teased him.

I have half a mind to give her a spanking.

Connor wrestled with the devil on his shoulder. He didn't want to let her go. She belonged in his arms. "I'm going to put you down on the bed. I don't know what game you're playing, but you've picked the wrong guy to mess with."

"Oh really? I'm not so sure." Ellie grinned. "For now, I'll be good."

Jeff interrupted, clearing his throat. "Uh... I hate to break this little soiree up..."

They both looked over at Jeffrey then to each other. Connor sat Ellie down onto the hospital bed and covered her with the cotton blanket. "I really need to be heading out. I have a shift." He turned around to her brother and extended his hand. "It's a pleasure, Mr. Richards."

"Thank you, Lieutenant Winslow, and call me Jeff."

He nodded. "You can call me Connor." The rubber soles of Connor's shit-kickers drug across the tile, as he slowly walked to the door.

"Will I see you again?" Ellie asked, licking her bottom lip as she ran her uncast hand over her wavy brown hair.

He glanced over at the card beside the flowers within his reach. "I'm not sure if me hanging around is a good idea or not." He stared at her and then over at her overprotective brother. "I accidentally brought you the wrong card." He snatched the envelope and slipped it into his pocket.

"Y"ou know you shouldn't be getting out of bed." Jeffrey rubbed his red swollen eyes. "Did you forget you almost died in that accident?"

"I'm sorry. You two were all the way in the hall, and I could barely hear what you were talking about. I... I couldn't let him leave without knowing what was going on."

Jeffrey stood still, his hand planted firmly on his hips. "Funny... you are on a first name basis with the firefighter who saved your life?"

"I was sure you were going to take a swing. You know, this isn't Connor's fault." Patting the covers beside her, Ellie waved her brother forward. "You look tired. Please, let's not fight. I'm safe now."

Jeffrey slid the chair beside the bed. In one swift motion, the bed rail went up, locking Ellie in. "Do I have to ask the nurse for restraints? Or will you stay here until the doctor gives us the all clear?" Jeff's stoic demeanor meant business.

She was not going to push further. Jeffrey exhibited a long fuse, but today was not the day. "I won't do it again. I promise." Ellie crossed her heart.

"You don't see it, do you? The guy's not here on a courtesy call for the department. There's some major crushing going on here, from both of you if you ask me, and I'm not sure I like it." Jeffrey stood to continue his back and forth patrolling "Since when is holding a vigil over an accident victim part of his job description?"

"You really think he's... crushing?" Ellie hoped he was right.

"Come off it, Ellie. You were playing it up for him, too. I may be overprotective, but I'm not blind."

"A little," she admitted. "But he's been here for me, and he saved me. I was so scared I'd die. And you've always been there, and I swear I haven't felt vulnerable. He makes me want to feel again."

"Why is he so important?" Jeffrey pushed up one of his sleeves. "Why do you like him?"

"Did you get a look at him? He's beautiful." She fanned herself. "But, seriously, I'm not sure why. For one thing, he's responsible for getting me out of the crash and to safety." Ellie ran her fingers over the laceration on her forehead. "Remember, oh brother of mine. I was scared, and he made me feel safe." She rubbed her hand through her hair. "But." She wrinkled her nose. "I know I swore off men in uniform, but there's something about him. Ellie shrugged. "I just can't explain the way I feel. Maybe a screw got loosened in the crash."

"Just because James wore a uniform you shouldn't lump the whole male species with the sick bastard. Besides, it's been over two years." Jeffrey's grip tightened on one of the bars on the bed.

Her brother's brows knitted together and the corners of his pinched lips turned down with the mention of her ex-husband James. Ellie knew where this was about to go. "I realize what you are saying, but I don't need a man— ever—thank you, very much." Ellie quivered as a shiver went down her spine. "No one can hold a candle to you anyway, Jeffrey." She gave him a sheepish grin.

His demeanor instantly softened. "No, you don't need any man, but you do deserve a good one. Someone will be lucky to have you one day. If it's not the firefighter, then someone else. It's time to move on with your life, don't you think? Though, I'm not saying I'm sold on the notion. I guess both of us need to let go."

Jeffrey stopped suddenly like his feet were glued. "Just because James took advantage of you and the law he swore to uphold, doesn't mean any other Tom, Dick, or Connor will do the same." Jeffrey smacked his fist into his palm with force. "It's a good thing he's dead, or I would have killed him myself."

He cradled Ellie's hand in his. "I'm no dummy, sis. I see the way you look at this Winslow guy. You two were throwing off so much heat, I almost needed to take a damn cold shower myself." Jeffrey sang a poor rendition of an old song by the musician Nelly, *It's getting hot in here.* He walked over to the thermostat on the wall and tapped it. "Nope, the heat's not coming from here, according to the temperature gauge. The firefighter and you were sizzling up the atmosphere."

"Stop! Quit teasing me." Fire spread across Ellie's skin, and she hated being so transparent. No matter how tough or calm she acted, her skin was always painted scarlet.

"Let's see what the Doc feels about your improvement." Jeffrey leaned in awkwardly with his hands in his pockets and his smile faded. "You're not looking so hot, El. Get some sleep, will you? I'll get out of your hair for a few." He walked toward the door. "I need to make some calls. Then we need to talk about the accident and why you were driving in the middle of a storm."

As Jeffrey left the room, Ellie reached up for the bandage above her left eyebrow and brushed her fingers across the big lump. The vice grip around her head had loosened in the last few days, easing the whopper of a migraine from the concussion.

The ache in her head had eased now the hum of the florescent lights was tolerable without the pain pills, before everything hurt. The dizziness and nausea would probably take time, and she was covered with cuts which were raw although the sharp pains all over became less frequent. Her cracked ribs were another thing all together; every time she moved or breathed it hurt.

Her memory of some of the details was still foggy. Random images of her car rolling down the ravine, the blare of a horn, the headlights, screeching tires, and her new car being demolished and dismantled by the fire rescue... Ellie shivered and pulled the blanket around her with her only good arm.

The gunmetal gray eyes that had stared into hers were her favorite recollection. The calmness he exuded. She swore for a mere millisecond the pain in his eyes had mirrored hers.

An intense buzz of heat had flowed through her entire system when he'd carried her back to the hospital bed. She'd never experienced something so powerful. Ellie didn't want to let him go, not for a minute. She felt so alive. She hoped it was the same for him.

CHAPTER 8

$\mathcal{C}$onnor arrived at the station after visiting Ellie at the hospital. Bill and Garcia were inhaling their morning caffeine and cinnamon rolls. Garcia's face was splattered with sticky icing and crumbs. Jax was lazily drawn back on his chair, feet crossed on top of the kitchen table, arms cradling his head. A new, but unfamiliar guy was doing all the talking. Connor knew there was going to be a visitor. He must be their ride-along on today's shift.

The new guy was a pretty boy with wavy blond hair, blue eyes, and a slow thick southern drawl and seemed nice enough. Connor was a pretty good judge of character; he wasn't so sure about this one. The guy's beady eyes followed Connor's every movement, as he continued talking to the rest of the squad.

"Welcome to Station 56. I'm Lieutenant—"

"I know who you are, Winslow." The guy stopped yammering and looked up before interrupting Connor. "You're quite the celebrity in these parts. No, wait, Thomas Winslow was your Dad. A decorated saint in the district, not you." His cocky smile oozed along with his syrupy twang.

He reached out to shake Connor's hand. *What is this dudes problem?*

"Evan Parker. I'm up for a Lieutenant position soon, and I'm checking out your station to see if you can handle another person on your shift. I'll tell ya right now this is where I want to be, and I usually get what I want." He puffed out his chest like a rooster. Connor turned to the faucet, filling a glass and snickered before shaking his hand.

Connor turned around to set his glass down before catching his cousins eye.

Jax mouthed the words, "asshole" from behind Parker. Connor snorted his water.

"Evan, we'll just have to wait and see if you're a good fit, but in this house, there's only one captain, and this shift already has two lieutenants, which is more than required, and more than most stations allow." Connor interjected his authority in case pretty-boy was unclear. *I'm going to have to talk to the Cap about this chump and his tude toward me, he's laughable. I've got a weird vibe on this joker already. You don't walk in here like you own the place. Not in my damn house.*

Nothing was going to ruin his day because Ellie wasn't married.

She hadn't seen or heard from Connor since his dramatic exit. Ellie sat on the bed, days later, waiting for release papers. She was finally in comfy clothes and out of the ugly hospital gown. Ellie's dusty blue t-shirt shouted the words 'best hair class of eternity' in electric pink letters across the front, which was so not true. Her hair looked like it had been caught in a rotisserie. Her oversized holey-paint-splashed navy sweats had seen better days but were the best Jeffrey could do when she forced him to go get her clothes from home It was bad enough to ask him to rummage through her dresser in the first place, so he must have grabbed whatever he could find from the wrinkled clothes in the dryer.

She heard a rap at the door and hoped it was Connor. Another man she didn't recognize peeked through the doorway. She tucked the loose hair cascading out of the wad on top of her head in her sloppy ponytail.

"Excuse me, for the interruption. I'm from station 56 ma'am. I understand you were brought in weeks ago from an accident." The man stood all casual-like with a tilt to his hip. "May I come in?" He swaggered to the side of the bed that her feet dangled from, barging in before Ellie had a chance to say anything.

"No." Her delayed reaction didn't deter him in the slightest.

"My name is, Evan Parker. I heard they're springing you out of this joint today." He hitched his thumb to the door.

He was about Connor's height, but thinner. More of a surfer boy. His blond hair twisted up around the edges, disheveled in disarray. His eyes were deep blue like the ocean, and his mannerisms out of place in Colorado. His golden skin would be more appropriate on the beach with flip-flops. Ellie's radar went ballistic, bouncing off this guy.

He slowly released her hand and smiled ear-to-ear; his gapped teeth added to his boyhood charm.

"I heard through channels no one has been here to visit lately. Reckon that's why I'm at your service." His eyebrows wiggled. "Just hoping you might need some company?" His lazy drawl stretched over his words.

"Actually, I'm being released today. There's no need for you to be hanging around." Ellie covered herself with her brother's jacket hanging on the edge of the bed.

Evan's eyes twinkled. "Do you need a ride then?"

Before she could answer him, Jeffrey walked in with rolled up papers in his hand. "Got your walking papers, El." Waving them above his head, Jeffrey stopped in his tracks. He shot Ellie a look, his mind seemingly reeling at the thought of another interruption. "The nurse is coming with the wheelchair." He tilted his head, motioning for her to do something about Evan.

"Hey, I'm Evan Parker." He flipped his Justin Bieber hair to the side and gave Jeffrey a what's-up sneer with his nose in the air and jerking his head back, before plastering his pearly whites loud and proud as he wiggled his flirting eyebrows over and over. "The guys at the station asked me to drop by and see how our little Ellie is doing."

"Oh, Evan Parker, our little Ellie is just fine and dandy." Jeffrey leaned against the wall, hitting his chin with the rolled-up forms in his fist.

Mr. Parker reminded her of James, but he wasn't her ex. He flirted way too much for her liking. Ellie's shoulders eased as she relaxed a little. The guy has to be all right if he worked with Connor. However, the constant undressing-her-with-his-eyes thing creeped her out. Maybe she was just being paranoid. He's not James—He's not James.

Jeffrey cleared his throat, loud enough to get Evan's attention, and Ellie knew her brother didn't buy the guy just showed up to check on her. Jeffrey always had a sixth sense. Jeffrey's head did a bobbing thing, there was obviously no warm and fuzzy vibe between her brother and Evan. Sometimes she wished Jeffrey's overprotective side would just take a chill pill, but he was usually spot on about people and his B.S. hackles were up on hyper drive. She had to be cautious. She was run off the road and he was still out there.

"Are you sure you don't need a ride?" Evan asked again.

"Thanks, but I have it covered. I'm her brother." He rolled his eyes.

"Mr. Parker, thanks for stopping by and please let everyone back at the station know we appreciate their concern."

"Hey, Jeffrey. I actually wanted to stop by the firehouse later this week to say thanks," Ellie said.

Evan stepped forward, and Jeff leaped off the wall to stand between him and Ellie.

"Great, Ellie. I'd love to escort you if I could? Can you come by Thursday? Connor and I work the next forty-eight-hour shift. I heard him talking about you; I'm sure he would be stoked to see ya."

Ellie looked over to her brother and then to the sunflowers sitting on table next to the bed. Heat spread over her skin before she fanned herself. Not interested.

"We'll discuss your transportation to the fire station later, sis."

The nurse arrived with the 'so called taxi' out of there. Jeffrey apparently wasn't moving a muscle until Evan left the room.

"Protocol, Miss Richards." The nurse prompted her into the wheelchair.

"So, Ellie, will I see you Thursday?" Evan questioned, twirling his keys around and around his forefinger.

"Yes, Thursday's super." Ellie nodded to Jeff, and he gave her his two thumbs up, and his smartass 'whatever' grin.

"Cool, here's my digits. Give me a call when you're ready." He handed Ellie his card. "Well, I'd better go, y'all."

He turned and exited the room just as smoothly as he'd entered. Jeffrey speared his hand through his hair. Under his breath, Ellie heard him mock Evan's accent.

"Yay." Ellie clapped her hand against her cast and the nurse helped her into the chair. "Come on, baby bro. Let's get out of here."

Jeffrey gave her a lack-luster grin. "I don't like the idea of this guy coming by our place, and I got a James vibe. So, I can take you to the fire station on my way to the office, and you can Uber back or call me when you're ready. I think he's up to something, and he is giving me the willies." Jeffrey scratched his head. "Do you recognize him?"

"Oh seriously, Jeff, stop it. Never seen him before. I'm old enough to take care of myself, and I wanted to go to the station. Besides, we are down to one vehicle, and you need to get back to work. I feel bad enough you had to take the time off. I messed everything up." She scooted to the edge of the bed. "Now listen to your big sis for a change."

"Who's bigger? I mean, really?"

"You do have a point there." She giggled. "Anyhoo, you're my absolute favorite guy, Jeffrey." Her lashes fluttered deliberately and she stuck her tongue out. "I can protect myself with this." She lifted her bright neon cast and gave him a karate chop. "Just kidding."

"All right, Kung Fu Panda, let's get out of here."

CHAPTER 9

*C*onnor ran down the daily inspection list, marking off everything Jax had tallied and checked. All the compartments on the rig had the right gear, the med bag was loaded with supplies, and the CO_2 tanks and respirators were next up.

He leaned forward into the bus, carrying the dive equipment. "Hey, Jax. How's the pressure on the gauges?"

"Thumbs up, my man." Jax tapped the Plexiglas over the dials. Bending the rubber hosing, he looked for cracks. "I just replaced these lines with new ones. Our gear's sweet, and the ride's up to snuff."

"Where the hell is the newbie? I haven't seen him this morning," Connor rumbled.

Jax shrugged. "Cap said he's coming in late. Some personal stuff to deal with." His gaze went out the bay doors. "Speak of the devil. Look who just pulled up. Parker's in the driveway talking to your Jane Doe."

"Say what?" Connor darted to the open garage door. Evan and Ellie were standing close to her brother's truck. "You're shitting me. What's he up to?" Connor scrubbed a hand down his face. Was this why he was late? And was Evans arm wrapped around her waist?

Mine. She's mine

"Winslow... did you just growl?" Jax punched his shoulder.

Had he? He wouldn't be surprised, considering the way he felt.

"You seriously just growled. Dude. No one is to blame, but yourself. You need to handle this and figure out what you want." Jax slapped Connor on the back and grabbed the list from him. "You went ghost on her and stopped going to the hospital. You're a mess man."

Connor shoved Jax. "I thought she was married, before, so that's my bad and then I was embarrassed the way I acted. Shit, I'm confused." *He's right, I fucked up, but I plan to make it right. I don't have a clue what I'm doing.* "Jackson, she's got me all messed up.

Ellie scrambled, doing a one-handed teeter with a tray she carried. Evan's arms were full of grocery bags, and Jeffrey followed with another set of platters. Connor hit the pavement at a jog to retrieve the tray from Ellie before it went splat. He didn't have a beef with Evan other than he seemed to have an issue with him from day one, but Connor despised him right now, down to Evan's ego-filled grin and his arm on the back of Connor's girl.

Ellie was dressed in a shimmering peach camisole; a multi-colored floral skirt fit snug at the hips then floated above her knees with a ruffle. She had the legs of a dancer and wore jeweled sandals looped over her ankles. The bruises on her face were gone, and the light pink scar above her brow was begin-ning to fade. Her wavy brown hair blew in front of her face as the golden highlights danced in the sun. Her full lips shimmered with gloss. She smelled of orange and vanilla. Connor paused in front of her as he settled his nerves. This woman had the capacity to undo him.

What a jerk he had been the last week. His damn pride was in the way, and he was a little embarrassed by how he'd reacted. Feeling this strongly was new terrain for him. He didn't need this woman getting in his head again, so he had sworn off the hospital and those coffee-colored eyes. If only he could stop the damn ache in his chest. If he hadn't called and gotten daily reports from Janet, he would have gone nutso.

"Let me get that for you, Ellie." He grabbed the tray of goodies.

"Thank you. I almost dropped it." Her gaze went over to Evan who was oblivious to her struggle. She smiled and furrowed her brows observing his behavior.

"Parker!" the Cap barked as he came out the front door with Bill and Garcia to see what all the raucous was. "Give the girl room to breathe. Can't you see she's got her one good hand full? And take the bag off her cast."

"Sorry, boss." Evan took a step back, slid the plastic bag over her cast, and pointed for someone to get the extra sack he set down on the concrete.

But the usual damn smirk that crossed his face was directed at Connor.

Evan was un-fucking-believable and what's he got against me? He was a threat.

"Hi, Ellie, you look beautiful," Connor spit out the words. She was absolutely breathtaking. He was in awe of her and how alive he felt being near her again. The days he hadn't seen her had been excruciating.

"Hi, Connor." A blush spread over her cheeks and trailed down her chest. She looked down at the pavement and covered her red splotches, a telltale to every emotion or feeling coursing through her system.

"What's all this?" The captain's voice projected over the noise of the handheld radio at his hip.

"Oh, I hope you don't mind. I brought everyone food. Just a small token of thanks for what you've done for me."

Jeffrey stepped up. "We're both so appreciative of what you did." He wrapped an arm around his sister and kissed the top of her head.

Ellie's gaze averted from Connor to her brother. The familial love they had for each other ran heavy and sweet through the air. Connor fell hard in her beauty. He licked his lips, suppressing the urge to take her in his arms and kiss her.

"Guys, let's get this stuff inside." The Captain turned to Ellie. "Come on in, little lady." He reached for the bag at Evan's feet. "I'm Dan. Nice to see you again."

Evan followed them all inside, saying, "When I saw Ellie the other day I asked her to come by the station. I could only do the gentlemanly thing and pick her up at her house, right? I knew you guys wouldn't mind a visitor." He turned to Ellie. "I've enjoyed our time together today." He grinned, spreading his arms wide. "These are our digs."

"Sis, how did he find our house even after you said you didn't need a ride?" Jeffrey asked.

Ellie shrugged and whispered back, "I don't know."

Connor studied Ellie over Evan's shoulder, the look on her face painted with confusion. He really wished he could read her mind.

When everyone relocated into the kitchen, five first responders of the B crew, Jeffrey, and Ellie stood around the table and unloaded the bags and trays of food, removing lids and opening containers. Garcia, Bill, and Jax piled their plates a mile high with potato chips, sandwiches, and salad. Garcia wore half his food on his face, shoving his pie-hole full of food.

Jeffrey stood wide legged and arms across his chest as his phone vibrated. He stepped aside and answered the call. Ellie leaned against the counter near the sink, one hand supporting her neon pink cast. A smiley face glimmered in black ink near the wrist of the cast—a little something Connor had drawn when he'd visited her in the hospital.

"El, I gotta go, there's an emergency at work." Jeff said in Ellie's ear. "You ready? I have to leave."

"Okay."

"Thank you again for all you do and for giving me back my sister," Jeffrey said.

Ellie's head tilted to the floor as she coaxed her brown curls behind her ear. She gazed forward to each and every team member directly, then uttered her deep gratitude. "The words 'thank you' are just not enough." She fought away tears misting her eyes and shook it off. "I know I stand here today because you saved me. I will forever be in your debt."

Connor rubbed his chest, pulled and antacid out of his pocket and popped it into his mouth. He couldn't deny it any longer—he was going after the girl. Although, doubt plagued him. Was he even good enough? Was the chemistry between them because he was the one who'd helped her in the accident?

Heads nodded around the room. "It's our job, ma'am." The Cap spoke up. "All in a day's work."

She mouthed the words "Thank you," to Connor, and then turned. "I'd better go."

"What about a tour of the station?" Evan lurched forward into her space. "Then I can take you home."

"Thank you, anyway. But, I really should go home with my brother."

Connor stepped forward as he cut Evan off at the door, jarring his full glass of grape Kool-Aid on the front of his uniform. If the moron only knew his teeth were sporting the purple hue. Connor snickered as he followed Ellie outside, when the alarm at the station blared. Each of the three tones were at different octaves and gaining volume.

Ellie covered her ears from the sound of the trills. Chairs slid back and boots stomped on the floor behind them. Ellie's eyes widened in a cartoon-like "Yikes," and she rubbed her temples.

"Are you okay? Connor asked, touching her arm with the back of his hand, smoothing it across her soft skin.

"How in the world do you get used to that noise?"

He continued to stroke her arm. "It's in the genes. My father used to blare it so much, it's like a heartbeat." He raised her chin and stepped in to have a good look. "Can we talk soon? I'd like to see you again."

"Winslow, get in gear!" Parker yelled from behind. "Stop dallying with the lady. You're working."

Connor glared over his shoulder, the garage doors creaking up and the engine roaring to life. He only had seconds to jump into his bunker gear. "Duty calls." He bolted across the parking lot to the rig and yelled. "Can I see you?"

She nodded as a blanket of scarlet covered her cheeks and chest.

Connor positioned himself in the passenger seat of the ladder truck and leaned out the window watching Ellie and Evan standing near his silver and matte black Silverado. He waved and pressed the pedal to resound the siren. Ellie's pink cast waved into the air before they turned the corner. He smiled, only to find Evan's crab-apple stare reflecting through the side view mirror of the rig. He was shooting him epic eye darts. If he wanted a pissing contest, this fly-boy had no idea what he was in for.

Connor slipped his headset on, and Jax's voice piped through loud and clear. The engine was always so loud they had to communicate solely through the mics. He figured Jax would have something to say. He knew his cousin well.

"Pretty good cookies, huh, Winslow?" Connor nodded in answer to the comment, and Jax shook his head. "Dude, you look like the frick'n joker right now. It looks good on you."

Connor knew he wasn't talking about the food. His cousin,

and the surfer boy, might have given him the extra nudge he needed. Yup, he was definitely going after what he wanted.

The rigs slowly pulled into the garage from behind the station. Evan sauntered up, scooting the wide broom along the concrete of the bays. The captain leaned out the window. "Parker, don't you ever pull your shit again if you plan on sticking around here." The captain's red face expressed his anger as he jumped out of the fire truck and walked over to Evan who started filling the water bucket to mop the concrete.

Connor had known Dan McClain since he was a boy, and he'd rarely seen him mad. But when he did, he knew the cap was at the end of his tether.

"I thought it was a good gesture bringing her here," Evan replied.

"It has nothing to do with what you did, but it has everything to do with the way you went about it. You are playing games and with people's emotions." The captain stroked his jaw. "Connor likes the woman."

Evan laughed. "Boss, I saw someone in the garage earlier. Some guy said he was looking around and was asking questions about that accident Ellie was in. I got the drift he was up to no good. Real big fella."

"Thanks, Parker."

The engine truck and crew waited inside watching the exchange before Bill and Garcia jumped out to direct the rig into position. Parker was getting a serious ass chomping.

Jax turned the engine off, and both Connor and Jax stood by the rig, watching the situation unfold. Connor pulled out of his boots and rolled his bunker gear down. "I was thinking about something from earlier," he said to his cousin. He took his helmet off and placed it on the hook. "How does Evan even know Ellie? He wasn't at the station or on our call. He wasn't even working here yet."

Jax slowly shook his head, continuing to eye the cap chewing out the newbie "I don't know, but this isn't cool. We need to have trust around here, so I'm keeping an eye on the beach-boy. Keep your head clear, because I smell a rat. And watch your back. He probably overheard some conversation about her, which means he has his nose in our private affairs."

Evan stepped up closer to the captain. "I was going over some duties when you guys were gone, and it looks like no one's checked the dive bus and equipment." Evan held the clip-boarded checklist before he showed it to his boss.

"You've been awfully busy."

Jax and Connor rounded the truck as their shit-kickers pounded the concrete. "We checked it before we left... with a microscopic eye as we always do," Connor defended.

"Every tank and hose-line were checked or replaced," Jax interjected. "We haven't used the equipment in a few shifts. It's actually the second time we've inspected everything."

"If you did, what's this?" Evan lifted the leading hose from the CO2 tank, bending it between his thumbs, opening a huge gouge.

Jax bolted forward, and Connor held him back. "Do you actually think we would risk our own lives? We are the damn divers breathing through the lines for air underwater."

"Honeycutt, Winslow, my office now," the Cap commanded, his thumb hitched toward his office.

"But Captain, we know our duties." Jax's face was beet red.

"Shut it, Honeycutt. And close the door behind you." The captain peered back in Evan's direction. "Parker, go clean the kitchen and then the toilets. In that specific order. When you're done with KP, get busy with the rest of your duties. You're behind for the shift."

Parker's forehead puckered as he stomped off.

CHAPTER 10

"*L*ina will be here soon. Are you coming with us tonight?" Ellie stood in the doorway of Jeffrey's office, waiting for him to look up from his computer. "I'm tired of being cooped up here. Lina only has this weekend off before her new job starts."

Jeffrey's eyes darted from to the screen then back to his sister. "I'm almost done with this email. Give me a second, and I'll drive."

Ellie checked the time on her mom's old Seiko. "Well hurry, I'm starving. I heard there's a new band playing at the bar on Lincoln. Lina said the food's delish, and this will be perfect for my *What's Eating Ellie* column."

"It will be great to see you doing what you do best—eat," Jeff teased. "But speaking of work…I'm really proud of what you do at the Solemn Creed Family Crisis Center. Mom and Dad would be so proud of you."

"I'm just doing what I can. You know I need them more than they need me." Silence filled the room with unspoken communication as Ellie weaved from side-to-side anxiously. "You're right about the food blog. I am starving, and I can try every dish.

Then post a review." Ellie's mouth watered in anticipation. "If I don't eat soon, my stomach will start a revolution."

Jeffrey looked up and down at Ellie's outfit. "Are you sure you're ready to go out?"

"I can't stay here another night. I keep replaying the accident in my head and then I start thinking about other things."

"You know, sis. I support you and I'll always be there for you. If you want to go out we will go out." Jeffrey winked at her. "Maybe a night out will lift everyone's spirits." He gave her a thumb's up. "But, you're not wearing that are you?" He crossed one arm over his chest the other palm up. "Your shirt's a little... shall I say... not covering enough."

"It's a halter style top, and it's covering everything except my arms. And the cast is covering half of one of those." She lifted her arm. "Geez. I'll bring a sweater if someone starts drooling over my shoulders." Ellie leaned over Jeff. "Love you, baby bro, but I think I'm old enough to know better and still young enough to have fun. Besides, you'll be there to give anyone the crusty look and scare them away." A horn honked in the distance. "Sounds like Lina's here."

Lina walked through the door. "I'm here and ready to p-a-r-t-y. Love your sassy top Ellie, love the teal on you." Her childhood friend squeezed her tight and sniffled. "I was so worried about you."

"I'm fine. Don't be a party-pooper."

She wiped a tear that had escaped. Lina's straight black hair fell to her mid-back. The emerald green of her one-shoulder top matched her eyes perfectly.

"I've missed you girl, how are you feeling? You look great. I was so worried when I couldn't reach you. I called Jeff, too. I can't believe you were in an accident. I flew back as soon as I got word. My job training was pretty intense.

Ellie hugged her best friend tight. "I'm so much better now you are here." Ellie went for a butter knife in the drawer to slide under her bright pink cast. "This thing is itching like crazy; I get it off in two weeks."

"Whoa sista', put the knife down and step back. I hope you know… I'm qualified in self- defense and I can carry a pistol now." Lina stood like Superwoman. "Can you bah-lieve I'm working for the city as a truancy officer? Best thing I've ever done."

Ellie set the knife on the counter and danced in a place like she was a contestant on You think you can dance. "I'm so proud of you." She high-fived her childhood friend. "I'm going cuckoo-for Coco Puffs staying home. Other than the shift earlier at the shelter taking calls at crisis hotline, I've been nowhere. My boss didn't think I should be with the women at the shelter because of my cuts and bruises." She looked away tracing the scar on her forehead. "Which reminds me—come on Jeff, I'm famished." Ellie checked her phone, new ID, and cash, tucking it all into her small clutch. "I really need a night out."

"Jeffrey told me you had company at the hospital." Lina tilted her head up inquisitively, her finger tapping against her chin. "Do tell."

"There's not much to tell. He came. He's hot."

Jeffrey entered the kitchen. "Ladies, your chauffeur is ready." He tossed the keys high into the air and caught them.

"I'm ready." Ellie straightened. Perfect timing to end the discussion about Connor.

"You're not off the hook for a second my friend." Lina pointed her finger at her best friend.

"What? Did I miss something?

"Never mind. Let's go." Ellie said.

Johnny's, right? I drive by it almost every day. Looks like a dive, though." Jeffrey twirled the keys around his finger waiting for a response, but Ellie just raised her head up and down. "Lead the way, ladies."

****

Johnny's was on full tilt, and the place was packed.

"Over there, at the back table." Cade motioned to the corner where Garcia, Jax, a few other guys from 56, and a handful of off-duty Denver's police were. The crowd was thick, which made finding a spot to sit dicey, but they got to a table in the back corner. Connor followed.

Connor could feel her presence before she appeared. His body changed every time he got anywhere near Ellie, heating up in seconds like a microwave. *Where was she?* His breathing became ragged, his blood rushed through his veins, and his mouth went dry. Connor felt more alive than he had in years. He was a drowning man, and she was his life force. He looked around the crowded room until his eyes locked onto her.

The waitress directed Jeffrey, Ellie, and another woman to a booth in the corner.

"Did you see her?" Cade asked.

"Yes, I did." Connor tracked her to the table.

"Not your Jane Doe, but the woman with her?" Cade shifted his jeans up, his posture straightening.

"I've never seen her before." He couldn't keep his eyes off of Ellie. She tripped on something and flew into the table, knocking the condiments over in front of her. Her brother righted her with concern. Ellie laughed. Even in the light of embarrassment, she beamed. She made clumsy look sexy.

"C, do us both a favor. Quit sitting on the sidelines and get in the game. You've been driving me crazy ever since you stopped going to the hospital." Cade pushed Connor forward. "I'll go with you for support, so you can introduce me to the looker with her."

Jax walked up and joined the conversation. "Parker's here and guess who he just spotted?" He pointed to the entrance.

Jax and Cade started pushing Connor from behind through the crowd, and he didn't resist. Jax left to try to distract Evan. Cade tugged at his arm, moving them toward Ellie's table.

He made it to where they sat just after the waitress delivered their drinks.

"Hi Ellie, how are you?" Cade plowed into Connor with another arm jab, this time in the ribs. He clenched his jaw trying not to be obvious at his last nerve.

Jeffrey stood with his outstretched hand. "Hey, Connor, what a small world. Do you come here much?"

Connor shook Jeffrey's hand. "We are part of the woodwork —kind of a department thing. We've been coming here most of our lives. We used to come here with our parents when we were teens, eating the colossal tenderloins and gigantor root beer floats the place is famous for."

"This is my brother, Cade." Connor introduced to the group.

Ellie and the other woman stared up at them from the booth. The dark-haired woman rolled her eyes, flicked her hair, and turned away. The men continued to talk as the friend kept her head turned to the opposite direction, only to turn occasionally and sneer at Cade. Connor could only stare at Ellie, as she did in return. Jeffrey took his cue, surveying Connor and Ellie in their stare down. He cleared his throat. "Does anyone need anything?" Then he got up and went over to the bar, where he joined Jax and Evan.

Ellie's friend stood up from the table, her arms wrapped tightly about herself, her back to Cade as he slowly approached her.

Connor waited a long time for a moment to be alone with Ellie, but before he could get a word out.

Ellie's girlfriend walked forward and jammed her finger into Cade's chest. Words amplified, grabbing everyone's attention. Cade stepped closer towering over her not to be intimidated.

Ellie got up and her and Connor approached the two. Her

friend shouted something like "Conan the Barbarian" and that Cade was a Neanderthal of some sorts. How could so much animosity happen in mere seconds? Cade was such a like-able guy. Connor and Ellie just watched stunned.

Cade sulked back with his hands up in defense mode. "Geez, Ice Princess, warm up a little. I didn't do anything."

"Maybe not, but guys like you are so full of themselves, and I have a boyfriend."

"You're seriously wound tight," Cade fired back.

"My boyfriend does just fine in the romance department, and if you must know… he's an accountant."

"Oh, I'm sorry. That explains everything. "

"You, Jethro hillbilly." The woman stomped her feet. "Argh," she roared. "Your brain is as small as a pea."

"What did I ever do?" Cade winced. What the hell crawled up your derriere? Stop attacking me. I don't even know you and sorry if I did something for you start calling me names. There's plenty of you around. Who don't find me so offensive. You must be on a power trip if you think you're God's gift to men."

"Don't flatter yourself." Lina's stance was total Power Ranger. Cade backed off from the woman and her serious attitude, mouthing the word "Ouch."

"I'll be back, if you don't mind," Connor whispered to Ellie. "I'll go see what's up and pick my brother's pride up off the floor." He ran a hand across Ellie's soft skin above her backless shirt. She laced her fingers through his.

"I'm coming along." They slid in between their two friends and separated them.

Ellie tucked the hair behind her ear and watched Connor as he walked away with Cade, his palm at the back of Cade's neck toward the bar where Jeffrey was.

"Are you okay?" Ellie asked her friend. "What was all that about?"

"Nothing really. He's harmless and oh, so, cute. I was testing a theory and using my training they suggested in class. I didn't do the role play good at all until I borrowed my inner bitch. I really hated doing this to the fire fighter's sidekick, but the instructors advised to go for the ego—or in his case, his libido—and don't back off. Go for the jugular."

"Apparently, it worked. You were heartless." Ellie stepped closer holding Lina's hand and whispered, "What did he say or do?"

"Absolutely nothing. I didn't give him a chance to. He looked like he was on the prowl, and I wanted to do a practical for homework." Lina bit at her acrylic pink and white nails. Lina shook her hair away and stood a little taller. "He was really cute and all, but a big-headed Boof, and I wasn't in the mood to be his latest conquest."

"Lina, seriously you shouldn't have been so cruel to him. I heard he's a cop and used to be military. Besides, he's Connor's brother."

"Oopsy, really? My bad." Lina shrugged as she looked in Cade's direction. "He's adorable."

"You didn't mean any of the names you were calling him, did you?" Ellie looked over to Cade who was crouched over the bar about to take a long pull of a tall dark liquid over ice. His eyes furrowed as he spit out his toothpick and straightened his posture.

"No." Lina tossed her hair over her shoulder as they took a seat back at their table. Lina looked up. A guy headed straight toward them. "Not again, Geez." Lina threw her napkin and began to slide off her seat.

Ellie grabbed Lina's hand to stop her. "Please wait, Lina, no need to crush this guy, too. Keep your claws and fangs in," Ellie said.

"Of course, I didn't mean any of it, but I'm trying really hard to have a gristly exterior for my new job. I'm just getting the hang of this robust side of me."

"You need to relax Cullen no more blood sucking." Ellie giggled. "I won't tell a soul you're really a softie."

"better not." Lina rolled her eyes.

Ellie took a sip of her margarita and melting peach Bellini then looked to the now cold quesadillas, buffalo wings, cheese sticks, wontons, and nachos she hadn't touched and there was more coming. *I'm starting to get Hangry.*

Evan slowly approached–*Am I ever going to get to eat with all this drama?*–but Jax intercepted him just in time. They blew by the table, but not before Ellie grabbed a few quesadillas and a cheese stick and ate them as her and Lina ran to the bathroom.

"Ellie, are you okay?" Lina looked under the stall." I'm not leaving until you come out and know you're not going to the bathroom because I see you just standing against the stall."

"This is all new to me, Lina. I don't like all this attention. All I wanted to do was get something to eat and spend time out of the house because I was going stir crazy." She blew her nose. "I'd rather be invisible, and I don't feel like dealing with any drama."

"Hey, I'm sorry, totally my fault. I didn't mean to upset you." Lina knocked on the door again. "Come on out, sounds like someone needs a hug." Ellie unlocked the door and exited. I almost died in that accident and someone rammed by vehicle causing it." She blew her nose again and flushed the toilet. "and to make things worse I can't stop thinking about Connor."

"Oh—my—god. You're shitting me. I didn't know that." Lina hugged her friend. "I can't believe it."

"For the life of me, I can't get this weird feeling about James."

"James was a prick, and I hope he's rotting for what he did to you." She squeezed her tighter. "You deserve someone who will treat you better. Taking the first step is always the most difficult, but hopefully, you can find the man of your dreams one day." Lina turned Ellie to the mirror and fluffed up her hair.

"I should say the same to you. Holding on to a relationship you are miserable in is a lame excuse," Ellie said.

"We are not talking about me."

"Lina, I'm not looking. I'm happy right now, except for the accident, and I certainly don't want another man who's in uniform or married to his job." Ellie stood in front of the mirror, smoothing down her hair, and frowned. "I just want to eat something and have some fun with you. We can dance the food off later, if I ever actually get to eat."

Ellie came out of the bathroom with her friend in tow, heading to their table. She sat down, her head lowered as her friend pushed food in front of her and stood guard. She looked like a cop with her arms crossed over her chest in defense.

"Eat up girl," Lina demanded.

Jeffrey moved to Ellie as Evan approached, but Ellie signaled him to halt. Evan asked her for a dance, but she denied his attempt. There was only one guy she wanted to dance with if she could only get past her fear.

As if on cue she saw Connor approach. Ellie rubbed her hands together then raised her non-casted hand. She leaned forward sitting at the edge of her seat. Her stomach fluttered along with her increased heartbeat. She became breathless as he stopped in front of her.

CHAPTER 11

*C*onnor's heart pounded against his sternum as he drew closer to Ellie.

"Hi, again. Ellie you have something..." He grabbed the napkin on the table and wiped the sour cream from her mouth. Every time he got near her he felt alive—more alive than he had in years.

Crimson spread across her cheeks. "Hey, I was saving some for later," she snorted.

He loved how she reddened when he was anywhere in her vicinity.

He wanted to say, "If I ever made you feel like you were a waste of time, you're not. No one else interests me." He was an epic failure at resisting her.

Ellie stood. Evan stepped closer and pulled Ellie closer.

*H*er mouth fell open and her posture stiffened. Connor wanted to punch his lights out before he said a word. Evan's meaty paws were on *mine. If he so much as touches her again, I swear I'm gonna pop his chicklets from* *his craw.* Connor stepped forward closer to Evan. He was glaring at him. Evan advanced closer.

Ellie held up a hand. "Chill the testosterone, guys!" Ellie wiggled in between Connor and Evan and pulled them back. Her voice shaky. "No fighting, please." She shuffled back a step. Jeffrey, Cade and Jax surrounded them.

The situation was not the way he wanted things to go down in front of her, but Connor wanted to wipe the shit-eating grin off of Evan's face. He was goading him and deliberately man-handling Ellie to get his hackles up, and Connor didn't like it one bit. Connor retreated. "I'm sorry Ellie. I wasn't going to hit him. I wouldn't waste my time, and I wouldn't do that in front of you."

She had to see who this loser was, he was definitely playing her to get to him.

Connor took another step and turned to her brother, and whispered, "Would it be okay with you if I could talk to Ellie? That is if you don't mind I stop by for a visit? "Is tomorrow good? Ellie and I need to talk, and this is not the time or the place."

"Absolutely, Winslow, but only if your intentions are for the right reasons."

"My intentions have never been so right."

Jeff beamed. "Better be."

First. I'd like to dance with her before I lose the chance. I'll be back and get your address."

Jeffrey nodded before Connor walked over to Ellie.

"Ellie, could I please have a dance?" He slowly reached for her hand and caressed it in his. "I'm sorry, please forgive for the confrontation with Evan." He eased her to the pock-marked, wooden dance floor. She followed with slow cautious movements. Her pink cast rested on his arm, the other stretched up around his neck. "I need to apologize for s much more."

"Apologize? What is with you men?" she said with careful words and a probing gaze. "Are you manstrating?"

"What did you just say?" Connor laughed at her unique way with words. Manstrating? Don't tell me I think I can guess."

"It's the truth just please don't go there again."

She looked down at her feet. "Apology accepted. You know you're putting yourself at great risk dancing with me." She bit her lip nervously. "I'll probably trip over my own feet, or step on your toes." Her cheeks warmed to a rosy hue. "I'm not kidding you."

"Don't worry. If you step on me, I'm covered. If you fall, we'll do it together." Her body relaxed, secured in his. He held her tighter. The closer they got, the less he knew where his body ended and hers began. Ellie simply fit, even if she was a lot shorter than he was.

The notion of dating scared the hell out of him. Sure, he'd had other women, but Ellie was different. She was more. With her the connection was so powerful and he wanted to explore a relationship, a future.

Her body moved closer, and he pushed her hair behind her shoulder, her wavy, soft tendrils ribboning through his fingers. She smelled of orange and vanilla and her skin was silky. He ran his fingertips across her shoulder and down her arm; goose bumps pebbled her skin.

Connor nuzzled closer, but hesitated. He gazed into Ellie's eyes. Her breath hitched, and he could feel the increased beat of her heart. She pulled him closer and ran her fingers through his bangs. He wanted to kiss her. He couldn't explain what she did to him and what turned him on, but all of his senses were in hyper-drive. He knew he would never be the same after day one with her or tonight.

The song ended with the audience clapping and people moving around them. They continued their slow, sensual movements on the dance floor. Connor bent down and gently kissed her soft lips. They swayed for moments after that kiss, but he didn't want to let her go. He moved closer and she looped her fingers into his belt loop. Yearning filled her eyes and his body responded. She tilted her neck welcoming his touch. He caressed her, planting kisses along her cheek, her neck, and those full fantastic lips. Time stopped as he closed his eyes and inhaled deep while his muscles laxed. He could stay right there wrapped forever in her arms. It was the first sensation of peace he felt in years.

CHAPTER 12

*C*onnor only had one stop to make on his way to Ellie's house, and it was to the nearby florist to do his visit right and proper this time. He pulled onto Highway 13, following the GPS system he had plugged into his Dodge Charge.

He identified exactly when he came upon the accident scene where they'd first met. The area was cleaned up, but the ground was torn up and remnants of the accident were still visible. The damaged landscape would take years to recover and that tree still stood but was permanently jacked up. Even though the car wasn't there anymore, he remembered every single detail. Every second was etched into his brain. Every moment with Ellie and the moment they met.

So much changed for him. A chance meeting unlike others he had responded to. Something in her first initial look spoke to him like she knew him in the deep recesses of his soul. Like she was the life raft saving him, something as simple as answering his prayers from before his parents' accident. He had purpose on a different level and he didn't feel so numb. The night terrors were fading. Connor knew what he had to do. And Ellie had to be in his life. With the app directions he comprehended that she didn't live far from the wreck at all. He was sick to his stomach just thinking of the horror she went through that night and the month-long recovery that followed from her injuries. Have the cops found anything else out about who could have run her off the road. Who would be so vile to run her off the road? There were eyewitness' and someone would have seen something.

Connor couldn't believe how his life had changed since he'd met Ellie and couldn't imagine her not being in it, a missing puzzle piece and they belonged together. The biggest hurdle was to convince her that he was worth the risk after walking away from her at the hospital. He was walking into unknown territory, and he could fail royally, but worth the risk.

His car tires crunched over the gravel road flanked by aspen and evergreen trees. The white house with green shutters sat nestled under several large silver maple trees with a big pond nearby. Ellie and Jeffrey's place were an updated version of Forrest Gump's house with a large wrap around porch that looked homey. A three-car garage and a barn sat in the back, and a full garden flourished near a small coop full of roosters and chickens.

There were a few trucks in the drive, and one Connor absolutely recognized. The annoying fucktard was here. Wasn't he supposed to be making up a shift?

Jeff paced the front porch glancing repeatedly toward the front door. He leaped down the stairs and came toward Connor when he pulled into the drive.

Jeffrey's jaw was hard set face was grim with compressed lips mumbling as he came to the window of Connor's car He leaned in. "Hey Connor, I don't know what's up with this guy, but he's in there with Ellie." He let out a loud breath. "I wouldn't leave them alone, but I heard you pull in. Evan said something about how she might have left an earring at the bar and he was returning it." Jeffrey ran his fingers over his stubbly chin, and then pulled the corners of his mustache.

"I recognized his truck." They walked up the steps and onto the porch, then Jeffrey said, "Come on in, I'll let Ellie know you're here."

Why was he here? Ellie thought. *Why does this guy keep showing up? I don't want him here. In my house.*

"Evan, why are you here again?"

"Ellie, this is a small town. Everyone knows everyone."

"But, Evan. I really don't know you." Ellie shifted from left to right foot. "I haven't even seen you other than the last week, and now you're everywhere." Alarm bells sounded in Ellie's gut, and she steadied her thudding pulse. She looked out the window and saw a big black truck. She closed her eyes and breathed deeply trying to calm her panic. Why did everyone drive trucks around here?

"I found an earring last night and thought it was yours; it looked like it could be special."

Ellie touched her earlobe. "No, I still have the ones I wore last night, but thank you." What does this guy want? He got some nerve. Why can't he be more like Connor?

Connor entered the house. The open space was large and the ceilings were high with old exposed beams and pillars. He loved the old charm and character of all the wood, not like the fabricated houses they made these days. The wooden floors creaked under his feet. The large stone fireplace took up half a wall and gave the space a warm charm. Ellie stood within a few feet of the front door, her body closed with her arms wrapped tightly around her midsection. Evan had a fixed stare and he sucked his cheeks sucked in and was a little too close to Ellie.

Back off dingle-hopper.

"Small world huh, dude?" He snorted with a dismissive laughter.

"I've seen you more out of work than at work lately." Connor inched closer. "What is it you do for a living? Don't you have a shift you're late for? I swear I saw you on the schedule."

"What's it to ya, Winslow? You're not my boss." He stepped away, moving slowly toward the door. "I was just leaving anyway."

"Actually, I do outrank you." Connor evened the distance again. "Why are you here?"

"I could ask you the same thing."

"I was invited by him." He pointed to Jeffrey.

"You better leave." Jeffrey said.

Ellie positioned herself between them. "Wait a minute you guys. Please stop it." She squeezed her eyes shut and rubbed her temples. "I don't know what your problem is, but if it has anything to do with me, I don't belong to either of you. I'm not anyone's property."

"Speaking of real estate, Evan," Jeffrey said, hitching a thumb toward the door. "I think you have worn out your welcome and this is my house. I think you'd better leave."

Parker clenched his jaw but softened it when he turned to Ellie and gave her a wink. "See you later, Ellie." Then he huffed out the door.

Connor stepped forward, acting like a barrier between Evan and Ellie. "I'm sorry, Ellie. I just keep running into this guy, and I don't get it," he whispered through gritted teeth.

Ellie trembled for a moment. "I'm starting to get uncomfortable. I don't really know him. Connor, you probably know him better since you work with him."

"Not really. He's only been at the station for a few weeks. I don't know him at all, other than he didn't like me from our first encounter. What I don't get is why he went to the hospital to see you on our behalf when he wasn't even a part of the squad at the time of your accident." Connor scratched his head.

Ellie looked to her brother in a way Connor couldn't put his finger on.

"Why are you here, Connor?" She peered deep into his soul as she questioned him.

"I invited him El, and I think it's time you two sorted out what's going on here. Jeffrey touched his sister gently and kissed her on the forehead. "I'm heading out for a bit. Call me if you need me." He held up his fingers in a wave without turning back.

"These are for you." Connor handed her the bouquet of sunflowers, coral Gerber daisies, scarlet roses, lavender, and stargazer lilies. The bright bouquet failed in comparison to her beauty. "I hope you like them; the florist hand-picked them for me."

She smiled. "They're perfect. I'll get a vase and some water for them." She dipped her nose deep into the bunch. "They smell like a garden. I love them."

Connor heard cabinets open and water running, then smelled the faint odor of something burning. A cloud of smoke rolled out of the room. He leaned around the corner to a huge kitchen with canary yellow walls and floor-to-ceiling white cabinets. A small round table and chairs were nestled near a sliding glass door attached was a wooden deck with the view of a pond full of geese and mallards. The property went as far as the eye could see. The morning sun filtered behind checkered blue and yellow curtains. Smoke billowed from the oven onto the four-burner stainless steel stove.

The blaring high-pitched shriek of the fire alarm filled the house. Ellie screamed as she hurried to the stove. "Ellie, what's burning?" Connor took hold of her. "I got it. Stand back." He flipped the switch to off. "Do you have a fire extinguisher?"

"Right there." She pointed to the wall with a shaky finger. "The thing gets used more than I care to admit," she yelled. "Crap, my casserole. I wanted to make an egg dish I saw on the food network channel. I guess...I forgot it. Figures. The show was about worst cooks ever." Ellie's pout was filled with disappointment as she plugged her ears to muffle the high pitch of the fire alarm.

Connor grabbed the hot pads on the counter, opened the door to the oven, and pulled the charred, shriveled remains of her attempt out. "Open the door, we'd better get this outside, and maybe we can clear the air, in a matter of speaking." Connor set the smoking dish on the wrought iron table outside and planned to dismantle the alarm.

Once back inside, he yelled over the noise and pulled a chair under the alarm. He reached up and removed the batteries. Ellie went to the sliding glass door, swooshing the smoke away with a towel.

"I can't even boil water, so it's useless." She coughed and continued to yell over the alarm at is silenced. She snorted. "Oh, my god I'm such a Lucy."

She seriously had no clue how breath-taking she was. She was perfectly—imperfect. Yes, she is the one. Most women take themselves so seriously, she on the other hand isn't afraid to laugh at herself. Connor didn't care if she couldn't cook, because he excelled in the art of making food and putting out kitchen fires, and he would gladly do anything for her.

"I like you, Ellie," he blurted, and her eyes widened. "I 'm an idiot. I'm sorry I bailed on you at the hospital."

Ellie's mouth momentarily unhinged. She didn't move from her spot near the sliding glass door. Connor jumped off the chair, erasing the distance between them. The air around them was suctioned up by their intense charge.

"I thought you were married. When I found out, my ego got bruised. I've never pursued a woman or a patient I treated from any accident—ever." He ran his hands along her soft skin. "It creeped me out a little, that I was so upset you were taken and I'm not proud of it." Connor's eyes burned from the haze.

She coughed again and placed the blue and yellow checked towel over her mouth. "Connor." Smoke filled the air.

Connor pulled Ellie out beyond the screened door to the patio. A quaint gazebo covered an antique round table and chairs of distressed white rod iron.

"Now we can actually breathe. Are you okay?"

She nodded.

"Take a few deep breaths to make sure."

She inhaled the fresh air and gave a thumbs up.

"Please hear me out. I have to say this." *I'm about to sound like a wussy, but here it goes.* "I've never felt this way before, about anyone and I didn't know what to do." He had to touch the smooth plane of her hands. "I can't take it anymore—I mean, being without you." *Way to go, you silver-tongued Valentino.* "Shit, I'm not good with this." He wanted to rip his hair out. His palms were sweaty, and his heart throttled so much he swore it skipped several beats. "The day of your accident... the day we met changed me, and no matter how hard I try, I can't stop thinking about you." Connor swore the temperature around them went up another thirty degrees. "I don't want to share you with anyone, Ellie."

He bottled up his breaths to try and calm down, and anxiously waited for her to respond.

"What do you mean share?" Her hand moved the cloth away from her face. Her eyes narrowed. "I don't understand. Share? With whom?"

"I know you've been seeing Evan." He grappled with what to say next. "I want you, Ellie, and I want you to only want me." He caressed her small hands with an iron grip. There it was... the elephant in the room. He did it—put it all out there. *Now, what?*

"I'm not dating Evan." She hesitated "I've seen him out, and he drove out here and escorted us to the station, but I don't know him—really." She crossed her arms over her small waist. "Didn't your captain tell Evan to check up on me?" Her eyebrows crinkled at the corners, and her brows furrowed.

"He didn't even work at the station when you were in the accident." The look on her face was pure panic as she started to tremble.

"What?" Her lip quivered.

Connor soothed her and made light of the situation. *Nothing. Other than the guy's trouble.* "I didn't mean to scare you, Ellie. I'm not wasting another minute thinking about the pipsqueak, if he's not in the picture." He stepped closer and moved her hair away from her face. "I don't like the fact that every time I turn around he's lurking around you like a creeper."

Ellie pulled Connor inside the kitchen again, closing the patio door partially. She stopped, looked up at him, and stepped closer. "So, are you going to kiss me, or do you want to keep talking?" Her hands went to Connor's hips, and she bit her bottom lip. Her irises dilated, and cheeks flushed.

She had a sultry look painted on her face, and Connor couldn't hold back anymore; he was so hungry for her. He had to touch her, feel her in his arms. He picked her up as she wrapped her legs around him. He pinned her against the wall, and she melted into him.

The kiss was weeks of frustration encapsulated in this very moment. It wasn't as soft as their previous kiss on the dance floor at Johnny's. She tasted of cherry vanilla candy. Connor wanted her, but he held back because he was afraid he would hurt her. She was still so fragile. Ellie unleashed a part of him he'd never experienced. His skin buzzed and was hyper-aware of everything. What was numb before was now in sensory overload.

Connor lost himself in the moment as his tongue entered her mouth. She was so damn hot as she moved against him, and he wanted more of her.

He wanted to rip Ellie's clothes off and be inside her. He pushed his erection against her center. She was molten hot. His zipper and his dick fought for dominance. The heat of her core pressed against him again as she moaned.

His sensible reasoning ruled out, but he didn't want to blow this thing. Connor attempted to set her down, but her legs locked tighter around his backside. Her arms squeezed firmer around his neck, and her kiss deepened. His hands slipped over her breast and the thin layer of her top. He had to pull away or he was going to be inside her against the wall. All he had to do was rip off her panties under her loose skirt. He had to control himself, so he pulled away.

"What's going on? Why did you stop?" She bit his lip as her hands ran through his hair.

He caught his breath. *Breathe dude, get a grip. Concentrate.*

"You deserve better than this." He looked around at the kitchen and tapped the wall she was pressed against and with the back of his hand. Connor tilted his forehead to hers. "I don't want to fuck this up. I want it to be right, and I need to know everything about you." He ran lazy circles over her jaw and down her neck. "Don't get me wrong, I want you so damn bad, my knees are weaker than shit, and I'm suffering a slow death right now. I'm about to take you down on the floor, woman."

She nuzzled closer, her breasts pressed firmly against his chest. "We are adults, Connor. I think we both want the same thing." Her lips pecked the tip of his nose. He held her against the wall and started kissing her neck.

"I'm not sure if you have any idea of what I want to do to you." Connor heard her stomach grumble. He paused. "We will have to wait; you're going to need the energy. Let me cook something for you." Her eyes lit up. He wasn't sure if she craved him or the food he mentioned. He closed his eyes and focused on controlling his breathing

"I guess you came at the right time. You saved my kitchen from a fire and my house from burning down and me from smoke inhalation, and I get a meal out of it."

"I do know mouth-to-mouth." His brows waggled up and down. "Food first." He walked her over to a nearby chair and eased her down.

"Looks like I'm the real winner here." Ellie laughed.

CHAPTER 13

"*I*'m seriously in heaven." The gold flecks in Ellie's eyes sparkled. "I burn water. And it's happened more than you would ever believe. Jeff's going to kill me. After the last time he had to get out the extinguisher, he said the kitchen is off limits for me, but I'm trying to learn to cook, but it usually doesn't work out so great as you can see." She pointed to several extinguisher's around the kitchen. "We have several just in case, just so you know." She shrugged and bit at her thumbnail.

Connor wanted to be her thumb so badly. "Good thing I'm pretty handy in the kitchen." He grabbed Ellie and kissed her, heart beating faster as her nipples pebbled against his chest. She tasted of honey and heaven, her skin scorching hot under his touch. Connor cupped her breast, outlining the peak under her silky camisole.

"I'll say," she breathed. Her rosy blush spread to scarlet. Blotches on her chest rose up her neck.

The last thing Connor wanted to do was let her go. He needed to calm the rigid boner down in his pants that needed release. He set her down on the floor holding her close. The smoke lingered in the air, but most had rolled out the patio door. He turned to start the vent on high above the stove. Connor focused on feeding her and had to concentrate, or he was going to pick her up, throw her over his shoulder, deposit her on her bed, then lock the door and not leave her bedroom for days. Unfortunately, she lived with her brother.

Focus... He ached between his legs to the point he'd rather sit down and give his bits some space than cook. He was about to lose circulation from the waist down, his balance was wobbly and he was light headed. He needed to think of something else or he'd go all hallmark.

"You don't have to do this." Ellie moved closer. Her stomach rumbled again.

"Oh, hell yeah I do." He wanted to feed her and take care of her.

"Knock, knock." Jeffrey yelled through the screen. "I was mowing the field when I saw smoke coming out of the house." Jeffrey walked slowly into the kitchen. "Was that the smoke detector, again? Hello? Ellie, please tell me you weren't burning, I mean cooking."

Her mouth did a silent, "Oh shit."

Her eyes hooded. She looked down at the ground, fidgeting with her hands and tugged down her tank top. Connor stepped farther back with his hands in his front pockets.

Dammit. Another few minutes and Jeffrey would have had something to really bitch about—he would have had quite the peep show. Connor walked to the refrigerator. "So, let me see what you got in here." He bent deep inside the cold air. "I can make something out of nothing. Do you mind if I make you two breakfast?"

"Are you any better at cooking than Ellie?" Jeffrey questioned. He rocked back and forth from toe to heel.

He was all tongue tangled. "I've got it covered. I cook all the time, and I'm not bad at it." There were a couple of eggs, onions, a little half-and-half, and a medley of ham and other stuff.

Looking around, he found avocado and tomatoes in a bowl on the counter. Connor beat the eggs, pouring the half-and-half for an omelet. He opened the bread in the plastic sleeve and emptied the last four pieces into the toaster.

Ellie went to the cupboards to set the table for three. "How did you learn to cook? Obviously, it isn't my thing." She smiled. "But, I love to eat more than anything."

Jeffrey chuckled. "We order out as much as possible. Or we eat a lot of peanut butter sandwiches. She does have PB&J's down pretty good, but with her food blog we get to try all sorts of restaurants." He refilled his cup of coffee. "Shall I make another pot?"

Connor and Ellie shook their heads in unison.

"I think I need something cold," Ellie responded.

"Something to cool off sounds great." Connor smirked in her direction. "A food blogs? Sounds like an awesome gig."

Ellie fanned herself with a canary yellow towel. "Is orange juice okay?"

"Absolutely," he said.

"The blog is a side-gig to my day job. Solemn Creed News hired me knowing I don't cook, and the fact that I get to eat is the real reason I do the job. I'm most passionate about my work at a woman's shelter and crisis hotline."

"She's great as a counselor there. They're lucky to have her," Jeffrey added.

"More like I'm lucky to have them. I need them more than they need me." Ellie pushed the hair around her ear and fidgeted in her chair at the table. "I love my job. I'm better at it than cooking." Ellie laughed.

"You should check out the freezer. There's tons of macaroni, spaghetti, and pizza rolls. Ellie eats all processed crap and doesn't gain a pound." Jeffrey pointed out. "I eat it and..." He grabbed his midsection and patted it.

Connor loved the sibling banter. It reminded himself of

Cade and their relationship. "Take it from me, most fires start in the kitchen. Listen to your brother; he's a smart man." He turned to Ellie waving the spatula.

Jeffrey taunted his sister. "See? Just what I told you, El. Connor's a smart man. You need to listen to him."

Ellie just rolled her eyes. "Whatever."

"I cook a lot at the station." He turned back to the burner, moving the spatula lazily around the pan sautéing the vegetables. "We all take turns. There are, usually, about eight of us there on each shift — some on the ladder trucks, and my team on the engine." His thoughts went back to Jeffrey getting an eyeful if he had come in ten minutes earlier. He looked to Ellie, and he chomped down on his lower lip. He could still taste her cherry vanilla lip gloss.

Jeffrey cleared his throat. "You were saying, Connor?"

"Oh yeah. We raise money for our fallen first responder's brothers, sisters, and their families. We also raise money for their spouses and children's education. Our fundraising event is this weekend, and I'd love it if you'd come and support the cause. We have an award ceremony for the firefighter of the year first, but the rest should be fun. This year we went with a carnival theme with all the works and games, bumper cars, and even a Ferris wheel." Connor pulled the skillet off the burner. "Besides, I was hoping for another chance to see you, Ellie."

"Sounds like fun." Ellie's bright smile gleamed. "Yay, I love the Ferris wheel... And the food. Wow, what a great cause, and we can eat hot dogs, funnel cakes, and cotton candy. Oh, I can't wait!"

"Geez, all you have to do is mention food, and look..." Jeffrey pointed in jest to his sister.

"Grrr." She growled at her brother, but her eyes crinkled at the corners.

Damn, Connor liked this woman—a lot. *Wait until she finds about the kissing booth.*

Ellie ran her fingers over her still tender forehead as she answered the phone at the crisis center. "Solemn Creed Crisis hotline, how may I help you?" She heard deep breathing on the other end and waited for an answer. "Hello, how can I direct your call?" The stitches had dissolved, and her skin under her fluorescent cast itched like crazy.

"Bitch, I know it's you." The callers breathing was erratic as he yelled.

"Excuse me?" she asked.

"I know it's you, and the next time I run you off the road, I'll make sure you don't come out of it alive."

She had an inability to speak but wanted to scream. Her limbs shook. Images of the accident flashed through her mind. She couldn't wrap her head around someone actually running her off the road. The big mean truck ramming the back bumper, not once, but again and again. Why hadn't the police found anything? It was not a figment of her imagination; the attempt was real. Why would anyone try to harm her?

Adrenaline spiked through her and her heart raced nearly exploding. She wanted to flee or hide. "I don't know who this is, but this is not funny." Her eyes darted around the room and behind her.

"I'll be waiting."

The call ended. She had a skewed sense of time and jerked up, but her legs froze…Rooted in one spot.

She darted to her boss. "Someone just threatened me. He said he ran me off the road."

Her boss Harold, replayed the call and tried to put a trace on it, but it was from a blocked number. "I'll call the police."

Ellie flinched and grabbed on to the nearest chair. She had never done anything hurtful to anyone except in self-defense, and only when her life was in jeopardy. Visions of James flooded her. That was a lifetime ago, and he was long gone. She only wanted to help people and do right for those who were put in the same position she'd been in. Why was it so hard for her to get past all the hurt, and why was it so hard to trust anyone? Why couldn't she close the past and lock the door and throw away the key forever? She wanted so much to fall in love.

Connor punched the button on his cell phone and got his boss's voicemail. "Hey, Cap. I just got a call from the Battalion Chief's office today. They want to see me, ASAP. Do you think they're calling for a mandatory psych session? Can you call me back, please?"

Hours passed as Connor fidgeted with the spark plugs on his ATV. He jolted to a loud rap at the outside wall of the garage.

"Knock, knock," the cap said.

"What's going on, Cap? Your visit must be something substantial if you came all the way out here on your day off." Connor wiped the grease from his hands with a red rag and threw it aside.

Dan came inside the garage. "Hey, whatcha got there?" He pointed to the torn apart engine. "Taking it out for a run?"

"Nah, I haven't taken it out in ages, but I thought we could use another at the mountain house."

"Awesome. Janet and I wish you'd come up more often. We used to have so much fun with the family."

"I was thinking maybe since Cade's returned I might try. Or head up there with someone."

"You don't say." Dan's demeanor was calm, but the spark in his eyes expressed interest. "Well, well, well... and good for you. Does this have anything to do with our lovely accident victim you been drooling over?"

"A little premature." Connor felt the captain's cool stare

dragging over him as he dodged the topic. "Cap, do you know anything about what the head honchos are calling me into their office about?" Connor looked at the time on his phone after pulling it from his back pocket. "I'm heading in there in about an hour. It would be nice to have a heads up. I already made an appointment with the counselor for next Friday."

"From what I hear, the meeting doesn't have anything to do with what you think." The captain walked over to the ATV and scratched the paint with his thumb. "There's been a complaint, but that's all I know. Other than that, it has nothing to do with any of our calls. All the paperwork is up to snuff." Dan wiped his nose with the back of his hand. "It's probably some small stuff, which should be handled on my level and not over my head. It makes us all look like pansy asses going to momma about who loaded the dishwasher or who ate all the ranch dressing."

"You didn't go to anyone about our conversation a few weeks back?" Connor pushed further.

"No, you mean the one where I told you time and time again to go back to the squad counselor? Nope, I didn't. I knew we could handle it, and that you would do the right thing. You always do." He patted Connor hard enough to knock him into the old etched leather seat of his ATV. He almost choked and swallowed his gum.

"You're straight up Winslow like your pa was." He winked. "I'm not worried, but it's protocol. If any situations arise, they need to be addressed sooner versus later."

"I'll take care of it. You can count on it."

"Not a doubt, son." He waved his key fob in the air. Without turning back, he exited the garage. "I know, but 'd feel a 100 percent if you took care of the counselor thing too."

Connors phone rang, it was Ellie. "Hey, you."

"Connor," Ellie wailed. "I need your help."

"I'll be right there." he said as he grabbed his keys and ran out of his garage.

"Tell me what he said" Connor asked as he looked at his brother Cade then to her as he lightly stroked her forearm. "It's okay." He gave her an understanding nod.

She covered her face with her hands "I don't understand." She fought to catch her breath.

"Ellie, tell me everything you remember about the phone call." He brought her a box of tissue.

"It was horrible and he said he wouldn't miss the next time." Her chin trembled.

Connor held her close and covered his ears before carving his hair holding it back and then releasing it from his grasp. "Who is it?" he pressed his temples.

"I have enough information from the call center, Ellie You should get some rest. I'll let you know when we find something out." Cade reached for his jacket as Connor followed.

"Is that it?" Connor asked.

"That's all we can do right now. Trust me I will do everything I can to get to the bottom of this. Cade reached for his brother. "I promise."

Connor embraced his brother and looked downward." Please."

"I got you, bro. I won't let you down." He nodded.

Connor turned and released an appreciative sigh before returning to Ellie's side.

CHAPTER 14

*E*llie looped her arm around her brother's, lifted her sunglasses, and looked around. She moved about unable to say still. The rural park near the old brick-paved streets of Lizbeth, Colorado, the sister community near Solemn Creed was adorned with fresh flowers. Old trees were lit up with clear lights, and the stage was set for the Scottish bagpipes around the gazebo. The Colorado First Responders of the Year Awards Ceremony was soon to be underway in the center of town. "Come on. Look." She raised u and bounced on her tiptoes." The carnival workers rigged the beer tents and assembled the rides. Volunteer firefighters and first responders from all over Douglas County were setting up booths for various games of ring toss and knock the wooden milk bottles over. An ample amount of teal colored port a-potties lined the street near the beer garden and music stage.

Ellie screeched in a throaty laughter. "Wow." Big pink, fuzzy bears and odd colored serpents were hoisted on makeshift walls of peg board and balloons were blown up for a game of darts. The annual event had everything from a kissing booth to face painting for the kiddos. "Oh, my, I have died and gone to heaven." Ellie moved closer to erase the distance. "Baby bro. I'm hungry." Cotton candy, syrupy snow cones, funnel cake stands, to turkey legs roasting in massive barbecue cookers were a thrill to the senses. There were museum quality fire trucks of past days and shiny new ones, each flanked the perimeter with ladders raised high with the Colorado state flag, and America's stars and stripes.

"Come on sis, this is what we both need today. I'm buying. We need a day to forget it all and stuff our gullet." Jeff gathered his sister in for a big hug.

Connor took in the view with pride. The months of preparation had finally come to fruition, and half of the event's proceeds were donated by the firefighters themselves or private donations from the community. The new event was so out of the box from the normal raffles, auctions, and golf tournaments, that it had to be a success. Four city blocks were barricaded with the local police and volunteer security.

"Go big or go home. You've done well." Cade raised his arms to the heavens. "This is going to top all your events."

"I hope so, and now that you're home to see it, I won't have to send you photos." Connor gave Cade a high-five. "I've done all I can, and Bill has been driving me crazy with the checklist." Connor dragged a pencil to rest above his ear.

"Did everything smooth over after your meeting?" Cade asked as he and Connor walked across the park.

"Yeah, someone at the station house said I'm shirking my duties. Showing favoritism, and even said some particulars that hit too close to home. I know we have a mole inside. I wish they would just be man enough, or woman enough, to come to me if they felt like I wasn't doing my job. You know how serious I take this shit. I have big boots to fill."

"Yeah, Dad never let anything slide. He was always by the book," Cade added.

"Not a complaint in years and then two inside of a month. I got a feeling I know who it is."

"The newbie transfers?"

"Yeah, but I was told not to talk about it at the station. This all started shortly after he arrived. The cap told me someone's probably got their Hanes in a wad."

"You didn't get written up, did you?" Cade cocked his head and arched a brow.

"No, but they said they wouldn't hesitate if the behavior keeps up. The whole team has to go to some sensitivity training. The Battalion Chief wouldn't go into particulars, but they're taking this seriously. We've never had an issue until Evan Parker showed up with his southern tan and ultra-big ego."

"Yeah, I don't trust the guy. I'm going to see what I can find about him." Cade said with stilted speech as he gripped one of his wrists.

"Let's not waste another second talking about the chump." Connor complained under his breath.

"Okay, but I'm still checking his background out. Now let's go have some fun. I'm heading to the kissing booth or the beer tent, and I'm not sure in what order yet." Cade winked and rubbed his palms together as he crossed the park. "I'll see you for the awards ceremony."

The new Fire Chief, Avery Jensen, presented the Thomas Winslow Overall Achievement Award under the gazebo Hundreds of first responders and their families filled the park, along with the nearby communities and small towns across the foothills. She tapped the microphone and cleared her throat to project her mellow voice. A dozen fine men and woman were called to the stage.

Connor surveyed the crowd from left to right to find Ellie. Her hair was draped in a side ponytail over her shoulder, and her black cat eye sunglasses covered her eyes. A red checkered spaghetti string top, cut off jean shorts, and white sneakers understated her prettiness. Connor clasped his hands to his heart. Even the balloon art hat the clowns made with a green palm tree, fishing rod, and blue fish hanging off her head didn't deter from her innocence or unique splendor She was drop dead gorgeous, and she had him.

His quick movements drew him near as heat radiated through his chest. His mind went to wishing he was the cotton candy until he heard his name being called over the loud-speaker. Jax and Cade whooped it up and pushed him forward.

Connor squirmed, wanting to disappear, but instead he made his way to the stage with the other recipients awarded with dark wooden plaques and personalized brass engravings. He didn't deserve this honor, especially one with his father's name on it. His mouth was dry, and the blood drained from his face. He could feel the sweat bead on his upper lip. The Thomas Winslow Overall Achievement Award presented was for first responders who supported the community. Bill and Connor spear-headed today's fundraiser, so it was only fitting they received acknowledgment. Except, he knew he didn't measure up to such an honor. He fell short years ago when it mattered most. The volume of the crowd elevated as he walked on the stage. He heard Winslow being chanted. He was an imposter.

Bill Fletcher raised his plaque over his head as if he'd just conquered Mt. Everest. The crowd cheered for the firefighters and first responders for their honor

Connor cringed, but thought long and hard about the name behind the award. His father, Thomas Winslow. His role model and the man he couldn't save when it counted. Did he really deserve the reward of this prestigious acknowledgment? He just wanted off this stage. *I don't deserve this award.* He hesitated and shrugged before pursing his lips. He had to get closer to her and get away from the award ceremony.

Ellie and her brother moved farther into the sea of people. Connor exited the stage, then made his way through the hand-shakes, way-to-go's, and pats on the back. He jogged across the park until he finally spotted her. She and Jeff sat on a picnic bench, eating funnel cakes. Ellie's lips were pink from the cotton candy, and her face was dusted with powdered sugar. He wanted to lick the sticky sweet stuff off of her. Dammit, anytime he got near the woman he got an instant hard-on. Puberty was never this bad. He couldn't control the damn thing when he was around her.

Cade and Jax came up from behind him to join in. Jeffrey and the guys did a knuckle bump.

"You came?" Connor said.

"This is so much fun. I feel like a kid again. Have I mentioned how much I love the food?" Ellie said.

"Obviously, Ellie." Jeffrey rolled his eyes at his sister. "I think you have more *on* you than *in* you, and that's hard to manage."

"Hey, a girl needs to eat right?" She stood, poured bottled water on a napkin, and wiped her hands off. She brushed the white powder off her shorts, her shirt, and then her face.

Connor watched her every movement. "Hey, you missed some." He brushed at her chin as his touch lingered on her skin. She gazed up at him innocently.

"Well, I think this is our cue to go get a brew," Jax chimed in. "All of us are off the clock, let's have some fun."

"Let's get 'er done, dude," Cade echoed.

"I think I'll join you guys." Jeffrey cleared his throat, bouncing his stare to Ellie then back to Connor.

Thank God. Connor had to be alone with her or he'd explode. "I remember you said you like the Ferris wheel, right?" he asked.

"I love it."

He slowly took her hand and laced it through his. "Later

Gators," he said to the guys. "Have fun and remember… spend your money—and lots of it—for the cause."

Jeffrey nodded with his over-protective stare. "Will do."

"I'll take good care of her," Connor said.

"Counting on it, Winslow."

Connor savored the slow shuffle, hand in hand with Ellie as they waited for their turn in line for the Ferris wheel. Her eyes glowed with excitement as she looked up at the ride. He handed the carnival worker the tickets and helped Ellie into the seat when it swayed, then jumped in beside her. The attendant clicked the safety bar in place, and they swung back and forth. The Ferris wheel slowly turned as the rest of the seats were filled.

"Dammit Ellie, I can't take it anymore." He reached for her mouth, and she responded with as much hunger as Connor did.

"It's about time." She bit his lip, easing closer. The seat rocked as her eyes darted opened, and she suddenly giggled.

Cupping her breast, he slid his tongue into her mouth. He could taste the sweetness of her and the cotton candy still sticky on her lips. "What if we get stuck together?" He ran his tongue along the outline of her lips. This girl was undoing him fiber by fiber, but instead of fraying, he felt alive, protective, and stronger with her.

As the ride started to pick up, the wind floated through her hair. Her laugh was infectious. She raised her arms in the air as if she were flying. Connor couldn't get enough. Life illuminated out of her, and she carried this unexplainable zest for everything. This had been missing in his own life for so long. A slow smile built as he leaned forward. He simply wanted only her and nothing was going to stop him, whether he deserved her or not. He held in breath and trembled.

"What's wrong?" she asked after a moment. "Aren't you having fun?"

He leaned in again and stretched his arm around her. "Oh,

hell yeah." He kissed her forehead as the ride came to a stop. "I'm really happy you 're here.

The two exited the platform and retreated down the stairs. They slowly rounded the corner ending behind the nearest shed where Connor pulled her close and kissed her. She jumped up onto him like she belonged there. Her legs wrapped around him, and she latched her sneakers at his backside. He pressed her against the old wooden building, blocking them from the crowd. She was fire and he was ice, and they melted together.

He nuzzled into her neck, feeling slightly breathless. "The things I want to do to you, woman…You have no idea," he whispered in her ear as he bit her lobe.

"I'd like to find out," she panted.

"We need time alone. We need to get to know each better. I have property in the mountains." He pulled away, trying to read her as he smoothed the hair that had come free of her ponytail. "I'd like to take you there. Can you get away for a few days?"

"Just us?" she whispered as she licked and sucked at Connor's neck. "Um… Alone?"

Connors skin flushed, breath quickened his lips parted and a slow smile builds. He mirrored her movements with a lingering touch. Desire. A desire so strong.

She looked up. "You're setting fireworks off, Connor. Seriously. I'm seeing fireworks."

Another explosion of bright pink filtered through the air. The fireworks looked like the branches of a weeping willow tree. A loud boom followed and then another above their heads. Ellie jerked back to see a sky full of explosive colors. Her eyes filled with wonderment, like a child seeing the beauty for the first time. She oohed and ahhed through each explosion. Her excitement brought back a Fourth of July memory when Connor had helped his father with all the pyrotechnics for the fireworks every year. He'd loved working with this dad.

"Where were we?" She wrapped her body tighter into his.

Her hands soothed his disheveled hair back. "God, you are beautiful." She ran fingers lightly over his eyebrows and looked deeply into Connor's eyes. "Your eyes are a unique color. Sometimes they are a stormy gray and other times they almost look blue. Like today, in your blue shirt, you are like a chameleon." She ran her forefinger along his cheekbones and chin. "Have you ever modeled?" Ellie cupped his face. "I think you should."

"Sort of."

"What do you mean?"

"Calendar stuff for charities." Connor winced.

"OMG, I knew it. You *are* on the firefighter calendars for the children's hospital." Ellie wrapped her arms closer around his shoulders. She repositioned her casted arm as it teetered on his shoulder. "That's where I've seen you. The call center where I work bought everyone a copy to put at our stations." Ellie eased back and outlined his full lips. "Can I have your autograph?" She batted her lashes and a smirk covered her mouth.

He laughed. "Let's change the subject. I'd rather talk about you."

"Psssh… What month were you?" she whispered. "I'm so getting you to sign my copy. I've never been so close to a celebrity." She held back a laugh but failed miserably and ended up making a weird noise instead.

"Back to our discussion about getting away together…" He pushed into Ellie, caging her against the wooden shed. His breathing hitched. "I don't think I can take this any longer. I'm aching for you, and I need to be inside you."

Her face and chest blotched crimson. "I think I can arrange it. When? Tonight?"

"I'm working tomorrow. How about Sunday? I'm off for a few days." Connor rubbed his nose with hers.

"Sounds great. I don't have to go back to work at the Center until Thursday."

Connor was feverish with the undeniable heat and he quivered with chills. He was fixated on only her. "Not until then? Darn." The smirk on her face played with him.

"Okay, I'll go. It's very clear or I think we both better take a cold shower," she joked. "I'll make it work."

"Okay, Sunday then." He stepped back. "I think we better get back before your brother gets too worried."

CHAPTER 15

*J*eepers creepers, Connor Winslow was a frickin' stunner. She was in awe of his oh-so- hotness. *What does he see in me?*

Ellie filled her suitcase with some clothes as she drew the bath water; it was time for some body prep and she wrapped the pink monstrosity on her arm in a plastic bag. The doctors said it was waterproof, but she didn't believe it.

The memory of Connor's touch trailed lightly across her, and the power when they kissed was like nothing she had ever experienced before. No matter how strong the attraction, she always found her way back to this spellbound moment of pure enchantment. She wanted him as much as he wanted her. Never had she been so captivated.

Butterflies rippled through her stomach just thinking about how he held her against the wall of the kitchen and then by the shed at the fundraiser.

What's up with him pinning me against walls because it's so darn hot?

Folding her undergarments and swimsuit into her suitcase,

she could hear Jeffrey's boots walk across the wooden floors downstairs as they creaked. Her brother approved of Connor or he wouldn't have invited him over, and she wouldn't be packing for a weekend even if she was a grown woman nearing twenty-nine. There was enough stress and nerves lately in the house from both of the siblings.

Connor was the first man she'd been attracted to since James, and there was so much self-doubt in making the same mistake. She had been so very wrong about James, and it almost cost her, her life. It was hard for Jeffrey to stop the whole over-protected, not-so-little brother thing.

"Will you stop, Jeffrey? You're probably wearing a path through the floors," she yelled. "You're making me more nervous, and my stomach is queasy enough."

Jeffrey hollered up the stairs. "Hey, I can't just turn the switch off after all these years when it comes to you. Being protective is ingrained."

Ellie leaned around the corner at the top of the stairs. "I know, and I love you for it." She shaped a heart over her heart with her hands and then blew Jeffrey a kiss. "I'm getting ready to take a bath. I'll be down later. And dear brother, please take a seat or watch some TV."

"Okay, I hear you. I'll take a chill pill."

Ellie eased into the bubbles and steaming hot water, thinking of Connor, again. His chiseled jawline and intense eyes. Not to mention his abs, and his arms. *I can't believe I'm about to go away with him.* He oozed sex, and what he brought out in her was so foreign. He was her drug. She'd never felt this way about anyone, not even James. It'd been almost three years since she had even kissed a man.

Ellie knew what this weekend would lead to. She couldn't get within his radius without swooning. She rubbed the soft shaving crème over her legs, and then let the blades of the razor slide across her skin. Her pink cast was wrapped and tied in an oversized plastic bag, as it teetered on the side of the claw foot tub. She quivered.

His lips, his clean heady scent, and the combination of CK One cologne and a whisper of smoke. Her skin was still sensitive from his stubble running across her skin. The deep gravel of his voice when he'd told her what he wanted and what he planned to do to her when they were alone had been totally erotic. Their chemistry was just passion between two consenting adults. Sex... and nothing more. A relationship between the two of them was doomed anyway, but why couldn't she have fun? Could she? Would she? He made her feel attractive like no one ever had, but she wasn't about to change her mind for any man, not even steamy Connor Winslow.

After the last ten years, Ellie wanted to believe in love... to have hope. Every girl wanted the happily ever after, but it was entirely different believing in it for herself. Romance novels were safer. James ruined the image for her and any trust she'd ever had. She didn't even know the depth of his manipulation, it started when she was so young. The little digs and comments began a downward spiral in her confidence. His jealousy and insecurities were cute in middle school, but then it became peculiar and when he got out of the academy and put his badge on he became controlling and toxic. He was never around because he was always working. Then he went rogue with the wrong people and then the violence...

She quaked and the water rippled. *But Connor wasn't James.*

He'd been there at the hospital and their lives kept intersecting for the last month and a half. Ellie really didn't know anything about him except he'd saved her and held vigil over her at the hospital. He was a firefighter who helped people and was good at his job. Her gut knew there was something dark and mysterious about him, she couldn't put her finger on it. She couldn't help thinking there was so much more behind his pain-filled eyes and calm outward demeanor.

Ellie motor-boated her lips and submerged herself under the water to wash her hair one-handed with a shampoo scalp swirl. The lavender and hibiscus shampoo made her hair soft and the conditioner allowed a little more control over the natural wave. Everything had to be perfect for this weekend. She hoped the trip would give her a glimpse into who the real Connor Winslow was.

J effrey yelled up the stairs as she zipped her weekend bag shut. "Ellie, your ride's here." She glanced another time into the full-length mirror and applied her vanilla sugared lip-gloss. She let out a breath she wasn't aware she was holding. Her white ruffled peasant blouse flowed over her matching light blue bra and underwear. She shimmied into her cotton teal skirt and it hugged every curve.

"Here goes. One big leap for womankind." She exhaled and dropped her shoulders. "Maybe it's time to try and trust in a man again," she said to her fragile heart. She slipped into her ballerina silver flats that matched the silver and pearl earrings dangling from her ears.

Ellie thought of the eerie call at work and wrestled her luggage until it bounced down the wooden steps. She trailed after it and caught the strap before her bag hit the landing.

Jeffrey ran across the room and looked up the staircase. "Don't hurt yourself," Jeffrey said. "Let me get that for you."

She nodded and whispered, "Thank you."

She rounded the corner; Connor's hair fell loosely over his forehead. His steel gray eyes were bluer against his electric blue oxford with rolled up sleeves that enhanced his taut forearms. Something about a man's forearm made Ellie go all gushy inside. His clean-shaven face and the intensity of his gaze made Ellie take a step back, and she settled against the wall as one of the pictures swung.

Jeffrey and Connor darted forward as she turned and righted the picture.

"Just call me Grace. I'm fine, just a little accident prone."

Connor's worn blue, diesel jeans hugged him perfectly, and his distressed Sketcher slip-ons gave a casual vibe. She drank him in. Connor and Jeffrey watched her. Should she rethink this trip? Could she just have casual sex and not pine over a man for an eternity?

Jeffrey cleared his throat and pointed out the huge picture window backed against the pond behind the property. Connor ran his hand through his disheveled hair. She admired his biceps strained under his shirt. Her mouth suddenly parched as if she'd swallowed a cotton ball. She almost choked, and when she coughed, both of them looked in her direction again. Connor walked to Ellie to try to grab her hand. She took a step and ran a hand over her skirt.

"Wait a minute," Jeffrey stated. "What's the rush?" His eyes bounced back and forth to them. He pinched his lower lip at the same time as he teetered his stance heel to toe. "We need to talk about what happened with that creep threatening you."

"Jeff, stop it." She knew he was stressing out over her going away, as much as she was. "I'm a grown woman and it's the 21st century." Her voice quivered over the jackhammer in her chest. "I'll have my taser."

"Where are you guys going?" Jeffrey inquired. "Don't forget your phone. If you need me, I can come get you anytime."

Ellie walked over to her big-hearted, handsome brother and touched his caring face. His eyes had a sheen in them. "I'll be okay, I promise. I have my phone if I need you." She stretched to her tip-toes. "Which, I always need you." She kissed his cheek lightly. "I'll call."

"Promise?" His shoulders relaxed as Ellie stepped away. Connor grabbed Ellie's luggage as they headed to the front screened door.

"I'll make sure she's safe. We have a security system. I've talked to my brother and they're looking into the threat and I'm just as worried about it as you are."

Ellie responded by a gesture of crossing her heart.

Jeffrey turned away and cleared his throat.

"Hey, Winslow." Jeffrey led his two fingers to his eyeballs and pointed back. "You have precious cargo, so I suggest you treat it kindly."

Connor obliged with his smooth assuring tone of respect. "She'll be in good hands. My parents' place is only about two hours into the foothills, near Breckenridge. I can give you the address and landline."

"Yeah apparently the hands part is what worries me, but I trust you will take care of my sister. Comprende?" Jeffrey followed them to the door.

"Got it." Connor shook his hand.

As they slowly drove away, Ellie mouthed, "I love you," to the most important man in her life.

I've never had any woman at my house or this cabin. No one was ever worth the risk or the time. Today was the first date I've really ever had.

"What are you thinking about right now?" Connor asked as he gripped the steering wheel. Driving straight was hard not to get distracted, but Ellie seemed so far away in her thoughts. Distance lingered in the air between them.

"Ellie? Do you want to turn back around and go home?" Connor brushed Ellie's shoulder lightly, feeling the softness of her skin.

"Hmmm? Oh… I'm sorry. No. It's so breathtaking. I'm just taking it all in." She smiled as she glanced out the window into the vast depth of evergreen and aspen trees littering the landscape.

"Look over there." He pointed to a herd of buffalo grazing.

"Seriously," she said. "Amazing."

"I know exactly what you mean." *Pay attention to the road, you dumb fucker, or you'll never get there in one piece.* He was sinking deeper and deeper the more time he spent with her. He needed to focus, or he was going to head-butt a boulder.

"I thought we could stop for a bite to eat. Not far ahead and around this bend, there's a dive called Kermit's. The place is just a hole in the wall, with dollar bills all over the joint, but their green chili is famous." He pointed up to the exit on the right. "It's down this way. Do you want to eat?"

"I'm always up for food." Her sultry lips puckered at the cupid's bow. Connor almost went off the road.

Kermit's was as small as a cabin with a fireplace and stone walls, some areas the ceilings were low enough that Ellie could touch them. And, as promised, there were signed dollar bills stapled to the walls and the ceilings. Connor led Ellie to a table near the picture window overlooking the foothills.

"Do you mind if I order for you?"

"Please do, since you're familiar with the menu," Ellie answered.

The waitress arrived and he ordered two small cups of the green chili with sides of flour tortillas and two large glasses of water. Ellie fondled her napkin and Connor leaned forward. The connection was so strong she was breathless. The employee returned with the order.

Ellie fanned her mouth after a few mouthfuls of the spicy sauce. "H-o-o-o-t –Yowie!" It was the kind of heat that built up slowly, bubbling as a volcano ready to erupt, straight up out of her stomach and into her throat. "Water," she croaked.

Connor spit out the mouthful of water as he gasped, watching as Ellie turned crimson.

"My tongue is on fire!" She yelped and grabbed a few ice cubes to stick on her tongue. It was numb. "I take it it's a hotter batch than most?" she rasped." My poor insides."

Connor smirked. He looked like he was trying to hold back another chuckle. Instead, he leaned over and kissed her.

"Hello! This stuff is hot. What are you trying to do, kill me off?"

Connor lifted his hand in the air to summon the waitress. "Could you please get us some sour cream, please?"

"Certainly," the waitress responded with a wink.

"My lips are starting to swell, I kid you not." Ellie dipped the napkin in her water to cool them off and wiped them. "Not helping. I need milk."

He got up and leaned over when she pulled the paper away, and his soft wet lips sucked at her bottom lips. Then his icy tongue swirled from top to bottom. Ellie suddenly felt another kind of heat race through her body. Her vision blurred, and she felt nothing but him.

He whispered, "Better?"

"What?" she murmured. Then the annoying hiccups started. She plugged her nose and chugged the water, but it was useless the onslaught got louder and louder.

Connor got up and darted across Kermit's to the bar. She couldn't hear what he was saying to the bartender through her sneezes, and ruckus, but it looked like he ordered a drink.

She shook her head to halt him from getting any closer as she squeaked again. There was no way she wanted anything else. Her hiccups grew even louder and now she had everyone's attention. She was so embarrassed she wanted to hurl.

"Here, drink this. It's bitter with lime juice." He inched it closer to her mouth. "It will definitely get rid of your hiccups. I promise. And your milk will ease the heat."

Ellie grabbed the shot glass of milk first from his hand and tossed it back. She prayed to the gods to give her a break and let this glitch pass. She drank the lime drink. Another hiccup escaped mid-drink, and she almost spit the liquid out. All she could do was pucker as the tart concoction assaulted her already ruined tongue and singed taste buds. She set the empty glass down and closed her eyes, just waiting...and waiting, muttering another silent prayer for them to please stop.

She opened her eyes and looked up. Then she smiled. "Hey," she paused. "What do you know? It worked." She took another breath and eased back. "Lieutenant Winslow, you've saved me again."

Connor straddled the chair, and his chiseled chin rested on his hands as his steel gray eyes bored through her. She could only stare.

"You okay?" he whispered.

Ellie wanted to wipe the damn smirk off his face, which he was obviously holding back, but he was so dreamy. "Yes, I'm fine now they're gone. But I'm not about to eat any more of this stuff." She pointed to the barely touched, fiery green chili.

"Wimp," he teased.

"Smart." She countered with a tap to her temple.

"Come on, woman. Let's get going." Connor threw a few bills down on the table as he thanked the waitress and pulled Ellie behind.

She loved how she felt with Connor. He continued to pull her through the front door and flipped her around to the side of the building, holding his strong, firm body against hers. She eased into his arms. Their bodies were firmly pancaked against one another, and she didn't want to let go. H is stubble scratched across her skin and she could feel his hard six pack under his cotton shirt. She held onto his derrière as he ground against her. He groaned and pulled away.

"Come on, let's go. Before it gets too late."

CHAPTER 16

Connor turned into a secluded gravel road. Ellie gazed at the structure as they inched closer. The place was a compound. The log cabin house was mammoth, and at one side there was an A-frame with an add-on from the original design that was nearly as tall as the surrounding trees. A second story wrought iron deck wrapped around as far as she could see. One side was all glass. "Wow."

The main level was surrounded by rustic stones and pavers in different shapes blended into the scenery. Tiki torches lined the walkways. Everywhere Ellie looked there were oversized but intimate sitting areas that were well thought out to fit the setting for small families or larger groups.

There was an outbuilding to the right and a three-car garage on the left. The property was flanked by humongous willow trees, and a lake off in the distant which had a boat dock where wave runners floated over the water. The landscape around the water was painted with massive evergreen, aspens, and foliage.

Wake me up. I'm dreaming in Technicolor.

Along the ridge in the distance were jaw-dropping mountains capped with snow. Ellie felt like she was in a surreal movie set in Wisconsin near Egg Harbor, but surrounded by the majestic Rocky Mountains, and it was breathtaking. The place was paradise, and she felt automatically at ease. The property was one of the most beautiful, peaceful, places she had ever been. She wanted to drink it in, bathe in it, and sleep for days.

Connor looked over and said, "Home sweet home." Connor pulled the car into one of the garages closest to the house.

"Oh, you have got to be kidding me." Ellie gasped. "Seriously?" Her mouth gaped open. "I—I thought you said it was a cabin. This is so not a cabin."

His hand went to her cheek and brushed against her chin.

"Is this place yours?"

"It was my parents'...." He hesitated as his head went downward. "Now it's the family's. My parents bought this place when Cade and I were kids. We've built on it over the years. My Dad loved working with his hands." He kicked at the gravel beneath his feet. "There was only a shed when we started, and it took about ten years. To build the house. Mom had a vision." He grabbed the luggage, an insulated cooler, and enough of groceries to feed an army, from the trunk of his Charger.

Ellie reached forward. "Here, let me at least take my own bag. You have enough to carry." She tossed it over her shoulder.

"I haven't been here in several years." He hesitated and sat a bag down as he fumbled with his keys.

"Why not?" Ellie slid her hand along the cotton shirt covering his broad shoulders.

"Haven't wanted to." His eyes shined with moisture as he looked away then back to Ellie...almost through her. Somehow, she comprehended his pain, and her heart ached for the cold, dark, cavern—one she recognized in herself. Almost breathless, she wanted to take every ounce of his pain away from him, absorb it, as she never wanted to before, but knew her own life depends on not fixing another man. The sorrow in his eyes tore at her soul. Ellie saw the same pain in Connor's eyes as the ones reflected back every day.

Gory details of James and the hell he put her through took over her thoughts. James could have left her for dead. He'd killed her spirit through the years, one she'd fought to regain. She would never be the shell of a woman she'd once been.

She pulled her hair back away from her face, touching the sensitive scar at her forehead. So much had happened to her over the years, and getting past old, fears, wounds and everything in counseling was a rebirth. She would never be the same. The recent accident had derailed her but wasn't going to stop her. She wanted to live every day and enjoy what life had to offer. This weekend might change everything. Connor sparked a fire in her she had once vowed to never re-awaken. She felt pretty, she felt desired...

Ellie set her bags down as she heard Connor's muffled voice in her distant thoughts and sketchy nerves.

"Ellie, where are you? Do you need to sit down? You look pale. Here let me take your bags to the guest room."

She hesitated. "I'm fine. Just point me in the right direction."

"First room on the right."

She pulled the luggage behind her and wheeled it down the hall. "Thank you. I'll be right back."

Ellie closed the door behind her as her breath burst in and out, and she swept her hand along her forehead to wipe off the sweat. She went into the adjoining bathroom and threw cold water on her face with her un-casted hand. She stood there in front of the mirror, wondering if she had the guts to take the plunge. Why did thoughts of James hit her here... now?

A light tap sounded on the door. "Ellie? Are you okay? Can I get you anything to drink?"

She fanned herself. "I'm fine. Do you have any wine?"

"Absolutely."

Good. She needed a little liquid courage right now.

"I'm coming." She ran the lipgloss applicator over her lips, took a deep breath, and marched to the closed bedroom door. "Do you have anything light and fruity or anything with bubbles?"

Connor rested his arm along the side of the door and waited for Ellie. "I have just the thing."

She opened the door, he palmed her hand and walked her to the kitchen, then opened up the large bottle of Verdi Spumante he'd picked specifically with her in mind. He grabbed two glasses and popped the cork. "Come on, let me show you around."

The house had so much warmth. Pictures lined the dark distressed mahogany mantel. A stone slab fireplace went to the pitched ceiling of the great room. She ran her hand along each red, white, and green picture frame of different sizes. The similarities of the smiles and each moment in the past drew her into an intimate time. Each picture showed love.

Ellie bumped against Connor and bounced on her tippy-toes to reach the largest frame. "Are these your parents?"

"Yes." He barely glanced at the photos, looking at her instead.

Ellie sensed she was intruding on something beyond words... so very special, but somehow untouchable and forbidden.

"Where are your parents, if I may ask?"

The man who stood beside her was darker, harder than the boy encapsulated in the photos.

"They're gone." He hesitated. "Dead."

A small gasp slipped through her lips. He was so matter of fact. Her heart ached for him.

She longed for her own parents. She missed them so much. Her father had died of a sudden heart attack and her mom gave up slowly on everyone and everything, then died less than two years after his death. Jeffrey and Ellie watched her go deeper into depression, then catatonic, so she'd really died when their father had. Ellie vowed never to give any man control over her life like her father had over her mother's. She loved her mom but felt sorry for her because she hadn't tried harder for her children or the beauty life offered.

A petite woman with soft eyes and a loving smile held a young Connor with his piercing steel gray eyes and dimpled chin. She was taken aback by the intensity of the warmth in each photograph.

He came up behind her and pointed to another picture. "This is Cade and me." Ellie looked at two small tan boys with ratty, mussed hair, no shirts and cut-off shorts. The two fishing poles they held were bigger than they were and each held a fish. In their hand. Their arms were looped over the other's shoulder. She could feel their bond leap out of the photograph.

The thick stone hearth created a centerpiece to the open floor plan, which was surrounded by floor-to-ceiling glass showing off the outside beauty. It gave an air of being outside. Ellie imagined many family dinners were eaten around the deeply distressed mahogany picnic table in the dining room. She imagined laughter once filled this place. How could it not? She wished she was a part of an earlier time. The environment was endearing, and it was an honor to be invited. Though, the man beside her swayed silently. He was miles away, looking through the glass wall ahead.

His eyebrows furrowed, and he appeared unassailable and forbidden. Ellie saw pained depths in his storm-filled eyes, almost cold and empty. She knew that pain and every cell of blood flowed through her as a reminder of what she'd gone through.

The old Ellie wanted to take his pain away.

I don't have it in me anymore to fix anyone. I have to take care of me first—live every minute like it's my last. I know what it's like to be near death. I want to live.

She questioned if her heart was ruling her head, and if being here was the right move, but something deeply rooted drew her to him. She was a moth to a flame. He'd captured her from the beginning and she couldn't deny her feelings it was oh-so grand.

"Can you tell me about your parents?" She held his hand, rubbing her nails against his palm, and eased closer.

"Sorry, Ellie. This is the first time I've been here since before they died. It brings back a lot of memories." He inhaled deeply, then exhaled, finally relaxing his shoulders. "There's not much to tell, but I'll try. They've been gone almost eight years. They died in a car accident. Cade and I were there. We barely got out ourselves."

"I'm sorry." Her heart broke at his sadness.

Connor stepped back with Ellie's hand in his. "How about a walk?" He pulled her across the room to the double sliding doors which led to a second level deck. The view was so beautiful it took her breath away. "Bring your glass. I'll get another bottle of wine."

She closed her eyes and took a deep breath, inhaling the fresh mountain air. This place had the ability to heal and cleanse the most fatigued.

Connor's faded jeans hung loosely at his hips as he leaned over the railing.

His backside looks fantabulous, if I do say so myself.

Ellie could see the navy-blue band of boxer briefs peeking out above his jeans. His white V-neck t-shirt showed a light sprinkle of chest hair, and his denim shirt gave him an easy, relaxed look. She stood close enough to breathe him in, and his woodsy clean scent was intoxicating. She teetered from side to side nervously. His brown hair casually fell over his forehead when he looked back. His gray eyes dilated to the point they appeared obsidian and filled with sexual intensity. Ellie ran her hands along the hard plains of his body and heat seared through her.

Dammit, this guy had me at h-e-l-l-o. Ellie Richards you're in major doo-doo.

Connor imagined his mother in the kitchen baking cookies and his dad reading the paper or tinkering with some project. The family gatherings with Aunt Janet and cousins Jax, and Journey. He loved spending summers here with Cade. He pressed the center of his chest. Would he ever get over the loss? He reached for his lifeline—her and moved Ellie in front of him, nestling his body against her as they looked out over the terrain. She rested her head on his chest. She mattered in the deepest way. He wanted to protect her, see her smile, hear her laugh, touch her skin. He didn't do the emotional crap. He'd given up years ago. Get too close, he'd get burned. He didn't have it in him to commit to anyone. *Not that she'd ever commit to me.*

He set the bottle of bubbles on a nearby table and wrapped his arms softly around her mid-section. He painted feathery circles along her stomach, and goose bumps spread across her skin. He pulled her hair away from one of her shoulders and nibbled her neck.

Ellie melted against him. He licked at her neck and kissed the top of her head. *Jesus Chriiist.* He wanted her in a bad way. He lifted her chin, lingering closer, softly rubbing his nose to hers. Her hands went under the tail of his shirt.

He groaned, and his lips touched hers. His tongue slid into her mouth. Euphoria encapsulated him. He lost track of time.

He was safe—whole. She matched his movements. He nipped and tugged at her bottom lip.

"Uh, dammit Ellie, you undo me." He panted to catch his breath, then closed his eyes, trying to keep himself under control. His head tilted to the blue sky above. He could feel the thumping of her heart in her chest. Or was the jackhammering his own?

"Let's take a stroll of the property before I rip your cute little peasant girl outfit right off you here and now." He raised his brows. "We need to cool off a bit, and I have a lot to show you." He directed her to the view ahead. "After that, I'm making you dinner since we haven't had an official first date yet." He wrapped his arm over her shoulder. "Protocol, right? An actual dinner dates. I want to get something right." He bit at her jaw, then nuzzled at Ellie's neck. His whiskers softly scratched her skin. "You know you are the first woman I've ever invited here?"

She arched back and titled her head to the side. "You've got to be kidding me. Never? "she giggled.

"You're the first."

"Okay... About a date. You made me breakfast already. Could that be considered a date?" she asked.

"I saved your kitchen from burning in your attempt to make breakfast, and then I felt sorry for you because your stomach was growling." He laughed.

"I'm always hungry, and I'll almost eat anything. Well, maybe not the atomic green chili again."

"Deal, no green chili," Connor replied. "We have all weekend to eat, be lazy, and enjoy the scenery. Besides, you will need your energy." He pulled back and peered deeply into her eyes, wiggling his eyebrows in jest. Ellie bit her bottom lip.

"I may just have to lock us in the bedroom for days." He wished more than anything something would happen.

She smiled and nodded. "Sounds perfect."

"Tell me what you want."

She swallowed hard. "I'm here, and I like the fact we are alone." Her skin heated red.

With Ellie, Connor wanted more, and he wanted her to be happy He wanted to be nowhere else, but with her.

CHAPTER 17

"*A*re you ready for the tour?" He handed her the bottle of wine. "I'll get the basket and blanket." They walked to the lake and spread out the multi-colored Spartan blanket and emptied the basket filled with assorted fruits and cheeses. He fed her until she was full and protested. They lay down, looking up at the bluest robin egg sky in each other's arms. Connor laughed as he watched Ellie intently while she purred in her slumber.

*S*he jolted upright. "I think I dozed off."

"You did. I've done it so many times myself. This place and the great outdoors has that effect." He twirled his fingers around her hair and along her forehead. "Do you want any more fruit or cheese?"

"No, I'm good." She nestled into the crook of Connor's arm. Her arm rose to shield the last of the sunset before it went behind the mountains. She covered herself with part of the blanket and turned over, anchoring her fists under her chin. She looked positively serene.

"Dollar for your thoughts?" she asked. Her lashes fluttered.

"I was thinking about some of the special times we had here." He hesitated. There was no time to walk backward down a path leading nowhere. The pain was always there, percolating under the surface. Having a guarded wall was easier, and to feel nothing was simpler. It was his armor.

"Please, Connor? I want to hear about you and your family." Ellie smoothed over the surface of Connor's hard-working hands and laced her fingers through his.

He had to think of something safe and distant. Detouring his thoughts, he concentrated on something other than the accident. "Do you know that Cade is not my brother? I mean he is... but not by blood. He was my best friend first." Connor looked away, agitated. He rubbed the back of his neck. This talking stuff wasn't easy, and he much preferred talking about her, not himself. He twisted his watch around his wrist. "My family adopted him."

"Really?" Ellie asked as she rose to sit and fingered her necklace. "Start wherever you like; I want to hear."

"I think he was meant to be my brother from the very start. Cade and I were best friends since kindergarten. We hit it off the first day. We were with each other every day, most nights, and then more and more weekends. The two musketeers.

"He was a runt and very skinny. Hell, we both were." Connor laughed. "He didn't talk about his family life much in the beginning, but through the years we noticed his parents became more absent, then they were never around at all. Dad suspected there was neglect or abuse and gave them an ultimatum. It took years to finally make everything legal. They kept coming around for money. The pond scum attempted to get money for him."

"Like sell him?" Ellie asked.

"Yes." Connor shook his head with disgust. "My dad told Cade's parents he'd put them both away if they didn't leave Cade alone, and my dad wasn't kidding. My mom gave Cade the choice to see his folks, but he said we were his only family, and he never looked back. All I knew was, we loved him, and he was ours. His mom was always riding off with some new man on a Harley, and the last we heard, Cade's so-called daddy was in jail on drug trafficking."

Connor had never told this story to another soul. He was screwed up and broken, but with Ellie he wanted to try to be open, and maybe pretend for just a little passage of time he actually deserved her love and a little happiness. This woman had so much sparkle, she was intoxicating, and he was addicted to her energy for life. There was a first for everything, and for some odd reason, the nightmares ceased since he'd started the pursuit of her. After all the years of reliving them, it's a godsend the worse parts of the accident had faded, for now.

"Wow." Ellie covered her mouth with her hand. "He's so lucky to have you."

"We were the lucky ones." The silence stretched through the air.

"What happened to your parents?" Her expression was sincere but pensive.

He eyed her deep concern. Connor's throat grew parched with every ragged inhale. He chugged the last of his wine from the glass, then filled another and offered her the rest. "We were hit by a drunk driver. Mom, Dad, Cade, and me. Dad was trapped in the vehicle when it exploded, and Mom died at the side of the road in Cade's arms. We almost didn't make it out ourselves, but I was thrown from the explosion. We were pretty jacked up from our injuries."

"Oh my god, how awful. I'm so sorry." Tears filled Ellie's eyes, and she stilled.

He looked away. "Don't pity me, please." He couldn't look into her eyes. "I'm okay now, and it was a long time ago." His throat thickened.

Her chin trembled. "There's no pity here, but you never get over something so horrifying. I don't care if you are King Kong, Freddie Krueger, or an alien. The heart never gets over losing a parent. Something so dreadful can haunt you." She wiped a single tear trailing down her cheek.

"You're shivering." Connor considered this sensitive, loving woman and only wanted her more. He ran his palm over her skin to warm her.

"We have events in our past which ultimately change our future." She sniffed wiping her nose. "Thank you for sharing what happened."

Connor could see the stinging pain in Ellie's eyes. Damn, he could love this woman. He fought with every muscle twitch and cell in his body not to feel the pain. He couldn't show the sadness. He halted for a moment and stared down at his hands.

"Okay, it's your turn" It was time to twirl this conversation around and stat. He had to control his breathing and switch gears.

"My father passed away, and my mom was never the same. She gave up after dad died and no matter what Jeff and I did, she wouldn't try." She shrugged her shoulders. "I guess she died of a broken heart." Ellie twisted her hands together and hesitated. "Her pain trumped her will to live for us. I'm not sure I ever got over the notion, but I've forgiven her.

"I also think you should know something else about me. I was... married when I was younger." Regret set her features.

"It's okay, you can tell me." Connor grabbed a nearby twig and heaved it into the air. He hadn't expected she'd been married. How could someone let her go? Connor hated the guy already.

"We were childhood sweethearts and married too young..."

She shivered again and wrapped her arms around herself. Something in her voice didn't sound right. Connor pulled the blanket around her and ran the pads of his fingers along her cheek.

"Maybe one day I will tell you everything, but right now he doesn't belong here with us. You and me only this weekend. He will not ruin this moment. I won't let him. He's done enough damage." She splayed her fingers into Connor's hair. "I'm here with you right now and that's pretty much all I care about. I don't regret the past, but I certainly won't relive my mistakes. I'm not going that direction." She eased against him, sliding her arms around his waist.

Connor pulled her body firmly on top of him, drinking her in. His cock stirred and strained against his zipper.

The daylight dimmed, and the fresh air became crisper as he pulled the blanket over them.

I want this woman to erase it all—the agony, and everything bad. Maybe, I actually do have a chance.

"Ellie, maybe we should go inside. You're trembling."

She looked up with her coffee brown eyes, the gold flecks muted as her pupils dilated. There was lust within them. Her breathing was almost erratic. She kissed him like no other woman had. Warmth radiated through his body, his muscles trembled and he almost lost motor control. Her movements were animated. She took a series of breaths. She was pure hot, and as excited as he was. Connor knew if they didn't get up he would lose all his inhibitions pressed deeper against her delicate frame to get closer.

"I'm not cold. It's you. You are doing this to me." Her lingering touch rushed up against his stomach.

Fuck—that did it.

Ellie's fingers fumbled as she undid the top button of his jeans.

"I want you, now. Take me." She sat up and pulled at the back of her cream-colored top, slowly sliding the zipper. Her hair fell over her shoulders, and he looped the soft waves around his finger. Goose bumps peppered her skin.

"I think we better get inside," he rasped.

"Shush. There will be no more talking, Mr. Winslow," she demanded. Her top slowly fell from her shoulders, but she cupped the fabric over her breasts. She hesitated, and the moment flared her cheeks with crimson.

A howl went off in the distance. "What was that?" She hissed, pivoting around. Her body went from languid to a statue in a split second.

"Yeah, I think it's time to go inside. Coyote. Mountain lions and bears around here, too." He rose to his knees and put the leftover plates and glasses into the picnic basket.

"What?" Ellie dove over Connor to get up, pushing him back down, and pulled the blanket around her. She stumbled to her feet. "Come on already. She shooed him forward and slipped on her flip-flops. "Hurry," she said as her teeth chattered uncontrollably. "I'm not about to get eaten alive out here."

He threw the bottle and glasses into the basket, stood up, buttoned his jeans, and eased the zipper over his cock. "Grab the basket, will ya?" He bent over, lifted her, and hauled her over his shoulder to the house in a fireman's carry. Her laughter infected the air around them.

"Put me down, you big brute," she yelped and squeezed his butt cheeks.

"You are going to get it, woman." He meant every word of it. Miss Richards was so going to get everything he had.

CHAPTER 18

"*E*l, it's Jeff. When you get this message, call me back. I'm just checking to see if you made it to Connor's place." He looked out the window again. "I just got home, and I swear I just drove by Evan's truck or one that looked similar. What color did you say the truck was that hit you and caused the crash? It was parked off the road in a ditch. I didn't see anyone in it, but I've checked the house and it's solid. My hackles are up. I don't like this one bit." Jeffrey pulled his right-to-carry pistol out of his case. He unlatched the safety of his Ruger.

"If everything's cool with you, just text me back. I'm probably just being overprotective, as usual. Maybe a little flipping paranoid, but it's my job to make sure you're safe. Old habits die hard," he said as he slowly walked up the stairs.

"We both know there are some weirdos out there. And sis, I hope you're having a great time. Try to relax; you deserve it. Love you. Don't forget to text. Call me back. K, bye." Jeffrey pushed the end button as he slipped around another doorway and flipped on the outside flood lights. Tires screeched nearby as he ran to the window, only to see tail lights and the truck disappear.

Ellie's skin was supple as Connor ran his palms up the backside of her thighs near her bottom She was languid against him. She plopped the picnic basket on the table as they walked by. The blood had to be rushing to her head by now. He bent on one knee and eased Ellie onto the microfiber sectional. Undraping her, he scooted her against the fluffy mound of pillows, but she slid off the cushions. Her hair was in disarray and looked absolutely incredible. She smoothed her chestnut strands away from her face.

"You are beautiful," he said.

The scarlet blush rushed into her cheeks and rose across her chest. Her hand floated to the scar at her forehead. She winced and her nose crinkled.

"I didn't hurt you, did I?" Connor asked, as he leaned in and lightly kissed the scar above her brow.

"I did it to myself. You will get used to it. If you haven't noticed by now I'm not very graceful. I'm kind of a Lucy."

"Grace is overrated. You're not trying to be someone other than you, and it's pretty hot."

"You're being serious?"

"One hundred percent." He smiled. "You barely see the scar anymore. You're gorgeous. I don't see anything but you, and *you* work for me." He trailed kisses along her face and neck.

Connor squeezed her thighs and ran his fingertips up under her shirt. "If it's not obvious, I can't keep my paws off of you. I want to be inside you, Ellie. You're in charge. Connor pressed against her core. I will stop if you want me to.

Ellie ran her hands over her arms and shivered.

"You're cold. I'll start, a fire." He raced the distance to the switch and flipped it on and turned the music on."

Connor gathered and threw a dozen pillows from the sectional onto the faux cowhide rug. He cradled her in close and started kissing her hand as she trembled. With the slightest tug her hand darted under his shirt again and along his stomach. He lured her to the floor. He kneeled over her, erasing the space between them. The heat radiated off her as she relaxed against his chest. Damn, he loved feeling her close.

Her fingers danced over his skin, running lazy circles above his navel. Every breath she took, the way her lashes fluttered over her hooded, dilated coffee colored eyes. She triggered something primal in him. Her red swollen lips had not been kissed enough, and he wanted to do the biting of that bottom lip instead of her doing it. Connor could feel the layers of his guard slowly disintegrate. Being with her was so different than all the other women.

Ellie's firm little round bottom was soft under his kneading. He gently eased her onto the scattered pillows and had to touch her hair again. The feel of her curls and the richness of her hair color shined against the flames in the fireplace and waves fanned over the plush rug.

"Connor I-I haven't been with anyone since my...ex." Her lids closed, and she took a deep breath. "I want this, but I'm nervous.

She was vulnerable and strong in one, and she was so captivating. She had him.

"Don't be nervous, Ellie, we will figure this out together." He lifted her chin and rested his forehead against hers. "I promise I won't hurt you."

He kissed her petal soft lips and lightly nipped at the bottom one. He traced her features wanting to memorize every angle, plain, and feel of her.

Ellie ripped open his shirt as buttons bounced and darted across areas of the wooden floor.

"Oops. I've always wanted to do that, but in the movies, they must use snaps." She looked around. "Sorry. Guess, I'll buy you another shirt," she snorted.

Connor laughed as he picked a stray button off her head. "I don't mind at all. You definitely keep things interesting."

She rested her head on his chest and scored his skin above the unbuttoned top of his jeans with her lightly painted nails. Tugging down at the loops of his jeans, she slid them below his hips, then snapped the waistband of Connor's boxer briefs.

Connor wanted her to enjoy this more than he cared about his own pleasure. He had to be closer with her.... *I want her to feel treasured.*

Connor lifted her up slightly. His elbows added support as he ground into her. Careful not to have her bear his weight. He didn't want to crush her, she was so small, but she pressed him against her instead. She too carried an underlying strength he couldn't quite explain for someone who looked more mouse than mighty.

Connor ran his tongue over the salty sweet skin of her neck as she giggled and bit his earlobe. She combed her hands lightly over his scalp and tugged at his hair. Every sensory nerve and cell in his body were engaged, and most of the sensation went directly south. Her breasts were full under his grasp, the taut buds of her nipples pressed against the silk of her tank top.

Connor's senses were raw, and he had to have this woman. He wanted to know every place she was ticklish, every hitch of breath when he found his way to her most sensitive spots, the purr in the back of her throat when she liked how something felt. Most of all he needed to feel her warmth around him as he went deep inside her. He wanted her to climax, over and over.

"God, you feel so good, Ellie." He was almost hyperventilating, and from the sound of Ellie's ragged breathing, she was too.

Tears welled into Ellie's coffee brown eyes as she looked at Connor. She pulled at the straps of her tank top, easing it down and off her arms slowly.

Her sheer white lace bra with the front closure barely

covered her pert breasts, and he could see the shadow of pink buds behind the thin fabric.

Her lashes fluttered, and when she blinked, a tiny tear rolled down her temple.

"Are you sure about this?" he asked as he wiped away the tear with his thumb. "We can stop.

"I'm positive. I want you so badly, but I'm really nervous." She closed her eyes, took a huge inhale, and her shoulders relaxed. "Please don't stop. I don't think I can bear another minute." She wiggled out of her bra and eased she stood in front of him as slid down the skirt. Her white sheer panties perfectly matched her discarded bra.

Ellie drew Connor's shirt down his shoulders. "I didn't know you had a tattoo." She ran her coral tipped nails over the tribal design with dark blue and jagged black edges. "Wow, it's huge. Didn't that hurt?"

"I might have gotten carried away."

She ran her fingers softly along his bicep, up over the shoulder, and down his pectoral.

"I'd have to say this area hurt the worst." He pointed to the red, orange, and yellow burst of flames near his heart. The meaning behind the tattoo, the pain in his heart and their loss, was worse than any of the ink etched could hurt.

She knelt down and planted her lips on the surface of the slightly raised inked skin. "Here? I think it's so hot." She blew wisps of air across his chest, making his skin prickle and his nipples pebble hard. "I've always wanted one but never did. I tend to hurt myself naturally, so it wouldn't make sense to pay someone to torture me slowly."

He laughed at how easily and lightly she poked fun at herself. The girl was unbelievable.

He laid Ellie back softly against the pillows, running his hand down her body as he stripped away the satin and lace barely covering her core. She crossed her arms over her breast and then in front of her femininity, which he was about to unveil.

"Stop, I want to see you. I want to see all of you."

She put her hands over her face with embarrassment.

"You are gorgeous, every inch of you." There were two small scars above the soft curls below her abdomen. He ran lazy circles over it, as it piqued his curiosity.

Connor wanted to let go, and he wasn't even inside her yet.

He reached for the foil packets out of his jean pocket, which was still puddled around his ankles, feeling like he was playing a game of Twister as he reached for them. He bit at the corner of the package and tore the foil open.

"Here, let me help." Ellie raised herself in the sitting position and reached for the condom and rolled it over his tip, sheathing him to the base. He eased her down, again nudging her thighs open. He trailed his fingers over her subtle mound as her body arched up to meet his, and she wiggled under his touch. Her voracious mouth welcomed his, their tongues mingled. He pressed against her entrance. He slowed his breath retreating as the pressure increased at the tip of his cock, slowly easing in and out. She tensed and her nails dug into his back. "We will take this slow." She was tight—too tight. He pulled away and fondled her as she moistened. His brow pinched in concentration, familiarizing himself with her body as her internal muscles squeezed. Her body relaxed. "Please, Connor. I want you. He slowly entered her again as her body accommodated his size and she gloved him and drove him wild. He slowed his movements flooded in her warmth.

"Why are you stopping?" she asked between panted breaths.

He inhaled deep. His heart panged. His nerve endings tingled. "Woman, I'm just warming up. I have died and gone to heaven." Their lips met as she raked her nails into his scalp.

"I want to kiss every inch of you."

"What? She squirmed with every feathered graze over her skin, her giddiness contagious. "Lord help me."

CHAPTER 19

*E*llie was wrapped around Connor like a vine and both were sated, but after three mind-blowing hours, they needed another few foil packs and sustenance.

"Ellie…" Pulling the hair away from her neck, he kissed the ticklish spot near her collarbone.

"Hmmm?" She burrowed farther against him.

"Are you hungry? I need to eat something. You're wearing me out."

She laughed, unwinding her legs from him. "Geez, I should be offended, but seriously, I thought you would never ask. I'm so hungry, I can't stand it."

Connor grabbed the nearest pillow and handed Ellie an afghan from the back of the couch.

"This looks homemade." She plucked at the yarn.

"My grandmother made it."

She wrapped it around her beautiful body as if she was suddenly shy, her chest stamped with scarlet blotches. "Sorry, Grandma."

Tires crunched over the gravel outside along with the purr of an engine followed by an eerie calm. In Connor's peripheral vision he saw the motion detection lights go on. The sound of heavy footsteps pounded down the wooden deck stairs out back. He threw on his diesel jeans and slid the door open and Leaped down the stairs two at a time. Someone was running down the drive. In the distance he could faintly see the dim tail-lights of a dark truck retreating like a bat out of hell spraying dust and gravel off the property and down the side access road.

Connor came back into the house, snatched his smartphone, and called 911.

"What's going on, Connor? What was that? A-a-bear?" Ellie's vocal pitch rose as her teeth chattered. She went to the stereo and turned down the volume.

Connor erased the distance between them, wrapping his arm around to comfort her, and pressed the send button on his phone. "I'm afraid not. It was a peeping tom or someone trying to break in."

Ellie's eyes widened as her casted arm held up the afghan and the other clutched her throat.

"It's okay. I got you." He cradled her tighter as the line picked up. "911 operator what is your emergency."

"This is Connor Winslow off of Revelry at Fireside. I think I might have stopped a break-in here, but they took off." Connor blew out a gust of air he was holding in, and he quickly gulped in another. "No, we're okay. I couldn't see the letters on the rear license plate, but the vehicle was a dark truck. The guy in dark clothing was at the patio door, but I didn't see his face." He ran a finger over Ellie's hair, along her forehead and down her tiny nose, smoothing across those freckles. She closed her eyes and relaxed against his touch as a deep sigh escaped her.

"No, you don't need to send anyone out here. Just tell the Sheriff. We're all locked up, and all the outside lights are on. Okay, I'll watch for them." Connor pushed the end button on his phone.

"They're going to send a car anyway and take a look around

and write up a report, but whoever it was is long gone by now." He kissed the top of her crown of brown waves. "We're safe inside, and they're patrolling. There's been a rash of break-ins, the Sheriff said. But we have a security alarm; I'll set it after they leave." Connor looked through the windows at the vast trees and brush and hoped to hell someone wasn't still close by. How could he not know someone was watching them? He was never careless. He was off his game with Ellie, he was weak. He couldn't protect her.

"You're so calm. Do you ever get rattled?" she asked. "I'm freaking out right now. What if he was watching us?" She covered her face and shook her head. "He might have seen us, you know..." She looked over at the scattered pillows and the floor where they'd spent the last several hours. "Oh, my goodness gracious how embarrassing."

"Well, I suppose we might have taught him a thing or two." He lifted and swung her around, her body barely covered by his grandma's afghan. "Let's get something in you besides me."

She slapped his arm. "Really? You seriously didn't just say that!" She rolled the words slowly over her tongue along with her eyes. "While you're preparing my sustenance, I'm going to go clean up." She licked her ruby lips. "Do you mind if I take a quick shower?"

"No, please go ahead." He pointed to the first door on the right down the corridor. "But, don't be too long. The Sheriff and Deputy should be here any minute. I don't like the fact that someone was trespassing on our property." He was territorial and wanted to protect her. "The quicker the police are out patrolling, the safer everyone is." He peered out the window to see the several cars with no lights or sirens in the distance coming closer to the house.

"Hurry up. I don't want any of them seeing you exposed." He squeezed Ellie on the rump and eased her chin up to kiss her swollen lips. Whisker burns etched her skin and neck. "I mean it. I'm not done with you yet." He tapped at the tip of her nose. She bit her lips, twirled her hair, and backed away into the nearest wall. He drew forward, matching her steps and holding her firmly against him.

She didn't need to flirt, her awkwardness won him over. She had no clue how refreshing and damn sexy she was just being Ellie. God, he wanted her again. He inhaled deeply, trying to control himself.

"Everything will be just fine; the Sheriff's department will check the property and we will be safe, I promise." He ran the back of his hand along the side her cheek. "You might want to put your swimsuit on, too. I don't want to risk anyone seeing you naked, but me. There are extra robes in the closet, next to the bathroom."

"Thank you, but should we be swimming after we eat?"

"I know CPR." He kissed her and licked her bottom lip. "I promise you won't drown after we eat. We're just going down-stairs to the hot tub." He winked.

"Oops, I almost forgot." She lifted her pink florescent cast. "Do you have anything plastic I can wrap this thing in?"

Ellie stepped into the guest bedroom where her things were, along with a box of Saran Wrap and an afghan wrapped around herself. She twirled around the rustic room with an end suite was pure mountain lodge aura. The king-sized bed was so high Ellie would have to pole vault into it. The headboard was made of horizontal wooden planks of earthy pine. She took a leap onto the burnt orange, taupe, and mocha sheet set. A heavy linen, striped, brown and rust coverlet was folded at the foot of the bed. She flung the afghan over the footboard made of old logs. She rolled over and viewed an old rocking chair in the corner of a nearby reading nook and was draped with an old quilt splattered with steer and elk. A wall-to-ceiling shelf filled with books was a reader's dream. Her heart palpitated over the literary dream.

The oversized picture window opened to the lake. The room was comfortable and had a touch of the old world. A circular chandelier hanging from the rafters appeared as warm glowing candles. She moved to the bathroom of rich warm hues and a copper basin designed above an old wooden dresser. She ran her toes over cool Travertine tiles on the floors. She opened the glass-encased shower. A copper soaking tub sat on another wall next to a double-sided fireplace with a stone hearth. "Wow, I could live here." Then she caught a glimpse of herself…

Her hair looked exactly like a tumbleweed. Her cheeks glowed like literal fireballs; she had road rash on her face from Connors whiskers. Her body was sore, but so…*alive*. She'd never felt this worshiped; she quivered thinking of the past few hours. What little makeup she had on was raccooning under her eyes. Alice Cooper would be impressed.

Stepping into the steamy shower as water trickled and comforted, loosening her taut muscles. Wrapping her hair into a top knot, she slathered the shower gel over her sensitive spots. The hottie firefighter knew what he was doing—she'd never known what she'd been missing. She rested her head against the coolness of the travertine.

She had never wanted any man again. *Well, well, well, you finally did it and succumbed to a man after all these years. You are such a hussy.*

Connor brought out something in her, which she'd never knew with James. She trembled. James usually did the deed with a wham-bam, thank you, ma'am.

More current flashbacks replaced the old—Connor lingering over her body as if he appreciated every nuance, and he'd made her feel revered.

The experience was a first. Connor had made love to her. She had never been made love to.

Every ripple of fiery water pulsated over her skin, easing the last of the muscle tension. After unwrapping the Saran from her cast and towel drying, she pulled the peach lotion out of her overnight bag and ran it lightly over her skin.

Her neon, hot pink bikini with fluorescent lime green bows fit looser than she remembered. She pulled the double X, charcoal gray, terry cloth robe from the closet around her, and it pooled to the floor as she cinched the tie before hoisting it up as she sat at the edge of the bed. Her phone chimed from her purse. She viewed the screen and spotted several missed calls from her brother and half a dozen texts. The last one read... *Why aren't you answering? Ellie, are you okay? It's urgent—call me.* She dialed Jeffrey, he answered immediately. "Baby bro, what's up?"

"Why haven't you answered any of my calls or texts?"

"Jeepers. I'm sorry. Can't I get away for a minute without you freaking out? Connor was showing me his property; we were outside near the lake and my phone was in the house."

"It's important, sis or I wouldn't bother you. This break is good for you, but I'm concerned for your safety."

"Why? What's going on?" she gasped.

"When I came home tonight there was a truck parked in the dense trees across from the ponderosa." Jeffrey's voice lashed.

"On our property?" Ellie pulled the towel off her head and looked into the mirror. "This can't be happening..." her movements jerked and flinched.

"What do you mean?" Jeffrey asked.

"Someone was just here at Connor's. A peeping creeper was looking in at us. He took off, and Connor's talking to the police right now."

"What did the vehicle look like?"

"I didn't see it, but Connor said it was a dark truck. He only saw the back of it and a few numbers on the plate."

"El, I think it was the same dark colored truck that was here; the timeline fits. You're about an hour and a half away, and I saw the truck here four or five hours ago. Tell the police to check and see if there were any cigarettes on the ground. Whomever it was chain-smoked when they were here. The smokes were camels, and the police took the butts as evidence. If you find any, it's the same person, and you're the link. You have to tell the police. Are they still there?"

Ellie ran to the door and looked out. "Me?" Ellie had to steady herself against the door. "Yes, they're still..." She clenched the opening of the robe.

"Sis, are you still there? Listen to me very carefully. You said the car that ran you off the road was a truck. What color was it?"

"It was dark. Evan has a black and chrome Silverado; do you think it was him?"

"He's not a smoker, and I don't think he would be so lethal. And this was bigger than his truck and everything was matte black—everything, rims, windows with amped up tires. But, I'll ask Jax if he was on shift."

"I'll talk to the police before they leave, and I'll let you know."

"Okay, sis, be careful. I'll talk to the police here."

Ellie ran out of the room. "Connor, I need to talk to the police. I just got off the phone with Jeffrey, and he shared something I think they might want to know."

The police left as Connor ran the tips of his finger along Ellie's shoulder and then he squeezed her neck and traps. "You did good, and I'm sure they will get to the bottom of all of this." Connor kissed the top of her head, grabbed her hand, and walked over to the sliding glass door. "Hopefully, the police don't find anything that ties these events together. Your safety is key. I promise I won't let anything happen to you."

"I know." She wrapped her arms tightly around his waist. "Let's leave them to do their job, and we have the rest of the weekend. Nothing will ruin our time together." She turned and inhaled. "Except food. I'm so famished I'm almost nauseous."

The delicious smell lingered through the air, assaulting her hangry stomach as it growled and rattled. She was sick to her stomach about what Jeffrey said and talking to the police. This couldn't be a coincidence. And... Why her? Her gut was never wrong.

She wasn't going to invite the past into this weekend—a weekend that meant so very much. The horrors of the past were buried deep and so was James and the abuse. She was not the same person now as she was then.

Connor scurried around the kitchen. A glass bowl of strawberries and assorted grapes were centered on the lavish mahogany picnic table along with a bottle of champagne chilling in a stainless-steel bucket. A glass goblet filled with chilled, peeled shrimp and a red sauce looked more like a centerpiece than something edible. Warm brie with slivers of candied walnuts and cranberries oozed on a platter next to assorted crackers and torn bread.

Connor was more than comfortable and at home in the

heart of the kitchen, but his right hand looked frilly and too feminine covered in the purple and green floral oven mitt, and somehow it didn't fit his rocking muscles and shirtless bare back. His low-slung jeans rested at his hips and his abs were not a six pack; she swore there were eight of those suckers. His V was a thing of splendor only ancient sculptors came close enough to getting right. He bent over, retrieving more food from the oven. His firm backside took Ellie's breath away momentarily. He was so intense, methodical, and stoic.

I've fallen in love with him, food or not.

He peered over something fancy on a baking sheet and padded closer.

"What smells so good?" Rich bacon and slightly browned cheese filled her nose.

"Prosciutto wrapped asparagus with parmesan." Connor pulled the snack from the pan with the silver tongs and placed it onto the large, white serving platter.

"I have died and seriously gone to heaven," she said as she wiped her now salivating mouth.

"Here's a plate. Be careful; they're really hot." He looked around. "I think I have everything... Oh! I almost forgot the champagne. It's chilled, but I need to uncork it." He started over to the bottle.

"Can I?" she asked. "I've never popped the top of champagne."

"Never?" he questioned and threw the oven mitt across the room. "Absolutely." He moved her in position, standing directly behind her and showed her how. "You need to point it away from you." She gripped the cork, and it flew across the room. Bubbles spilled over the neck of the bottle of Spumante before Connor poured the sparkling golden bubbly into two flutes. He pulled out the wooden seat at the head of the table.

"You should sit there," she said. "I'll sit on the bench."

"No. I never sit here." He pointed and stalled his movements.

"Dad's chair—Dad always sat there." He paused. "Or there." He pointed to the other end of the table. "Never mind. I'll just sit here." His head went down, and then side to side., slowly tilting it from left to right. "Please sit there, Ellie. You are my guest." He nodded.

She didn't know what to say, so she walked closer to the chair and sat down. What just happened? One minute a hint of a smile lifted only to sink to a frown. He was an array of clashing emotions, mirrored in her own reflection from the past.

His brooding made him sexy. Maybe at first it was the attraction, but somehow when he held her and kissed her. He was a contradiction of emotions. He captured her soul and not because what he had done to her on the floor the last several hours, or that he was smoking hot and could cook. He was a dream for any woman, and she was surprised he was single. The idea of any other woman with Connor killed her. Whatever this was between them, he was hers for the weekend, and she didn't want to think of anything beyond their time here together.

CHAPTER 20

"*I* can't eat another bite." She plopped the last handful of grapes onto the plate beside her. "Well, maybe another." She tilted her head back, savoring the succulent fruit like Cleopatra.

"Hmmm, can I have a taste?" His mouth moved over the sweet juices left on Ellie's swollen, well-kissed lips.

"Come on." Connor stood in front of Ellie and wrapped his arm around her waist. "Are you interested in a hot tub?" He moved and swayed against her. "It's outside under the deck." Connor grabbed Ellie's casted hand and stopped before pulling her to the stairs for the lower level. "Wait just a minute. I almost forgot something." He ran to the kitchen and held up the Saran Wrap she'd laid on the counter earlier.

"Are you sure it's safe with a peeping tom out there and all the coyotes and bears?" Ellie asked.

"I won't let anything happen to you, and the police are doing rounds. Whoever he was, he's long gone by now." He looked down at her arm. "We need to wrap this again to make sure it doesn't get wet."

"Oh, right." She laughed. "How could I forget this neon monstrosity? I wrapped it earlier, but most of the time I just hold it up and do everything one handed. No matter how I wrap it, somehow it still gets wet, so it's easier to keep it out of the way."

Connor flipped on the music system that surrounded the six-person hot tub. Approaching Ellie, he leaned in and kissed her neck as he spiraled his forefinger around one of her damp tendrils. He stepped back and untied the oversized robe. "You look great in this, but I like you better out of it."

She took his hand in hers and placed it on her heart. "You make me feel..." She paused.

"I know..." Connor eased the terry cloth material off her shoulders and let it drop to the floor. He trailed kisses across her silky skin, swept her up, and sat her on the edge of the hot tub.

"God, you are so beautiful. You make my heart hurt."

For a fleeting moment, Ellie almost believed him. She bit the inside of her cheek. He could have any woman he wanted What did he see in her?

She was glad she had her swimsuit on because she was definitely not an exhibitionist, especially with a creeper eyeballing them earlier. Ellie rose above the vibrating jets pummeling her sore muscles, wedged in the corner she walked her plastic wrapped, pink hand weight along the side of the hot tub. She scanned across the darkened landscape, looking for anything suspicious. "Are you sure we are safe?"

"Come here." Connor pulled her inward. "Turn around." Holding her against his chest, he massaged her tense shoulders.

"This cast is a real pain." She splayed her fingers wide, as her elbow balanced the cast on the lip of the Jacuzzi. "This feels great." She exhaled and fell languid against him, closing her eyes. He ran his fingers through her mass of golden brown waves and kissed her temple.

There was no conversation, only a comfortable ease, relaxing to the sound of bluesy jazz as they both looked up at the stars for how long it was unclear. They leaned into one another and sighed. Enjoying the company of one another.

"Yeah, I think it's time to go inside. I think we're all pruned." Connor moved to stand, then picked Ellie up with one arm and cradled her to his chest. "I need you, Ellie."

"Again?" She looked into his steel gray eyes and his super-hero charisma. Ellie nestled in closer, holding up her cast as Connor plucked her out of the whirling waters. He ravaged her lips and carried her carefully to the house. He locked the doors, setting the security system alarm behind them.

The birds whistled and chirped as the morning sun rose over the horizon. Ellie woke to a light snoring behind her and the feel of Connor's warm breath on her skin. She looked around the upstairs room where he'd brought her. He said it was his room. Similar to the one she changed in the night before.

She laced her fingers between his, kissing the top of his hand softly, feeling the charge of his body flowing through his protruding veins. He was a piece of art—the timeless brush stroke across a canvas.

Connor's grip tightened around her, and the rigid length of his manhood pressed against her backside. The man had an appetite for sex, and she was getting schooled. He ran his free hand between her inner thighs and lifted her leg. He kissed her along her back as he entered her from behind. Slow deep methodical strokes raptured her. She started seeing stars as he filled her over and over again. An out of body experience apprehended her as waves of her own orgasms imprisoned her to this man.

Connor never spent time with the same woman more than a night and now he had spent days doing exactly that with Ellie, and he wanted more. He'd never wanted anyone like he craved her. She was special, and he was different with her. He needed to be so close to her even the act of sex didn't satisfy his thirst. He wanted more than sex with Ellie, so much more. He wanted her until she was tired of him. She had all the power, but in the deepest recess of his gut, he knew he didn't deserve her and wouldn't have her beyond what they shared this weekend. She would start asking him questions about his past—questions he would never answer.

Connor suddenly stopped and jerked away abruptly. "Dammit, what a dip-shit," he said aloud. How could he be so ignorant to risk such a foolish act? He was in over his head and being so irresponsible and careless solidified it. A baby with Ellie made his stomach turn. He couldn't allow himself to love anyone. If he did, he would risk losing them like he'd lost his parents and would be his definite demise.

Ellie whipped around and pulled the cover over her shielding herself. "What's wrong?" she asked. "What happened?" She sat up and leaned away. "Look at me, Connor. Talk to me." Her voice raised another octave. She rolled her eyes as color rose in her cheeks. She crawled to the other end of the bed where his back was turned and fisted hands cradled his head. Her thoughts jumbled all she wanted to do was diffuse the situation What was wrong with him? He tore away from her grasp, retreating farther. She watched as he moved to the dresser across the room and slipped into an old shredded pair of Levi's and a V-necked white t-shirt.

"I messed up" He paced across the room and almost appeared to be rasping for air. He ran his hands across his face. His tan skin was paler than before. "I wasn't thinking, and I forgot a condom. Shit!"

"Oh, no." Ellie gathered her legs and rocked as a tear slid down her face. Horror gripped her, and no words came. She just rocked back and forth She wanted to find the nearest exit and escape. "We just both lost our heads."

"I don't lose my head." He paced back and forth running his forearm over his forehead each step pounding heavier as he paced. "What a moron. I swear to you. I wasn't thinking." He pleaded. "You have to believe, I'd never do anything to hurt you. I've never been so careless; I've never forgotten protection before."

"Oh.no." Ellie's voice quivered, her body shook as she wiped her tear-stained face.

"I think we're done talking. You better get dressed," he said.

She flinched. "Right." Ellie slid off the bed, wrapping the camel colored sheet around her. She wrestled with the plastic wrap hanging from her cast She wagged a finger. "Why are you being so distant?" She wrapped the sheet tighter. "It was a mistake. I think we really should discuss this civilly. "He gazes darted away.

"There's nothing more to debate. I don't make mistakes. Not one of epic proportions like this," Connor said as he stalked around the room.

"I'm just as upset as you are, but you don't need to take this out on me." Ellie whipped her casted arm in the air trailing the Saran Wrap over her head. "I didn't do anything wrong, and you don't need to be such a jerk."

The temperature was escalating in the room just as the conversation. Ellie opened the door to the bathroom and stood in the doorway across from him. "I knew I shouldn't have gotten involved with you." She snorted a dismissive laugh.

"What do you mean *involved*?" Connor backed away in defense. "We both knew what was going to happen this weekend. We are two consenting adults enjoying each other's company." His words bit hard.

"It was a heck of a lot more than sex, and you know it." Ellie stepped closer, her hands clenched into two tights balls. "Every single thing we have done since we met has always been more than chemistry and more than sex. Go ahead and con yourself if you like, but I'm keeping it real."

"Was it, Ellie? Hmmm… Are you sure?" he asked. His eyes vacant and fixed.

"Was this a game to you?" Ellie stomped her foot. "From you watching over the poor accident victim in the hospital, and then to you having a testosterone fueled beef with Evan? Huh? Answer me. Am I a pawn in your twisted, egotistical competition?" She quivered as her voice shook. "Connor, you are missing a sensitivity chip." Not again…oh, god, not again. Not him. *How could I be so terribly wrong? I must have stupid stamped all over my forehead.*

She took a deep inhale through her nose, closed her eyes for a second, and a power-filled sense came over her. "Mr. Winslow, apparently you got what you wanted. Congratulations." She tapped her hands together. "You broke my heart. You took it and shattered it into little pieces." A single tear escaped and trickled down Ellie's cheek before she brushed it away. "I shouldn't have trusted you. I thought you were different."

She inched from the icy-chill in the air Connor projected. She didn't want anything to do with this side of him.

"Ellie, don't cry. I'm not worth your tears." Connor crossed his arms over his chest.

"News flash, these tears are not for you." She straightened up, her back going ramrod straight as she threw her shoulders firm. "Funny, part of this ridiculous charade is… I thought you were worth it. My bad." She shoved past him to get her bags. "Take me home right now, or I'll call Uber myself. You're not the only one who's been to hell and back, and back again, but you don't see that. It's all about you and you have no concept. We all have pain. I've had my fair share, but I chose not to limp through life. I thought you were more astute."

Connor rubbed the center of his chest. "I don't want to talk about the past. It's dead and buried along with them." He paused, scrubbing his chin as he inhaled deeply. "We've... had a great time. Can't we leave it as is?"

"As is? So, you just shut down? Lock it away like nothing ever happened?" she asked.

"Pretty much." He closed his eyes. "It's called self-preservation. We had fun."

"Self-preservation." She shook her head. "Sounds like being masochistic to me." She gritted her teeth hard. "But I will drop it." She drew herself inward, one hand clinched the base of her throat and the other protected her heart. "You are emotionally unavailable. And that's not who I am." Her breath hitched with a groan. "I want to feel every bruise and every cut." She touched the scar above her eyebrow awkwardly with her bright pink cast. "I want to feel heartache and loss. I want to know what love is and feel what love is. At least I know I'm fricking alive." She paused, and her voice slowed and iced over. "Unlike you. You may have a heartbeat, but you are not living."

"Yeah, well join the club everyone says that anyway. Ellie, I can't miraculously do an illusion like Houdini and start feeling, it's too risky. It's not in my DNA."

"I will not do this again.... Not with another robot. I can't fix you; I *won't* fix you." Ellie turned and walked near the door.

"I don't need anyone fixing me."

"No, you are not peachy-keen, Connor. You've fooled yourself." She held back a sob that escaped beyond her quaking stance. "You don't see it do you?" She shook her head as another trail of tears streamed down her face. "I could have loved you." Her chin jutted up. "Your loss. Take me home, please. I'll go get my things and wait outside."

CHAPTER 21

*H*e hated to hurt her and see her cry, but he wasn't going to talk about anything he felt—he didn't know how to. He replayed the argument over and over again. *"Yeah, well join the club."* He eased against the wall to get away from her hurtful words, but it wasn't the first time he'd heard the exact verse from his counselor, co-workers, or family. Coming from Ellie's bladed tongue sliced deep...too deep.

Ellie's glare maimed and pierced him like a dagger. Connor's chest cramped with an undeniable mourning as the regret swallowed him whole. He couldn't transform who he was, no matter how he longed for it. How had things switched so fast between them?

The ride was maddening and the silence cloaked him. He was hollow. She turned and stared out the window all the way home, and Ellie last her fingers together around her cast. Her posture was board stiff. Connor could only see her profile, but he didn't know what to do. They were over. There was nothing more to say, and a clean sever was best, but he hadn't thought it would happen this soon. No one was going to make him to talk about something he never mentioned to anyone, and sure as hell wished never happened. And why was he such an idiot not using a condom? What was he thinking? Loneliness encapsulated to his core pushing him further into a dark abyss.

They pulled up to her farmhouse. The golden light of dusk warmed the entrance. She wouldn't even look at him. He opened the trunk, grabbed her suitcase, and ran to the passenger side of the car to reach for her, but she darted away from him.

"Goodbye, Connor." She whipped around and brushed the makeup smeared under her red swollen eyes. "Don't come around me anymore." She sniffed and dabbed her dripping nose. She clomped her feet across the gravel to the front steps dragging her bag behind her. "Have a nice life in your misery."

There were a million miles between them. He jolted when the screen door slammed behind her.

"Dammit." The woman had guts. She called him out on his shit.

Connor's phone vibrated, alerting him that he had a voicemail. It was from Jeffrey. "Winslow, you'd better answer the phone. I am not taking no for an answer. I need to talk to you about Ellie. It's been two weeks too long, and I can't bear to see my sister cry another tear for your sad self. Your pansy ass needs to hear me out until I've said what I have to say. I don't know what happened between you two, but I think it's time to get something long overdue off my chest. Either you call me, or I'll find you. I know you're working a shift and you're off before nine, so I'll meet you at the diner across from the fire station at nine."

Connor knew he had to face Ellie's overprotective brother sometime, and he had a few things he needed to say, too. The phone vibrated as the text showed up on his screen again. This guy was not about to give up. *I'm here at Ruby's. I'll see you in a few, you better be there.*

I'll be there. On my way. Connor texted back.

"Thanks for meeting me," Jeffrey said. He walked behind Connor as they took a table in the corner and sat.

"Like I had a choice. You've been calling nonstop." Connor held up two fingers when the waitress started over and she brought two cups and a carafe of coffee.

"You look as miserable as my sister does."

The waitress sat the cups on the table, poured the coffee to the brim, and set the decanter down. "Here you go. I'll be back for your order."

Connor nodded and thanked her. "Just coffee today."

"Appears you aren't getting much sleep either," Jeffrey said as he spooned the sugar into his cup. Connor watched and cringed at the amount he put in there. He occupied his thoughts with anything other than Ellie's brother's pep talk. This was not going to be the highlight of his day, but he knew he deserved what was coming.

"I don't know where you and my sister stand, but I think you love her and I know she loves you."

"She told you that?"

"She didn't have to, but neither of you are kidding anyone. I don't know you well enough, but I know her." Jeffrey tilted the cup back for a long pull of caffeine. "So, do you? Love her?" He waited for a response, but there was none. "Because, if you do, you'd better get off your sorry ass and tell her."

"It's not so simple." He shifted in his seat. "I do care for her, more than I've ever cared for anyone, but I fucked up. I'll admit she deserves better than I can offer. I have some nasty gremlins tormenting me. I can't even deal with my own shit, let alone

155

Ellie's." He squeezed the back of his neck to ease the tension then tilted his head to his shoulders from right to left. "No matter how much I want her in my life, she doesn't need my crap."

"Winslow, I get the PTSD, and I'm sorry about your parents. Ellie told me you're holding on pretty tight to the past. I drilled Cade and he told me you two lost your parents in a horrible accident at the hands of a drunk driver when you were younger. From my observation, you are all janked up with regret and think the whole thing is your fault."

Connor straightened in his seat. "You weren't there. I was. So, you're pushing where you shouldn't go."

"Maybe so, but I came here to say something, and it might just penetrate the concrete cranium of yours." Jeffrey knocked at his own skull and shot Connor eyes darts. "It's not always about your demons; we all have demons. Crap, I have a few ghosts in my own closet, but that's a season of Jerry Springer shows." Jeffrey smirked to lighten the mood looming over them.

"Ellie had her own bad hand dealt to her and a full house of heartache. My sister taught me at the end of the day you have to move forward and try to repair the past and make a better future. She taught me to live each day like it was your last." Jeffrey tilted his head and cleared his throat. "She's smarter than the two of us."

Jeffrey tapped his fingers on the table. "Let me start by telling you a little story, and I need you hear me out. Please just listen. Don't interrupt or I won't be able to get through this." He cleared his throat and shifted in his seat.

"I'd never betray my sister's trust to another soul, but I can't stand by and watch this misery for another day. She been happier than Iv3 ever seen her when you're together. Like she used to be when she was young. There's just been too much. It's killing me, and I believe in my gut instinct this is the right thing to do. And I wouldn't interfere if I didn't think you were worth

156

it, Winslow. If you get my drift," Jeffrey said as he nodded. "She would have me hung by my sacks if she knew I was talking to you. Neither of you has to tell anyone how you feel about each other; it's obvious to everyone, but you and her." Jeffrey shook his head again in disgust and took a long inhale followed by an even longer exhale. "Ellie told me she shared with you that she was married?"

Jeffrey looked like he was going to straight up hyperventilate any moment. If he didn't feel like he was going to yak himself he'd feel sorrier for Ellie's brother. Connor answered, "Yes she did." He braced his arms over his chest and eased back in the booth.

"Ellie and James were married a few years out of high school but were together since they were in their early teens. He was a self-centered prick. Ellie was smitten with the notion of the happily ever after." Jeffrey leaned forward with his elbows firm on the table as he pinched his lower lip. "The ass hat was jealous of everyone, including me, and occupied all of her time. Anyone close to Ellie was a threat. I think he started to control her from the start. She was stifled and didn't see it coming. The bastard smashed her spirit." Jeffrey gripped his cup as his hand shook.

Connor could feel anger swell inside. He clenched his teeth, and he could feel his veins pulse and twitch. He cracked his knuckles, glued to Jeffrey's every word.

"He tore her down time after time, but Ellie fought to regain her life back. He snatched it back because he was a major manipulator and she couldn't escape him. After our parents died, and I went off to boot camp, she was all alone and they eloped. The stakes kept getting higher, and he became more and more controlling. I regret to this day that I wasn't there for her. I tried to get out but was sent overseas." Jeffrey wiped his mouth, took a huge swig of water, and downed the whole glass. "He worked as a low budget private investigator and a bail bondsman and he was a badass. He wouldn't let her finish college. Forbid it."

Connor bit his hand and growled. "Fucker."

Jeffrey put his hand up. "I haven't even scratched the surface. You can't make this shit up. She rallied and came back stronger and stronger until she got her confidence back. A warrior. She's a warrior plain and simple. I did everything I could, including hiring some of my old buddies to follow him until I got back." Jeffrey hesitated and clenched his jaw tight and then smacked his fist against his hand. "She was a victim, but you don't see her acting like one or feeling sorry for herself. Ellie has more willpower and might than the both of us put together. She doesn't blame herself anymore, and believe me, it took some time."

Connor's muscles twitched, and he pulled at his collar. *I can't breathe.*

Jeffrey's nostrils flared, and he struggled to continue. "James became physical, and she took out a restraining order against him. He forced himself on her more than once, and she lost a baby." Jeffrey wiped the moisture from his forehead with the back of his hand.

"No..." Connor jumped up from his seat. He couldn't control the fury and rage he felt inside. He wanted to rip his hair out and bust the place apart. He stomped across the black and white tiles, shaking the cups and dishes on the tables. He flung the door open with such a vengeance it shimmied on the hinges. He lifted a large green trash receptacle wanting to throw it down the street but set it back down as he saw Jeffrey standing near the large picture window of the diner.

Connor waved off imaginary demons so he wouldn't black out. He wanted to take away any hurt Ellie had ever experienced. Debris littered the street as he kicked cans, hurling them into the alley. Connor kicked a metal newspaper stand with his steel toed boot, but the thing was secure in the cement. He wanted to destroy things, but he swore to uphold property. It was her abusive ex-husband's head he wanted to pummel.

Anyone ever hurting Ellie makes me die inside. Where was the anger coming from?

He picked up the debris and composed himself and walked back into Ruby's, stretching his neck front right to left. "I'll pay for any damage, Ruby, or fix it myself." Connor pressed against his temples, facing Jeffrey.

"You're the one, all right. Her knight in shining armor," Jeffrey muttered. "No man ever looks like this except an alpha male in deep shit over his woman. But you need to curb your temper. Feel better after kicking the garbage around?" He motioned for Connor to sit back down, but Connor stayed planted.

Jeffrey took a step forward eye to eye. "Sit down, Winslow. I'm not done."

"I don't want to hear anymore," Connor murmured through clinched teeth.

"Sit. You need to hear this, please." Jeffrey guided him forward.

"I don't think I can, not if it involves Ellie. I can't."

"Yes, you can. You're solid and I get it. I'll help you through." Jeffrey pointed to the seat. "Sit"

Connor slid in and interlaced his fingers to stop from biting through a digit. His brain waves were whacked, and he needed to concentrate. He wiped the sweat off his forehead and was about to go postal if he didn't take a deep breath and get in touch with his inner Zen. If anything, ever happened to Ellie, he'd die a slow miserable death.

Jeffrey continued his dialogue. "She filed for a restraining order and got divorced from the blow-hole. Went back to college with a degree and got a job at the crisis center. When I got home, I moved back in and kept my eye out for the prick. I guess she was smothered in a different way, but at least she was safe. That I could live with."

Jeffrey struggled to continue puffing his cheeks out, then swallowing the air and releasing it.

By the look on Jeffrey's face, he didn't want to even relive what happened next. "Go on, Jeffrey, this can't be easy for you. To talk about." Connors muscles bunched up under his skin.

"Nothing was going to happen if I could help it, but I failed." Jeffrey jumped as a dish and silverware was dumped into a nearby bus-tub. "I was only gone for twenty minutes one night, before the guys I hired to protect Ellie were in route." Jeffrey picked at the skin around his thumb. "James broke into the house. He must have been watching our every move. He broke in through a window in the basement. He had no idea what was in store from a woman scorned, and she was a ninja after taking self-defense classes at the crisis center. She fought him off, scratching at his eyes, biting his nose, and kicking his privates." Jeffrey's infuriated voice was slow and low. He cleared his throat.

Connor moaned while vice-gripping the tabletop.

"Makes you want to hurt someone, huh?" he asked Connor.

Connor nodded only to see fury and rubbed his temples, trying to alleviate the pounding.

"She was bloodied and bruised, but she was the one who dialed me, and then she called the police before she passed out. We found her lying in a pile of both of their blood. She still had a handful of James' hair clutched in her fist and a cast iron frying pan in the other."

Jeffrey stilled and pinched his lower lip. "I took him to jail myself, and he begged for me to take him. Guy crapped his pants as I waited until he confessed to every gory detail." Jeff's voice projected drawing back to the present. "She was a victim and not by choice, but you don't see her feeling sorry for herself ever. You wouldn't know by looking at her that she'd have that kind of past or power to move on from something so horrific."

Connor shoulders curled over his chest and he ripped the napkin to shreds. "I know the power she possesses." He'd heeded every horror he'd ever dreamed of, but this had happened to Ellie, and he couldn't bear what she had been through, or what his own recent behavior had been toward her. He prayed to himself for forgiveness. His chest burned from front to back as he kneaded the agonizing pain in his shoulders and he dragged in a calming breath. He'd rather be bludgeoned than feel what he was experiencing now. His head pounded. Pure rage engulfed him as he spat out venom. "Where is he?" he spat through flattened lips. "I'm going to kill the bastard."

"It's way too late for James. So, cool your jets." Jeff looked at the table and then to Connors hand. "Can I finish? Or are you going to have another Hulk moment and tear the table apart in your fist?" Jeff said as he jack-hammered his legs under the table.

Connor loosened his grip clutching his palms together and said, "There's more?"

"James spent time in jail. Skipped out on bail before his trial. He got mixed up with some bad people and they ended up killing him, so they say. I guess he played both sides of the law and got messed up in drugs and snitched on the wrong people. Lucky, they did the deed because it took everything I had not to wring his neck myself." Jeffrey's voice shook as he cracked his knuckles. "They never found his body. I'd spit on his grave if they did."

"Karma's a bitch." Jeffrey winced and lowered his head. "I'm just saying, at the end of the day you have to move along like she did. You can't change the past, but you always have an option in the future. We should all learn from her.

"So, Connor. I know you love, Ellie. Who wouldn't?" Jeffrey wiped his mustache with the napkin. "I can't take watching her love you; it's killing me. She's earned her happily ever after. If you're not it, stay the hell out of her life." Jeffrey stood and threw a few dollar bills on the table.

"And… Do me another super epic courtesy as you're mulling over my words. Get your own life figured out and deal with your past. You appear to be a nice guy and I kind of like you." Jeffrey crossed his arms with a hollow laugh. "Even though you're not exactly my type."

There's a lot to like here, but again and again, the reader is shown reasons why Connor and Ellie aren't a good match when you want your readers to be rooting for them. Showing him shaking, sweating, and barely holding himself together would maybe help. Showing Connor forcing himself to not break things b/c he needs to learn about Ellie would also help the reader understand why they're a good match, and how even when they're not together, she's helping him be better. Just a thought.

CHAPTER 22

*C*onnor brushed the debris of twigs and leaves off the cold marble stone. A row of a few dozen small rocks of different colors and shapes lined the top of the headstones that marked his parents' final resting place. The old cemetery was located at the top of a ridge, nestled only a few miles from the home where he grew up. For years, he never could bring himself to take the road and turn to finally come here.

"Mom... Dad, I'm sorry it's been so long. I hope you aren't any more disappointed in me than you already are." He leaned against the tree between the plots as he inched his way through the thick green grass. The dates of their deaths engraved in the granite scored deep into Connor's heart as if it were yesterday. He couldn't remember the last time he had been there. His night terrors had amplified over the last week, and last nights was the worst that he could remember. He couldn't shake the feeling he was on a ledge and about to fall into despair. Would he ever get through this?

A tapestry of helplessness, horror, and the loving memories of his childhood were woven into his core. The intensity of the dreams coming back had everything to do with Ellie, and what she'd been through killed him.

Horrific scenes replayed over subtle memories of love and laughter from his childhood. The dreams were so vivid last night, and there were things hanging over him he needed to remember. Why was he compelled to be here now? And what drew him to have this long overdue conversation with their ghosts?

Peace surrounded him, and the words just came.

"I've met someone." He unloaded his feelings as the wind kicked up around him. "I've been a total fuck up." He felt the hairs on the back of his neck prickle down his spine. "You would love her, I know it, but like always, I've messed up so bad she'll never see me again, but I can't stop thinking about her." His insides twisted and wrung. He reached into his front pocket, pulled out a partially opened roll of antacids, and popped one into his mouth. He chewed on the chalky grit that would settle his stomach.

"The house just isn't the same without you there, and the garden is full of weeds. I'm afraid to eat the last of the raspberry preserves in the basement because your handwriting is still legible on the lid, Mom." A lump formed in his throat the size of a walnut. "I'm afraid I'll forget everything—I'll forget you and Dad. Or I'll forget who I used to be. I can't erase the moments that led up to the accident or what I saw. I relive every moment over and over again. Sometimes, I think I'm going to go mad. I wish I was able to see the other driver coming and stop him. I hate that I couldn't. And that I just ran away and left you there. Like a coward." He cradled his head, pulling at his hair. "Your screams, Dad... I can't stop hearing them."

Connor rested against the rough bark of the old weeping willow tree. He closed his eyes against the warmth of the sun descending behind the foothills, casting a sienna and powder blue trail. The dark gray silhouette of the Colorado Rockies looked as if they were kissing the clouds.

Connor swore he heard a familiar deep voice. *"Son, I'm proud of you."* He heard his dad's voice as if he were standing right behind him. *"It wasn't your fault, and I wish you would stop blaming yourself. I'm as proud as any father could be and your mom is, too."*

How he longed to have his parents back.

"Be happy, son ... Find love."

Connor's thoughts were back at the accident scene, but this time, he heard the words he never remembered before and his dad trapped behind the steering wheel of the car in the driver's seat. "You need to get out of here. Run to safety. The car is going to blow, and it's too late for me. You need to do what you were trained to do...Run and get help for your mother. Where's Cade? He's going to need you, be there for him. Forever." His dad shoved him away, but Connor wouldn't leave. Pain and sadness gripped his features as he shoved harder. "Run!"

He ran as he heard Dad's trembled words. "I love you, son, promise me you will be happy." The car exploded, throwing him across the pavement asphalt as it shredded his flesh. The sound was so loud his ears rang, but he heard Dad's screams. The metal dropped from the sky around him littered the pavement. Fireballs of debris and stench filled his nostrils.

Connor must have replayed the moment over and over through the years, but he'd never recalled the words his dad said, and now they were clear as day. There were so many voids in his memory from the accident. How could he have not retained his dad's last words? The last sentence he spoke to him and the loved he'd shown. How could he have not remembered them until so many years later?

My father saved my life because he loved me.

He wretched for air, his palms fighting for more memories. His eyes stung as he gained clarity. He thrashed back and forth, digesting the emotion he'd guarded in the cavern of his turmoil for eons. He was weak and exhausted from fighting a fight he was never going to win.

Abruptly he rose and sat ramrod straight. "Dad, I'm so sorry I couldn't save you and Mom. I know I can't erase what I was unable to do, and the pain of losing you is more than I can bear at times. I know it's my penance for not doing more. I had to make up for it all these years, and I can't save enough people to make up for not saving you." He howled in anger. "I don't remember who I was before the accident. I'm walking along the perimeter of life, on the outside looking in. I'm so tired. We were so happy. All I wanted was to follow in your footsteps and make you and Mom proud." He couldn't stop releasing his anger or the verbiage.

"I'm in love, and I don't know what I'm doing. I can't figure out how to get past losing you and Mom. I want to be happy, but the guilt is tearing me up." His father's words echoed in his head again.

"Be happy. Find love. I'm proud of you, son, and Cade too. It's time to stop dying a slow death of regret. You must live each day like you were dying. Life is so precious. Take the happiness you deserve."

Connor cried for the first time since the funeral. He didn't know how long he sat there, but it was dark, and he was startled by a hoot of an owl in a nearby evergreen tree. There were no more tears to shed. Connor needed more counseling. If it wasn't too late…

Connor turned back to his parents' graves as the silvery full moon illuminated in the landscape.

"Mom, I miss your cookies. The snickerdoodles were my favorite." He remembered.

"They were mine, too," a voice from the tree line rumbled.

Connor twisted around to see the familiar shadow. "What the—Shit, Cade. You scared the living crap out of me." His brother used to lie in wait and sneak up on the enemy. He could hardly see him in his all black ensemble of jeans, t-shirt, shit-kickers and coal black hair. "How long have you been out there?"

"Longer than I probably should have...Sorry," he said. "You were sleeping like a baby and I didn't want to disturb you, but then you started talking, then shouting, and it creeped me out a little, so I came closer to make sure you weren't being attacked by a snake or having a seizure or something." Cade stepped closer. "You were you sleeping, right? I thought someone else was with you at first." Cade eliminated the distance as he placed another rock at their parents, Thomas and Beth's memorial.

Connor got up and brushed the grass off his jeans. His brother lined up another cluster of small rocks directly beside the other rocks on the marked steely granite "All of these rocks are from you?" he asked.

"Yup, I've been carrying rocks in my pocket for years and when I find something special I always bring it here. I have rocks from all over the world." Cade stood there, repositioning the rocks methodically. "This is the first time you've seen my rocks?" Cade asked. "Dude, how long has it been since you were here last? I've been placing them here for years until I went away to Iraq. I have some catching up to do from when I was gone." He shifted back and leaned against a nearby tree with his arms across his chest.

"I'm really not sure I can remember how long, but... too long." Connor got up and stepped closer to Cade. "Why the rocks?"

"Haven't you ever heard of a gratitude rock before?" Cade snickered.

"Can't say I have. Rocks have been rattling around in your pockets? No wonder you have trouble keeping your pants up."

"Don't be posing on me. And bring your own rocks now." Cade inched away from the tree and slapped Connor on the back. "I have a lot to be grateful for." He wrestled an arm around his brother and best friend. "You hear me? A helluva lot to be grateful for, and it all started with us." He pointed to the graves and Connor.

"The Winslow's." Connor nodded and said, "I do." He embraced Cade. "I need to go back to the company counselor and work some long overdue things out. Do you mind going with me?"

"I thought you'd never ask."

Jax pulled the fire truck out of the garage and to the driveway of station 56. "Cap, do you have a few minutes to talk?" He sprayed the hose on the ladder truck and wiped down the sides.

The captain picked up a rag from the pile. "Yeah, sure. What's up?"

"It's chafing me not to call Connor, but how's our boy doing on furlough? Been weeks. How much longer do I have to deal with Parker on my rig?"

"Honeycutt, I think Connor's going to be just fine. Janet's been dropping food by, and Cade says he's been hanging with Connor up at the cabin every day off that he can. They're catching a lot of fish and working on their cars. We're having dinner this weekend. The counselor says he can come back whenever he's ready."

"No shit? I'm stoked. It just hasn't been the same around here since he's been gone. I've worked with him all my career, and I kind of miss his mug."

"Yeah, me too." The cap slapped him on the back and pulled his phone from his front pocket and looked at the text.

"Speak of the devil. You'll see him on Monday's shift. So, Parker will be off your rig and back on mine." Jax jumped down off the rig and ran to give the captain a high five. "Woo-hoo!

Ask and you shall receive. I call the news a day maker." Jax raised his fist in the air. "Yes."

Jax, Cade, and Jeffrey decided to move things along and interfere as they peeked out the window of Johnny's, dodging and weaving behind the beer sign in the window as Connor's black Charger pulled into the driveway. Ellie's white rental car followed slowly behind, but she hesitated to get out when she eyed Connor. She looked around for her brother then slowly got out and leaned against her car.

Connor walked over. "Hi, Ellie. What are you doing here?"

"My brother said he needed a ride."

"I'm glad you're here. It's great to see you." He wanted to touch her but kept his hands in his pockets. "I hoped I would see you again."

Her eyes had less sparkle than he'd remembered. They were deep pools and dark shadows rested below the skin underneath them. She was thin—too thin. She stood there, jittery, shifting from foot-to-foot and looking around.

I want to hold her in my arms and never let her go. Tell her I would do anything for her. Love her until my dying breath if only I had the nerve.

"I can't begin to tell you how sorry I am. Your strength and courage have helped me get the help I needed to deal with my past and to learn to stop blaming myself, finally."

She looked into his soul and the years of the walls he'd built crumbled inside of him, brick by brick.

"I know you won't forgive me, and I can't blame you. I was an asshole."

She nodded. "Can't say I disagree."

He laughed. "The statement is not a first."

He stepped forward and reached for her hand, but her body language made him rethink. He had no right to touch her, so he shoved his fists back into his front pockets.

"I truly get it. Our timing wasn't right," she said, as she ran her hands over her chest, nervously rolling her necklace around her forefinger. "I was wrong about us, and I shouldn't have pushed you to open up with me so soon."

"I never intended on hurting you, Ellie, and I'm sorry for everything I said. You were right. I'm a self-serving butt-tard who's emotionally unavailable." He smiled and looked down. "I deserved you giving me the honest truth, but I'm clear now. I wasn't dealing with my parents' death," he said as his voice shook. "I didn't want to face it, for fear of losing their memory. Maybe, I checked out." It was easier to not feel anything than to feel the loss. He curled his arms over his head.

"When you pleaded for me to help you when you had your accident, everything rushed back. Maybe I desperately needed a do-over, and I had no right to involve you in my twisted reality. I just couldn't stay away from you. I tried. So unfair to you. I guess I felt I could right a wrong." He leaned against Ellie's car as close to her as he dared. "I can't explain this, but I'll try. When you look at me, I feel stronger than I've ever felt before, and I thought I could be the man you deserved." He stopped and rubbed his chest where the ache would not go away. She looked up at him, not saying a word.

"You have more fight and zest for life than anyone I've ever known. You're contagious, and I wanted who I used to be back in my life, like before my parents' accident. I just didn't know how to do it or how deep I actually was. I know I've lost you already, and you've had your share of losses, too."

Her eyes narrowed and her mouth opened but nothing came out.

"What do you mean?" she asked. "What I've lost? My parents?"

Connor turned and faced Ellie as he held her hands in his. "I'm so sorry Ellie, can you ever forgive me. I didn't mean to hurt you. I never wanted to hurt you. I care about you."

She moved closer and held him. "Thank you and I accept your apology, if you will accept mine. For pushing you when I shouldn't have."

They held each other. Connor didn't want to ever let her go as he ran his fingers through her hair, wrapping the tendrils around like ribbons as his hand shook. "I had no right to think I was the only one with loss and pain. I know you have had your own. How could I be so narcissistic or naive?"

"What exactly do you mean?" she asked, then inched away and looked up, her gaze clouded, going distant.

"Jeffrey told me about James and what happened to you."

She retreated further and stared at her palms. "He did?" She winced and covered her mouth. "He had no right." Her voice raised and her cheeks reddened. "No right at all. Why would he do that?" Her posture slacked as she stepped back farther.

Connor moved closer. "I'm sorry, Ellie. He felt he had to. I'm glad he did." Connor lifted her chin, and her face was blank, but her eyes were icy.

"I'm not, and I don't want anyone's pity." She lifted her chin, shoulders moved back. "I have to go now; I'm late for my shift at the crisis center. If you see my brother tell him he's a traitor." Her tone deepened. She stamped away.

Connor followed. "Ellie. Please don't go."

She threw herself into the driver's seat. "I don't need saving, Connor."

"I'm sorry!" Connor yelled. He squeezed his eyes shut and pinched the bridge of his nose. When he finally opened his eyes, wishing the whole meeting with Ellie hadn't ended the way it did, he saw something in his peripheral vision in the window of Johnny's. Three familiar jug heads with their nose holes planted against the glass before they ducked, dived, and weaved not to be seen.

Connor kicked at the gravel and pebbles sprayed around.

"Dammit!" His voice thickened. They'd witnessed the whole encounter.

Jeffrey led Jax and Cade outside. Each held their heads down keeping their distance. Connor's ego hit a new low.

Connor dragged his palms along his pant legs. "I have a feeling this wasn't a chance meeting between Ellie and me?" He shook his head. Connor wanted answers, and he wanted them now. "This was a set-up, wasn't it?"

Jeffrey stepped closer, hiding his face, and his voice cracked. "It's my fault. I couldn't take it anymore, and you two were literally killing me after we'd talked, so I took over as I always do. And recruited these two." Jeff hitched his thumb back at Jax and Cade. "So, if you are going to blame anyone, blame me." Jeffrey took a deep breath and rolled his shoulders back. "I called Ellie and told her to meet me here because my truck broke down. She's my damn Achilles heel, and I'm dying a slow miserable death as we speak. I know my sister, and she's in deep shit right now. You are the only one who can change things for her. I know she loves you."

"Yeah, and Beavis and Butt-head wanted me to meet them here precisely at a certain time." Connor looked over at his brother and friend who'd betrayed him and shook his head in disgust. "You two sold me out."

Jax stood back with his hands in his pockets, averting Connor's stare.

Cade shifted about and started talking way too fast. "We put up the closed sign to stop you from coming in if she didn't arrive yet, and I don't regret it either. You both needed to get within ear shot to get past whatever happened at the cabin. I'm not selling you out; it's caring for your sorry ass enough to help the process." He looked pale and harried as he rubbed his nose, then his ears.

"Hey, wait a fuckin minute here. Don't you think I could have done this another time when we were both ready? Or ,when I figured out what to say before you planned this heist?" Connor swallowed hard as he pressed his temples. "And don't you think you could not have hatched some hair-brained plan for us to meet in a bar parking lot of all places?" Connor anchored his fist on his hips pacing back and forth. "As you can see, it didn't go over so well." He scratched his chin. "She just bolted, and I don't blame her. I was a blubbering doofus. I'm just getting my head on straight after all these years, and it took round three with the shrink for it to finally sink in." He winced.

Jax shuffled forward, kicking the dirt. "Dude, can't you see she's in love with you?" Jax shouted and then shook Connor. "Wake up and smell the coffee, stubborn ass. And if I were you, I wouldn't stop until you got her back because your life is over if you don't."

"Watch it, Honeycutt. I'm still in a sympathetic mood." He removed Jax's hands from his shoulders and scrubbed his face. "I practically begged her to forgive me. She at least forgave me but left me standing here for you stooges to have a big laugh on me. I can take it, but Ellie's feeling betrayed. I shouldn't have said anything."

"Not so," Jax replied. "None of us are laughing."

"We're as sick about this as you are," Jax and Cade said in unison. They looked at each other. And then said, "Jinx, mo-fo."

"We've never seen you this way, bro. You're killing us," Cade added.

"Ellie is the one you should be worried about, not me. I'm solid for the first time in years." He pointed to his temple. "Well... I'm getting out of here. Sorry to be such a hassle. See you three amigos later, and by the way, the matinee is over." He turned waving his middle finger up and punched it into the air.

"Later. The woman's made up her mind, quit interfering in my life. You owe her the apology."

Connor looked to Jeffrey who was pacing and pinched his bottom lip. "Oh yeah, by the way, Jeffrey. I told Ellie about our talk and you may have some explaining to do yourself. She was pretty hurt about you telling me what happened with James."

"Oh crap. Now I'm in deep pig slop, Winslow." Jeffrey let out a controlled moan. "I guess misery loves company. You haven't seen her when she's really peeved. Her wrath is worst with the silence. She says a lot without saying a peep." Jeffrey ran around the corner to his pickup truck, put it in reverse, and rolled down his window. "I'd better get my punishment over with. Yikes." He saluted the trio and fired up his engine, pulling his ball cap down.

Connor flipped his key fob out to unlock the car. "The performance has ended boys, with the not so happily ever after." Connor shook his head and ran his hand under his nose. "I need to catch some z's before my shift. See you two later and get the puss off your faces. There's definitely going to be a sequel if I have anything to say about it." He high-fived his friends, started the engine and spun his tires. Connor looked in his rearview mirror at the guys as the gravel left them in a fog. Jax and Cade ran away from the spray.

I know I blew it with her, but I said what I needed to say. From this day forward, I know things will be different. I want to love. I need Ellie, and I am not going to give up without a fight. A life without Ellie Richards is not an option. I'm a Winslow, and I never quit.

Ellie couldn't sleep, she couldn't eat and she couldn't stop thinking about Connor. She still loved him. When she saw him, she wanted to hold onto him and not let go. How could everything between them change so fast. She drove away from Johnny's heading for her shift at work. She looked into the rear- view mirror and witnessed a truck speeding from behind. Was she being followed.? Not again. Memories of her accident replayed over and over. The truck swerved around her and the horn blared. She slowed to let the truck move far ahead, but it slowed. She memorized the letters and repeated them over and over. She slammed on her brakes and did a u turn towards the police station. When she knew she was safe in the parking lot of the Solemn Creed police station she locked her doors and called Jeffrey. "I'm still mad as hell at you, but I was followed again by a truck. I'm at the police station. Could you please meet me there?" Ellie looked around and had difficulty breathing and she couldn't focus. She opened the car door and though she was trembling she ran into the station.

CHAPTER 23

*T*he call came in for a four-alarm fire at a furniture warehouse with people trapped inside. Columns of black vapor rolled out of the five-story structure, and visibility was going to be worse because of all of the combustible materials.

Pumper and tanker trucks were already on site with their ladders extended and tapped into the hydrants. Several departments busted out the windows on the upper floors and blew lines inside to taper the blaze.

The men stepped over anaconda-like hoses to find a closer position.

"Winslow, keep alert. I need you to review the building specs." The captain laid out the building blueprints and pointed at the stairs to the floor where they needed to go. "There's a team on the fourth floor and another team going to the roof." The captain pointed to his ear. "Is your radio on and active?" he asked. "And... be careful, son." He gave Connor a thumb's up.

"Garcia, you ready, rookie?" Connor pulled the fire retardant Nomex material over his head. "This is the real deal. Anywhere I go, you stick close enough while you're eating my boots. Get as low as you can as soon as we get inside." He flipped his 02 and secured his mask and helmet into place. "People are counting on us."

"Got it, Lieutenant. I'm chewing your boots."

"Fletch, you ready to do this?" Connor asked.

"Yup, let's do this." Bill nodded.

The temperature inside the building was intense, perhaps several hundred degrees. Adrenaline coursed through Connor, and he felt super aware, but everything was in slow motion. He jumped up and down and swung his arms. "Let's head in, men," he said through the muffle of his mask. Sweat trailed down his skin while a laundry list of things bounced around in his head... *What if the ceiling collapses, and what if our oxygen runs out? What if we don't find any survivors? What if we can't find our way out?*

The midday sun was shining, but all they saw was darkness. Black smoke almost always dictated the fire was the most dangerous for a flash over.

Dammit, this is going to be a shit show. I hope Garcia has our back because there's no time to panic.

Connor could taste the rubber from his mask, but his breathing was soothing. At least, he could control something.

Garcia was stable and well-trained, but this was his first fire of this magnitude. His eyes were huge as he struggled for composure. The plume of black smoke billowed from the building. The choking smog obscured everything. They were going into total darkness with zero visibility, so they had to depend on other senses and could only feel their way around.

They are depending on me to get them in and out safe.

"You got this, Garcia. Keep sharp." Connor knocked on his helmet. "I'm just ahead of you, and Bill's got your ass. Are we clear boot? Keep moving or your PASS alarm will go off."

"Got it, Lieutenant, you can count on me."

"I know, Michael, I know." Connor inched forward through the veil of darkness, and the shower of sparks. The ceiling above was a fury of crimson devouring everything with its wrath. Connor signaled for everyone to get down. Raging flames leaped, hissed, and rolled in waves over their heads. Glowing embers roared and crackled before licking up the walls. The ceiling bellowed with ferocity.

Garcia and Fletcher anchored Connor from behind when he went to his knees, pulling the lever of the hose line to release the force of water toward the fall-colored inferno. A rumble quaked the building as drywall, sections of HVAC, and huge puzzle pieces of ceiling tiles torpedoed down on them. Rivers of water poured over knee-deep debris from the upper floors as they picked and axed through the maze of dilapidated scorched furniture.

"South Metro Fire and Rescue! Is anyone here?" Connor shouted out before he signaled for the men to follow. "Over there." The temperature escalated. He tugged the hose line through the fire as it devoured everything within its path until it diminished. Black fluffy columns turned into blinding white smoke. Connor's heart revved behind his sternum, exactly where his father's pin was; the metal was burning his flesh along with the trails of sweat leaving steam burns. Toxic fumes and gasses threatened as they crawled farther into danger.

Winslow, keep it together. Don't hold your breath! Move forward and keep breathing.

Another explosion shook the entire floor and rang through his ears. Connor stumbled back before he righted his boots and reclaimed his footing. His breathing echoed into his apparatus; there was something soothing about his breathing—it made him feel alive, lulling his brain to focus. He signaled for Bill and Garcia to follow as they struggled through the debris of charred and molten furniture.

"Winslow what's your status?" the captain's voice piped loud and clear into Connor's helmet.

A fireball tore across the room, leaving behind the stench of burning flesh. A man was engulfed in flames, his face black and scalded. Skin hung from his torso like an aged shredded curtain in a horror movie. His once shattered screams were faint as he whimpered before crumpling to the floor. Connor knew the man had to be moments from death and in immense pain. Soon he was going into shock but breathing the fumes and the intense heat damaged his airway, and that was something he couldn't come back from. There was nothing he could do for him here. All he needed to do was grab and go and get the hell out.

No, not again. I can't watch another person die. I just can't.

It was easier feeling nothing, so he didn't feel the pain. Connor focused on his breathing instead of the horror unfolding in front of him. There was a thick black haze ahead as shadows of glowing embers were fueled by the materials in the warehouse. The farther they crawled, the more isolated they were, but they had to help the survivors and put this firestorm out.

A second person flashed past him and almost hurled himself out the window. He pounded on a huge pane of glass, gasping for air through the rolling black smoke until it breached. Garcia dived for the man and pulled him inside before he plummeted to his death. They both fell backward into a heap.

"Help!" the voice screeched in horror.

Glowing embers floated down like dirty snowflakes. The black smoke was the Grimm Reaper, teasing them with their probable death. The fire swayed, accelerating above their heads. *This doesn't feel right.*

Connor pressed his radio button. "Cap, do you read me? We're in trouble here. We have one injured and another in critical condition." Connor checked the man's pulse, but there was none. "He just expired, Cap. He's dead on the scene."

I could have saved him if only we'd gotten here sooner.

Connor shielded himself as a huge section of the ceiling

caved in. Beams toppled over Bill and trapped his friend face down. He wasn't moving.

"Winslow, get everyone out of there! The battalion chief said it's too dangerous. A few floors are collapsing, but we are still soaking the fire from out here. Everyone needs to pull out," the captain yelled through the radio. "Get out of there now."

"Cap, the ceiling caved on top of Bill and he's pinned by a beam." Connor looked over at the deceased man with the horrid burns. *Help...* *"I'm not leaving Fletch. Not a chance."* He could hear the piercing sound of Bill's PASS alarm, signifying his man was down and now he was dodging furniture, debris, and water pouring through the open ceiling. Connor had to get to Bill.

Garcia aided the surviving victim, putting an EBSS tail and plug oxygen mask over his mouth and connected to his own air supply. The man fought off the attempt as he choked and gagged. Garcia muscled it over the man's head anyway. He looked back as Connor saw self-control and alarm spun together in his eyes.

Connor waved Garcia over as he pulled the man along.

"Garcia, we need a Rapid Intervention Team to come back in and bring us more tanks. Take him with you, so he can get medical attention." He pointed to the elderly man with the sooty-inked face and burns blistering his arms.

"What about him?" Garcia yelled over the crackling hellhole and pointed to the other man.

Connor shook his head and waved the signal that it was too late for him, he was deceased.

Garcia's eyes bugged out of his sockets with terror. Connor pulled him closer and stilled him helmet to helmet, lasering his true grit. Determination and gut instinct were the only way out of this. "You're a dead man if you don't focus, so listen to me. Get out of here." Connor gritted his teeth and swallowed, trying to suppress the contradiction. The honor of firefighters was leave no one behind, but he upheld his team's safety first. "Leave. While you can. I'm staying with Bill."

Violent popping sounds exploded around them as light bulbs busted from the temperature. Garcia flinched. Connor knew what was happening around him. Memories behind the cloak of the brutal fire beast fueled by plastics which liquefied and vaporized. Ceramics were roasted and coated black as tar. Wood bubbled, and paint curled from the walls. Sprinklers rained down and water gushed from the fire hoses on the ladder trucks in defensive mode at all quadrants of the structure.

Garcia jerked back. "But, Lieutenant, I'm not to leave anyone behind either, right?" Garcia shouted.

"That's a direct order. This isn't a grab and go anymore. I need you to go get help." Connor clutched the rookie's shoulder with his gloved grip, never letting go of Bill's artery, monitoring his pulse. "Listen to me and pay close attention."

Michael Garcia looked over at the weak and feeble man whittled into his side. His lips trembled then his posture straightened as he took a breath of determined courage.

"This is what you were trained for and why you are a fire-fighter—you must keep your hand on the hose at all times and follow it down. If you don't, you will get disoriented like you did in training." Connor knocked the rookie's helmet hard. "Don't you let go of the fucker, not for a second, because it will lead you to the truck and to safety."

Garcia nodded like he was having tremors.

"You got this."

"Connor, get out of there." The Captain screamed the order through his headset.

Connor knelt over his gauge to read the amount of oxygen he and Bill had left. "Mayday. Mayday... RITT Crew engine, 43, 56, 31, Alpha, I repeat Mayday. Mayday. I need all hands on deck." There were no more tanks inside to tap into.

"Cap, I'm sending Garcia out with the injured... solo."

"No," the Captain howled as the communication ceased.

"Hurry, Garcia. Haul ass." Connor looked at the dial. "We don't have much air, so you need to bring help." He shook the rookie hard and pushed him away with his steel-toed shit kicker. "Go! We're counting on you."

Garcia turned away, slipping and sliding through the rubble with the hose line and the injured man draped over his shoulder. He skidded down the stairs in the flow of water.

Connor could see the reflective name on the back of his bunker gear as it disappeared in the darkness.

Connor checked Bill's pulse again as he stirred. He reached and extended for his pike pole to get some leverage to move the beam away, but the more it rocked the more Bill screamed in pain. He put all his weight into it but there was no use, the beam was too heavy. "We're fine, buddy. Help is on the way. Don't move." Maybe another few seconds of air could also save their lives. "You know we are sitting ducks until someone comes in with tanks and help." Connor looked around and there was no one. His low air bell chimed, and his light came on in his mask.

We are both dead men. What happened to our tanks?

In the calmest voice Connor could project, he said. "Fletch. I need you to focus and follow my lead. We need to skip breaths to conserve our air. I know you are hurting right now and help is on the way, but we need to do our part and save the minutes we have left. As we trained, I need you to take one breath in, then another in, and one exhale. Keep the pace. Two breaths in, slow, and then one exhale. Everything is going to be okay. Do the best you can. We will see Trish and kids soon." He shifted closer to Bill. "Can you tell me where the pain is?"

Connor wished he could help, so he rocked the beam again as Bill hollered and padded along Connor's bunker gear.

"Winslow, I'm royally fucked, and I don't think I'm getting out of here. Something's broken and not right, near my lower back and my legs are starting to go numb." Bill grabbed

Connor's jacket with as much strength as he could muster. He grunted out, "You need to promise me something—you and the station please take care of Trish and the kids." Horror and sadness filled his eyes.

"There won't be any need." Connor's reassuring hold on Bill's arm didn't need any words, but he dialogued them just the same. "Help is on the way, partner. You will see them soon."

Bill's alarm blared and reacted. He only had 15 minutes of air left. "Winslow, you need to leave now and get out of here before you can't." Bill just relax and concentrate slow your breathing.

Connor looked around to see if help was coming. Garcia had to be out by now. He slowed his own breathing down to conserve 02. The charred man lay lifeless beside him.

Fireballs fell like hail around them. Connor swept the cinders off before they burned through their bunker gear and waited to look for any movement.

Bill gasped for more air as his bells warned his oxygen was near out and yanked away his mask.

It's my job to save my team, and Bill has a wife and kids.

Connor took his helmet off and started for his breathing apparatus then leaned closer to his friend, but Bill fought him off.

"No!" Bill's slur pleaded as he held on to the sleeve of Connor's bunker jacket.

Connor inhaled and took his last gulp of lifesaving air, then laid over Bill to protect him. The men held on to each other, thinking they would be found soon, but they wouldn't be alive. Connor ran his gloved hand over his father's helmet as he started to struggle for air but held his breath.

Bill deserves it more than I do. He has a family and they need him.

Toxic fumes and poisonous gasses would fill his lungs if he took off his mask. His last thought was of Ellie... *I love you. I don't want to go.*

CHAPTER 24

*G*arcia tore out of the building to the waiting paramedic. She grabbed the man hanging on him. He'd hauled ass and slid down a few flights with the rush of water. He gasped as he pulled off his face mask and shouted, "They're running out of air. Get the extra tanks in there!" He inhaled again screaming louder. "Help! They don't have much air left."

The paramedics grabbed the injured man before he fell to the ground.

"They're on their way in, Garcia," the captain shouted.

"Your dumb idiot," Jax shouted, as he reached to shake the living shit out of the rookie. "You never leave a man behind... Ever. Haven't we got this into your pea brain?"

"Lieutenant Winslow ordered me to get help and he called the response team." Garcia paced. "It's bad in there and they're running out of the air. I had to..."

"Cap, I'm going in!" Jax ran for two extra tanks of compressed air and hoisted his gear on with the Denver tool over his shoulder.

"No, you're not. Someone has to operate the rig and protocol. You're the engineer, fool; you stay on deck and await orders."

"Cap, several other units can stay on deck and watch the rig. Connor needs help." Jax whistled and waved over the other engineer from another unit and took a few steps before pulling the rest of his gear on. "Watch my rig, you got the controls, and nothing better happen to it or you will be singing soprano. If I don't come back, take care of my baby."

He ran back to the Captain. "Cap, come on. Kill me later. Hang me up by my nads, but I'm going in. We have to get our men." Jax' face was tormented.

"You're not going alone. The RITT already went in, but I'm sure they're going to need help getting Bill out from the collapse." The cap scurried alongside Jax. "We are both going in. Let's get our boys out." He looked back to make sure the new Battalion Chief didn't see them.

The cap pointed to the ambulance. "Garcia, go get checked out and get some air. We'll be back."

"Cap, they're about fifty paces in above the stairwell on the third floor, near the southwest corner," Garcia said.

The cap threw a thumbs up and nodded. Then pointed over to the bus for him to get checked out himself.

"I'll deal with you later, Rookie." Jax threw up a knuckle sandwich in his direction.

Dan McClain and Jackson Honeycutt placed their air masks and tanks, securing their gear, then grabbed the Halligan and a pike pole and headed into the structure.

"Help!" a woman screamed from a second story window.

"Come on, Parker, I need you to get to the second floor and get her out of there while we retrieve Winslow and Fletcher," the Captain ordered. Evan hesitated and looked around before he ran behind three other firefighters in the pursuit. Water from plugs to hose lines on ladder trucks was being dispensed into the blaze at four different angles. They retrieved the woman to safety. The building was cleared except for Connor and Bill and the fire was almost out except for a few hot spots. Everyone was accounted for except the three still in there and the victim who'd perished.

Garcia stood at the bus, inhaling the fresh oxygen when he heard a car screech to a halt behind him. He turned, hearing Cade yelling at the top of his lungs as he ran through the crowd. He burst in pursuit of Garcia still tethered to his oxygen tubing and almost taking the tank with him.

"Where's Connor?" Cade lashed. "Tell me my brother's not in there."

Before Garcia could answer, Cade took off, plowing over someone to get some bunker gear on.

"Stop. Cade, you can't," the rookie pleaded.

"Like hell, I can't."

"The captain, Jax, and a few more firefighters just went in there for search and rescue."

Cade twisted out of the group of men holding him back and punched the side of a rig. " I can't just stand here and do nothing. My brother's in there."

"You can't go in. Calm down. First I need you to look into something." Garcia shook him. Cade spit on the ground and jerked out of the hold the first responders had on him. "Bullshit!"

"When we were in the building there was another firefighter in there, too. I yelled at him to help us, and I thought he heard me. He turned and bolted. I thought he looked over at the lieutenant, but he kept running down the stairs and out of the building. I was yelling for him to stop, and I kept after him. I'm not positive, but I think it was Evan Parker from the station."

Cade yelled at the top of his lungs, "Parker, where are you?" Everyone turned around looking at each other, but there was no Parker in sight.

"Parker went back inside. I saw him go back in!" another first responder shouted over the noise.

Jeffrey turned on the television. "Sis, great job on getting the partial plates from the truck earlier. The police are looking for the idiot driving it. I hope they catch them before you or anyone else gets hurt and put them in jail for reckless endangerment."

"I did my civic duty and it can't be a coincidence." Ellie froze.

El, are you ever going to talk to me?" Jeffrey yelled from the kitchen as he made a sandwich. Jeffrey rounded the corner. "I swear I'd never tell another soul, but Connor is different, and the man loves you. So, I made a judgment call. One I'm sure you may make me regret, but I'd do it again to see you smile. I hope one day you can forgive me." Jeffrey stepped farther into the great room to see if Ellie was still there. He walked up behind her. "Did you hear me?" he asked. "What's this?" He looked and pointed.

The television was on when the late-breaking special news report interrupted some WW2 war movie Jeffrey was watching. Ellie stood in front of the television screen as the news crew shot live from the furniture warehouse that was ablaze. Several fire trucks from South Metro Fire and Rescue with surrounding precincts were on the scene and from the looks of it, a bad one. Entranced, Ellie's stomach assaulted her as she walked closer to image and sat in front of the screen, sliding to the floor. She perched on her knees and tore off the twisted towel from her wet hair wringing it in her fists as she stared ahead.

"What's happening?" Jeffrey took a sip of his morning coffee then set it down.

She turned and looked up. "I just saw the station 56 engine and ladder truck on TV." Her brows furrowed as she chomped on her bottom lip. "Do you know if Connor worked last night?" She cringed and brought her knees to her chest and rocked forward. "Was it his shift?" Her voice was hysterical and louder than before.

"He said he had to work a forty-eight-hour shift with the next ninety-six off," he stuttered. "Calm down; we can find out for sure." Jeffrey took a deep inhale. "You're pale and ashy, sis. You're going to have a coronary. Just breathe. Relax, I'll try to call Cade." He kneeled in front of her and placed a hand on top of her head. "It's okay. Don't you worry. I'll find out for certain." He tapped her nose.

She crab-crawled away. "Jeffrey." Her voice escalated. "I know he's there. I feel it." She whaled. "Oh my God, it can't be." She cradled her head into her fists, clawing at her dripping curls. "I know he's hurt." She darted across the room and relayed up the stairs. "I have to go there. I need to be there," she demanded, breathless.

Jeffrey stomped across the room and shouted up the stairs. "Stop, Ellie." He pinched his lower lip. "Don't panic. I'm calling Cade."

Ellie was breathless and couldn't think.

"Pick up damn you, Cade, pick up," Jeffrey whispered through gritted teeth.

"What?" a grated voice bit.

"Cade, it's Jeffrey Richards. Where are you? Ellie's freaking out right now. Is Connor okay?" Jeffrey's steps pounded back and forth across the living room as the floor creaked. "Is he at the fire they have plastered all over the TV?" He hesitated and could hear Cade's loud breathing, earsplitting sirens, blaring intercoms, and a hell of a lot of noise, but Cade was silent on the other end of the phone. "Cade! You're there—aren't you?" Jeffrey stopped at the bottom of the stairs.

"Yes...Connor is trapped in the building with Bill."

Jeffrey stared at the top of the stairs to see Ellie clenching a towel in her mouth, holding back her screams. Horror filled her eyes and tears trailed down her cheeks. She looked so fragile and scared. She trembled and wailed. "Connor. Oh, please God. No!"

"Cade! Dammit, what's going on…?" Jeffrey shouted before the line went dead. "Holy shit."

Several firefighters retreated from the building and none of them were his brother. Cade caught a glimpse of Evan Parker taking his helmet off, standing behind one of the fire trucks. "You mother fucker." He tore off after him in a sprint. Parker saw Cade and turned to run, but he tripped over one of the hose lines on the ground, and Cade tackled him flat. "Tell me, Parker, or so help me, sweet Jesus, I'm going to throttle you. Did you bail on your team?"

Evan's hands went up. "I didn't see them, or I would have stopped. I heard the captain's orders and got out of there when I was told. We were on the roof. I just went back in, but they called us out again," he said behind his crossed arms as he flinched.

A group of firefighters surrounded them. "Yeah, he was one of the first to leave but went back in to save the woman on the second floor. He just brought her out."

"Yeah well, we will see if this pans out. I've heard different from another firefighter who was in there. Until we get all the details, you're mine." Cade spit with the threat.

Evan fought to get out of his grip. "I swear to you. If I'd known he was hurt, I would have helped."

"We will sort this out when my brother comes out safe, and not until then. For now, we have an eye witness saying you didn't stick around to save a fellow firefighter. You broke the code." Cade pulled Parker up and pushed him against one of the rigs.

"If anything happens to one hair on Connor's head you will deal with me. I'll personally press charges." Cade shoved him forward to one of Denver's finest police force barricading the perimeter. "Hold him for a few minutes, but he's not under arrest."

"And you are?" the officer asked.

Cade flashed him his badge on a chain around his neck and showed him his Walther P99 in his sidearm holster. "I'm your boss for starters, and this guy has been nothing but trouble since he arrived in my city, so he's under suspicion. Keep a close eye on him until the ashes settle." Cade scrubbed his face and cracked his neck to get a grip on the situation "If anyone gets hurt or dies up there, so help me, Parker. Garcia said you bailed on your team." Cade shoved Evan into the officer head first. "I will see to it myself you pay for this." The other men standing around anchored Cade back. "You will rot in the state penitentiary." Cade turned to the commotion behind him.

"I did my job. I always do. We have witnesses to prove it," Evan retaliated. "You will pay, Five-O, for doing this." He tried twisted out of the officers hold with no use. "You just wait. I'd never do that to anyone. I swear to you on my sister's life." Evan collapsed against the side of the police car exhausted.

"I'll apologize if I'm wrong, but I'm the temporary judge and the jury is still out to lunch. When you started trouble for my family, you barked up the wrong tree, Parker. I did some investigating on your past. We will have a conversation when all of this is over. I'd like to know what happened back home in the fire."

Evan hesitated. "The fire..." His head drooped, and a tremor shook his chin.

CHAPTER 25

*C*onnor couldn't wait any longer. His O2 was seconds away from empty. He had to suck face into his mask but the high temperature made inhaling excruciating, and the face of his mask started to bubble. He had no more air and couldn't hold his breath another agonizing second. He was teetering on blacking out. He was near the end...he was dying. The victim near him was dead, and Bill wasn't moving anymore. This was it.

He could hear the piercing sounds of their PASS alarms, then everything blurred. He thought of Ellie as he struggled. He gagged and coughed. His lungs constricted, and he was strangling for a breath. A life with no more pain.

The ceiling above shot down furniture and debris. The pain comforted him, knowing he was still alive. He was dying, and he had so much to live for. He loved Ellie and he couldn't bear anyone having her other than him.

Everything went black.

The PASS alarms blared, warning them they were close to their fallen comrades. "Over here," Jax called out. He felt his way over two bodies piled in the corner; the glowing patches of their names and South Metro Fire and Rescue on their uniforms verified they'd found Connor and Bill. Connor was huddled over Bill, but neither was moving.

Jax signaled the team forward as he waited for the captain's orders. "Come on, guys, let's get this off." A beam pinned Bill's face down to the floor. Jax and the captain ripped away the ceiling debris, chairs and furniture that were on top of Connor. He was curled into a fetal position with one arm over his head and the other over Bill. His blistered mask was still on. Another team of firefighters held the hose line and shot water from the spout at the burning embers around them. Soon the entire fire would be nothing but ash and smoke.

Jax eased Connor over and pulled his blistered mask off, replacing it with an oxygen mask, but nothing happened. Panic set in as he continued to revive him. Still nothing. Connor wasn't breathing. He pounded on his chest. Jax reached to pull his own mask off, but the captain shouted, "Are you trying to kill yourself, you flipping idiot?"

The captain felt for a pulse, but there was none. He started chest compressions on his lieutenant, who was like his own son. "Come on, kid," he ground through gritted teeth.

Someone from the intervention team squawked, "We need to snatch and go." They strapped on another oxygen tank to Bill so the air could fill his mask also.

The other firefighters continued aide on Bill. Several fire-fighters swarmed the area with a pike pole and their hoses, each of them knowing the risks to their own lives to save their fallen brothers.

There was a man near them who was deceased, so he was

covered with a yellow tarp, boarded, and placed into the 'stokes' basket. His hair was singed off and the burns on his body were so severe he wouldn't have made it. His skin was melted and falling off. Two men transported and carried him away while one of them gagged at the sight.

Jax pounded on Connor's chest as he and the captain took turns pumping air and continued even repetitions of CPR to revive him. They pushed everyone else aside as they would be the ones saving him. The intervention team tried to pull the captain and Jax off of Connor, but they didn't budge.

"Back off," the captain shouted. "Don't you die on me." Connor was motionless.

"Come on," Jax said between gritted teeth and a clenched jaw. Tears ran down his face, clouding his mask. Jax worked tireless to get a heartbeat. The captain shouted, "Hey, Bill, don't move! They're putting the neck brace around you and then were getting the hell out of here."

Bill's screams grew louder. He mumbled his wife's name. Then shouted, "Winslow."

"We'll call your woman," the Captain assured. "We got you, and we plan to keep you safe until the docs can fix you up right. So don't move a muscle."

The captain's words blared through the radios. "We need two buses and we need an airway and the AED ready. Two critical and one DOA exiting the building."

"Out," the RITT team commander demanded. "Now! Not in here assholes. Load Winslow and Fletcher up. We have to get them out of here or he's not going to make it."

Jax felt for a pulse—anything. "Don't you dare die on me, dude." He, the captain, and two other firefighters lifted Connor and carried him out as the other responders secured Bill for transport.

"Hang on, son," the captain yelled, and blared orders as he

and Jax shoved them as fast as they could, flying down the stairs. Jax threw his helmet off once seeing the light through the open door before chucking his mask. He settled his ear on Connor's chest. "I still don't have a pulse."

A ragged cheer came for the fearless team to the onlookers when they exited, but it soon became silent as they watched. Connor was laid on the ground near the stairs, outside the exit in the safe zone. They worked diligently to keep him stable with fluid through an IV line. The captain and Jax wouldn't move from his side.

Connor's skin was a pale cement gray, his eyes were only slits, and he was still limp. Jax unsnapped Connor's bunker jacket as someone else hooked up the monitors. The captain ripped open the AED defibrillator from the case and placed the pads on the sides along Connor's ribs. Oxygen was placed over his mouth.

Jax yelled as he started chest compressions. "1-2-3-4-5…"

The captain felt for a pulse, but there was only a faint one, so he flipped the switch to charge to the defibrillator. "Jackson, clear." An electric jolt traveled to Connor's heart, and his body convulsed. "Nothing? I'm hitting him with another shock," Captain Dan said. The monitor reacted. "We have a heartbeat. The rhythm isn't good, but it's something."

"It's getting a little stronger, and we've got a better pulse." Jax leaned back and jumped to his feet. "Hold on another minute, buddy."

The Captain hollered, "Let's go." They lifted Connor and placed him on a gurney. "Get our boys to the hospital."

Cade stood next to the radio and heard the captain. He pushed through the barriers to get near the door of the warehouse, but he could just stand there; his boots were leaded weights and he had a heavy heart as he watched his brother fight for his life.

"Cade! What the heck do you think you are doing here, and why is Parker being held by the police? Tell them to let him go right now." The captain pulled at Cade's black t-shirt, almost tearing it off his back. "Give us some room." He shoved him back and ran alongside of his men. "We have this under control." He shouted with authority, but slow and sure. "Look at me, you can ride with him by ambulance to the hospital, but right now he may not even make it there." The captain's face was deep and marred with black ash; his hair dripped with sweat.

Cade's stare was vacant as he nodded to the officer holding Parker. "Let him go," he mumbled and turned. "Damn it, Dan." Cade gritted his teeth and clenched his fists into balls. "C doesn't deserve shit. He deserves a break."

Dan's empty monotone voice quaked. "Yeah, he does, it's about time don't you think?" They didn't hide their tears. The men turned back to Connor. "And right now, he needs everyone's prayers and a few guardian angels to help us out here. Tom and Beth, we need your help." He looked up. "We can't lose him." Dan covered his face with his gloves.

"Cap!" Jax shouted. "He's coding." He lept on top of the rolling gurney and resumed compressions, then blew into Connor's lungs. The paramedic pushed Jax away as he continued mouth-to-mouth. The captain grabbed Jax by the back of his bunker gear, pulling him off the gurney so the paramedics could insert a breathing tube.

"Fool. You're not a one-man show. Let them do their job and save him."

Jax slumped back. Cade ran alongside the gurney to the waiting ambulance. Jax and Cade's eyes connected. He wiped his nose with the back of his glove as tears threatened his eyes.

"We need a second bus," the cap's voice cracked into the radio. Bill was carried out of the building. "We have another injured firefighter on his way with possible trauma to the spine."

CHAPTER 26

*E*llie's finger shook as she dialed the hospital to reach Janet only to struggle several times dialing the number. She clenched her hands into fists as her nails pierced her flesh before making another attempt. She couldn't focus enough to get her brain to compute how to call for a number. Her breaking heart and pulse hammered through her body. She got through to the hospital and started to see spots as she waited on hold for them to page Janet. She weaved from side-to-side, feeling light-headed.

"This is Nurse Winslow," the familiar voice came over the line.

"Janet, it's Ellie Richards." Taking a deep breath into her lungs, she tried to calm herself. "Janet, please tell me... Is Connor okay?"

"I'm afraid not, hon. I just got word he's in route to the hospital, and it's pretty bad." Janet's calm composure broke as she blubbered uncontrollably into the phone.

Ellie dashed across the floor, pulling a sweater over her head. "I'm on my way."

"Wait." Janet's voice hitched but was softer than before. "Why?"

"I love him, Janet, and I need to be there." She caressed her neck. It was the first time she said it aloud to anyone other than when she implied it to Connor at the mountain house. "I love him. I've always loved him." Tears poured down her cheeks.

"Sweetie, we all do. I'm not sure if Connor will make it, and I can't bear it if we lost him. He's so young, and my heart aches."

"He has to… I—"

"You're in no condition to drive here alone," Janet said.

"Jeffrey's waiting in the truck. He's driving me."

"Ellie, I need to go. The ambulance will be here in a few minutes, and my trauma team is ready and awaiting the arrival."

She hung up the phone, and Ellie slung her bag over her shoulder before scooting into a pair of slip-on, camel colored moccasins. She was disoriented staring at her trembling palms. Jeffrey started the engine and ran around the truck to help her as she closed her phone and looked around in a panic taking drunken steps as spots clouded her vision and she leaned against the house for stability. The horn blared, bringing her back into focus.

"Sis, come on." Jeffrey yelled. He leaned over, hoisted her into the seat by her waist, and slammed the door shut. Jeffrey grabbed a wad of tissue and blotted the tears.

"Thank you, I'm sorry. I'm a complete mess."

"No, worries, sis. I'm here and I'll get you to Connor." The truck's tires peeled over the graveled drive. "I'll get you to the hospital as fast as I can but get your damn seatbelt on."

The sirens blasted and horns blew as the paramedics worked tirelessly on Connor, trying to get him stable. In transit, Cade looked ahead, watching intersections pass. He yelled over the blaring siren and behind the paramedics keeping his brother alive. "Bro, don't you give up on me." One hand clutched Connor's leg while the other beat and pounded the bench underneath him.

Janet and several doctors waited outside the emergency doors. She ran to the ambulance like her hair was on fire as it pulled in. She wouldn't be able to work on Connor, but she was sticking to him like gorilla glue. She would watch every move, and if Nurse Winslow didn't like she wasn't able to assist and if anything happened to her nephew the hospital would hear about it. She would bark out as many orders as she needed to save him—or anyone for the matter—but emotions could hinder his care, so she didn't say one syllable.

"Get out of the way, Janet. You're too close to this one," Doctor Tallyn called out. "We got this." He looked at her. "I promise you. I'll care for him like he's my own. I know he's Thomas' legacy and your nephew. You have my solemn word. There's nothing you can do for him but pray. Connor wouldn't want to put you through this."

Janet scrutinized her team and the ER staff over her shoulder. "You damn well better give it your all, because I'll hold you to it." Her stern voice became sobs. "Please... please, I beg you. Save him."

"Janet, please, get out of here before you get hysterical. We know it's Connor. Calm down and let us do our job."

There was soot sketched on Connor's face, and he had a bluish hue to his complexion. His was clammy and his hair was plastered in sweat. Small blisters littered his face, and his body was limp. She didn't know how long he'd gone without oxygen or if he'd suffered brain damage. Heart monitors were already taped to his chest, and his heart was beating, but not enough. Tubes were everywhere. The paramedics continued to shock and push the vital air into his lungs to breathe for him. They were keeping him alive.

Her heart lurched. She wanted to move, but her feet were rooted to the ground as the crew pushed Connor's gurney through the emergency doors. Cade embraced her, and they wept. Then she could feel Dan's familiar arms around her as his uncertain whisper said everything was going to be okay. Jax ran up behind them and joined in. They huddled there, frozen in time, praying aloud.

The second ambulance arrived as another ER crew ran to it. Bill was conscious, but in excruciating pain. Jax, Cade, and the captain ran to the back of the ambulance as the rear doors opened and the paramedics eased the gurney out.

Bill pulled his oxygen mask off; he panted and winced through his pain as he spoke. He was secured to a back board. "He saved my life. Winslow attempted to save the other guy, but it was too late. I was almost at two percent 02. And he gave me the last of his own air." Bill clutched at the captain's arm. "Mother fawker risked his life. To save mine." He cried out.

"Easy, boy. Don't move anything else until you get x-rays," Jax said.

Cade and Jax followed close behind before moving to the waiting area inside the emergency room doors. The staff wheeled Bill into a private bay for assessment.

Still outside, Dan walked back over to Janet, holding her tight. "He's a fighter, Janet. Stupid shit took off his mask and buried himself in his bunker suit to save Bill. Didn't I teach these guys better?" His face was sullen.

Janet turned and pounded on Dan's chest. "Stop, honey. You taught them to do their jobs and to save people." They leaned in, placing their foreheads against each other's, and closed their eyes. He caressed her as she sobbed.

"Why-why-why… Connor." Janet whimpered in a subtle whisper. "I lost my only brother, and I won't survive it if I lose his son, too."

"Babe, I don't think I can survive it either."

"There they are!" they heard in the distance.

Dan and Janet turned to a beefed-up truck screeching around the corner and into the lot. "Idiot drivers," Dan muttered. The door opened before the truck stopped. Ellie flew out, tripping to get to the front doors. "Oh my god, it's Ellie." Janet wailed.

Jeffrey killed the engine. "Ellie you're going to get yourself hurt, hold up!"

Ellie met Dan and Janet's gaze, then ran to them. "Am I too late? Is he… is he gone?" She crumpled to the ground, passing out cold.

"Sweet Jesus, El." Jeffrey ran over her but she hit the pavement. He swung her up and into his arms.

Janet ran ahead. " You're kidding me. I'll go get a wet towel. What else is going to happen?"

"Are these two doomed to be together, or what?" Dan said.

Jeffrey responded, "I surely hope so, for their sake. I pray Connor is going to be okay."

Dan patted Jeffrey's back. "Me too, son… me too… We need everyone's prayers right now."

The waiting area and hallway were already filling up with firefighters, first responders, and hospital staff who knew Bill and Connor. Some gathered in groups, but most stood silently, deep in their own thoughts. Two of their brothers had fallen, and the outcome on both was very grim.

Ellie stirred on a gurney and woke to the smell of antiseptic. She was reminded of her previous hospital stay. Her head pounded, and she could feel the sting on her shin. She looked around; she was in the hall next to the trauma area. A wet cloth hung askew on her forehead. She looked over and saw her brother as he stroked her hair nervously.

"Dammit, what am going to do with you?" he teased, his eyes tired.

She pulled the cloth off her head, dropping it to her side. She felt the scrape at her knee now covered in gauze, but it wasn't anything compared to her broken heart.

Cade stood against a wall across from her, staring holes through her, and she wasn't sure if he was actually looking at her or performing some kind of exorcism. His pain mimicked hers. She couldn't stand it. She had to see Connor. She sat up and pushed herself off the gurney in a not so graceful landing. She stumbled through the crowd, but Cade stepped in front of her, blocking her path.

"Where do you think you're going?" His arms were crossed firmly over his wide chest. He was still packing his holstered sidearm. His biceps were etched with scars, and a 'Special Forces' military tattoo of a skull, rattlesnake, and dagger painted his skin with the words Motivated-Dedicated-Lethal under it. He mimicked a bodybuilder. If he was intimidating and he aced it. Ellie swallowed deep, inhaled through her nose and out for any extra courage.

"What are you doing here? Haven't you given the guy enough heartbreak?"

Just breathe… You got this. "Get out of my way, Cade. I need to see him." She stepped forward, her nose about to his chest and looked upward.

"No one can see him." He leaned in. "I'll ask again. What do you think you're doing here? You're not family; didn't you make this clear a time or two?" He leaned in farther, his brows furrowed over green eyes that were dark and intense. He growled with the edge of a warrior.

"You don't scare me a bit, you know." She trembled but pulled her shoulders back and stood a little taller. "Cade, I have to know if he's going to live." She fought the tears clouding her vision.

I'm not backing down and even the big brute was not getting in my way of where I should be.

"Mama bear trying to protect her cub? A little late for that isn't it?"

She bit at her lip so hard it started to bleed. "If need be. I will protect what is mine. I hope it isn't too late. I need to see him."

"You're not getting anywhere near him. He's not man-candy." He stood solid, mirroring her every attempt to pass.

"You're not stopping me," she growled back.

"Why is it so important to you? Why do you even care?" Cade spread his arms out. "You going to kick the man when he's down again? He's dying, Ellie."

"No!" The force of her shriek echoed in the hall, and she could feel all eyes upon her. She pointed her finger up into his face and spoke what was in her heart. "That is my life in there. My future husband if he will have me, and if I'm lucky enough, the father to my future children," she said fiercely. "My everything."

"Whoa… what makes you so damn certain of that?" Cade questioned.

"I'm not—not certain at all. I can only wish he'll have me. But, with every breath I have in me, I will not stop trying." Her hands covered her trembling lip. "So, if you don't step aside this very moment, I'm going to deck you in the kisser."

"Determined lass, aren't you?" Cade's chin jutted out as he looked up into the fluorescent lights. "It's about time you admitted it to yourself." He snatched Ellie's petite frame with all the tenderness he could and shifted her toward the room

Connor was in. "Bring our guy back to us... I have a feeling you're our best chance and the only one who has the power."

Cade stepped aside, almost bowing as Ellie walked closer to the emergency personnel who were trying to save her love. Her pulse was an agonizing staccato as she drew closer. Her heart would rupture at any minute. If only she had a chance to repeat the very words to him.

Ellie lifted her head. What had it been... a day? Two? She looked at the hands of the clock on the wall. No, it was exactly thirty-six hours and forty-three minutes since she arrived. Jeffrey came in and told her, Bill Fletcher the other guy that was in the building with Connor just got out of surgery and immobilized in a back brace. His pelvis was fractured, but all his injuries were not life threatening, and he would be able to walk after a long stint in rehab. He was very lucky to be alive after the ceiling beam fell on top of him and he could have run out of air.

She nodded and a smoothed back Connors hair and kissed his cheek. "Please wake up. I'm begging you. Don't leave me," Ellie whispered.

Connor remained unconscious in the ICU on a ventilator in critical condition.

"Sis, come on; you must take a break. Someone can call you when he wakes up."

She held tight to the guardrail of his bed. "No, I can't. I want to be here when he wakes up." She stood and ran a wet cloth over Connor's forehead. "Thank you for getting everyone overnight supplies from the store. I really appreciate the toiletries."

"That's the least I can do." Jeffrey squeezed her shoulder. "I worry. El, you haven't even been outside this room in days.

There are firefighters and emergency personnel lining the halls from all parts of the Solemn Creed. So many that they're setting up posts out in the parking lot. Everyone is taking turns in the chapel. Jax and Janet are in there now. Cade and Captain Dan are a mess. Wives and partners have been bringing food. It's everywhere. We could eat for weeks. They even brought in a two-gallon coffee dispensers and water. You really need to eat."

"I'm not hungry. I can't—I won't."

"Dammit, sis. I get it, but you need to keep your strength up. You're not eating, not sleeping... Connor may have a long road if he pulls through, and you need to be strong for him."

"If?" Ellie turned and wept in her brother's arms.

CHAPTER 27

*C*onnor wasn't sure where he was. His lungs burned. He drifted somewhere between heaven and hell. He heard his dad's words over and over. *"I'm proud of you, son. Live, love and laugh. Go, it's not your time."* Those words were loud at times and other moments... only a whisper in the air. His pain became fiercer, almost to the point where he couldn't tolerate it. Barely lucid, the wrath of pain in his sternum and broken ribs seized him. He craved for something to take the agony away, but he wasn't sure if he was in hell itself. Was he alive?

Memories of the accident he was in eight years ago were paired with happy memories of his childhood—how much love he felt and the laughter. He couldn't remember feeling anything but guilt and heartache over the years except when he was with Ellie. His heartache softened with waves of hope. God, he loved her, and he swore he could hear her, touch her, and knew she was near. What would he ever do if he couldn't have a life with her? He fought to gain strength before he melted into his solitude of darkness. He never wanted to go back to the past eight years of self-loathing. He wanted to feel like he'd had when he was a kid, like he could conquer anything. Or when he was with Ellie, making love. She made him herculean.

"What's that smell?" Cade asked. She didn't care. But they didn't stop, and she finally caved.

"It reeks in here. Ellie is that you? Connor's definitely isn't gonna dig your essence," Jax chimed in. Dan and Jeff held their noses." Pew."

She looked around. "Geez. Your tactics are dirty." Ellie rolled her eyes at Janet and lifted her arm and bunched up her nose. "Can you show me where to wash up?" Janet, Dan, Cade, and Jax needed time alone to say their goodbyes if the worst happened and Connor declined. She wasn't about to say goodbye, and she prayed he would awaken soon. She kissed his forehead.

It had been over seventy–four hours, and there was a very little improvement. He wasn't breathing on his own, but the treatments were improving his lung function and healing the effects from breathing in toxic fumes. Each test was coming back a little more positive than before, but he still wasn't waking up. She feared he would have brain damage or stay in a vegetative state. "I'll be right back."

Don't go.

Cade finally got the alone time he needed to say things he hadn't. Memories of his happy childhood at the Winslow's drowned out the barely moving figure on the bed. He couldn't bear to lose his brother. Every time he came in, he couldn't speak. He could only watch as Connor's chest rose and fell. "Bro, you can't leave me, there so much I have to say. I... I never have."

I love you too, Cade.

Cade wiped away the moisture rolling down his three-day-old facial hair. "I'm not sure if I ever told you what Mom said to me the day of the accident." He stuttered, holding back the sadness. "She told me to take care of you, and no matter what I'd never be alone because I was loved and you'd always be at my side."

Dad said the same to me.

He could barely continue. "My eighth birthday." He hesitated, wiping his tears away. "The day you adopted me into your family was the happiest day of my life. I finally had a family, someone who was mine, people who loved me for me. And I finally had the brother I always wanted, and you were my best friend. I couldn't believe it. I seriously hit the damn lotto."

We all did, bro.

Cade looked closer, and Connor had tears streaming from his eyes.

"So, don't you dare give up now. Don't you leave me. Please. I promised Mom." He cupped his head in his palms. "Who's gonna hand me the wrench when I still need to get the damn Mustang up and running? And you still owe me a case of beer from the last bet, so don't think you can weasel out of it now."

Cade heard the knock on the door and turned away to wipe the last of the leakage spilling out of his sockets. "Yeah, come in." He stood, looking over his shoulder to see Jax stride in. "Hi."

"Hey cousin, how's he doing?" Both men turned to Connor who was now flailing on the bed. He was arched and almost elevated as he struggled to pull at the tubing down his throat. He gurgled and gasped to breathe. Jax headed toward Connor, but Cade bowled him over, pushing him to the door to get help. "Nurse...Doctor...someone. We need to help."

"Help!" they yelled in tandem.

Connor fought and pulled the wires and tubes connected to him. His eyes opened then rolled back as he struggled to breathe. Everything was blurry, and he couldn't catch his breath.

He was choking and needed to pull at whatever was down his throat. He fought for words and air. Was he still in the fire? Was he dead? Confusion encapsulated him.

Several medical staff surrounded the bed, one pressed the call button as another pushed more fluids and watched the monitors. Another fought to control his flying limbs.

"He's trying to breathe on his own; we need to get the tube out." One medical staff stated.

Connor's eyes opened wide in a panic as he looked around. A hospital employee flew into the room and went to work, removing the tube as another staff member injected something into his IV line. Warmth filled his veins.

"Get out of here," the doctor shouted. The four of them—Dan, Jax, Cade, and Janet stood fast. They weren't budging.

"Not moving," Captain Dan McClain stated with grit.

The doctor pulled out the breathing tube, and Connor coughed uncontrollably as the oxygen tubing was placed in his nose. His vision blurred and everything went all wonky. He fell deeper more relaxed. He was breathing on his own, finally. The huddled group at the doorway let out their breaths, but he couldn't make out their faces.

CHAPTER 28

"Good, you keep breathing. Just like that. In and out." Jax paced back and forth across the space of the room where Connor now rested peacefully. He raked his hands through his spiked hair and clawed the annoying growth on his face itching him half to death. "Dude, I can't believe we sucked face. The worse part of it, I didn't think twice. I didn't even put the mouth piece in. I just went for it. Seriously, man, all I thought about was saving your damn life. I think we're going steady now, go figure."

A raspy deep voice resonated in his ears. "Jackson Honey-cutt, I could kiss you right now, you know. I can't get those lips off my mind." Connor coughed and laughed at the same time, he winced, holding his chest and ribs.

"What?" His best friend was talking to him and giving him shit. "Did you say something?"

"How long?" Connor asked in a whisper, smacking his parched mouth.

"You've been out about four days." Jax's iron fist gripped the end of the bed.

Connor paused… "Hmmm… No, I mean how long have you been wanting to kiss me like that?"

"What the f… You're kidding me," Jax bellowed. "Seriously, Winslow, you're going to be just fine." Jax walked up and kissed the top of his bud's head twice and pivoted. "I see your faculties are in order Just thought you should know I was the one who saved your life, so you owe me." He laughed again. "Unbelievable."

Jax heard snoring and looked back as Connor was out as quick as he was alert. Sound asleep. "I'd do anything for you cousin." He walked away, making sure the door didn't make a sound. "Thank you, God, for answering my plea. I owe you. And I promise to pay it forward." He placed his hands together in prayer.

Jax's shit eating grin met the eyes of Janet, Dan, Cade, Jeffrey, and Ellie in the waiting room. Bill was wheeled nearby in his hospital bed. He'd threatened his care team that if they didn't move him, he'd move the bed himself down the hall to see his friend. Jeffrey stood behind Ellie, squeezing her shoulders.

"Hall- effing- ujah, folks." Jax clenched his fists and hit the ceiling. "Connor Winslow has returned to the land of the living and gave me a heaping handful of shit like always." Jax strutted across the room, pulling at his Levis. "But, he couldn't handle the heat, as usual, so he's sleeping like a baby. He said he'd never be the same after I kissed him like that with the whole mouth to mouth scenario." Jax hoisted up his pants again with a swagger. "Yup, that's what they all say."

J anet and Dan embraced. There were gasps, sighs, claps, and roars of the celebration. Bill kissed his wife. Ellie hugged her brother then pivoted toward Cade and smiled.

"Ellie," Cade said. "You've got some work to do. Go get your man." He nodded and waved her forward. She nestled into his side and gave him a partial squeeze because her arm didn't quite go around his bulk.

"Thank you. I'll give it all I got." She pulled up on her tippy-toes as he leaned down. She planted a kiss on his cheek and whispered. "You don't fool me a bit, you softie."

Cade retaliated back. "Don't blow my cover, woman. I have a reputation to uphold."

"Your secret is safe with me." She winked and retreated.

Ellie peeked into Connor's room. His coloring was finally coming back. He unequivocally took her breath away. He was so still just lying there, but he looked more peaceful breathing on his own. So, did she, knowing he was going to live. Whatever they had to face, they would do it together. There was so much she wanted to say.

She wound her hair around her finger and into a chignon on top of her head. She went over what she needed to tell Connor. She had never been in love before.

Ellie, don't blow this.

"I'm not sure if you can hear me right now." She scooted her chair as close to the bed as possible and took an inhale of courage. "But, I'm saying it anyway." Her stomach did a somer-sault. "You are the most beautiful man I have ever known. Inside and out.

She grazed his stubble jawline, then along his ear and through his mussed-up hair.

"Hmmm." She cleared her throat. "You scared me to death, my love." Her fingers danced over the light golden hair on his arm. "I couldn't bear it if anything happened to you." A catastrophic hurt she couldn't measure. "I fell in love with you long before I opened my eyes in the hospital after my accident. Do you know I heard you talking to me? I wasn't sure who you were, but I knew your presence. You calmed me. You were the peace in my soul I never knew I lacked. A missing puzzle piece I required in my essence.

"I know I have my hang-ups with trust, and I'm so sorry for not giving you a chance another chance. I just wanted to know everything about you. I've never felt this way about anyone before. You scare me, and I'm afraid I'll lose myself again like I did with James. Though, I know unquestionably you are not him. He was a monster. He was a mistake. You are not. Losing you would destroy me."

She paused to breathe. The adrenalin and lack of sleep had taken a toll. "You're my promise of the happily ever after I never knew I wanted anymore. I'm sorry if I hurt you. Please. Please, forgive me." She ran her nails across the width of Connor's chest, dancing and swirling over his pecs and the decorative tribal ink. He was still the poster boy of all of the best romance novels rolled into one, and he was hers.

"I don't have a chance without you, I know you may not ever love me back now, but I promise you this, I will never leave you if you accept me in your life. You are meant for me, Mister Winslow. I will go with you to counseling. I will even learn to cook. I don't think I will be much more graceful, but if there's a class for that, I'll take it. You made me believe in love again. It just took my pride an eon to catch up."

Ellie couldn't fight it; she was crashing. She rested her arms on the side rail. Her eyes drooped and her head bobbed as she lost the fight to stay awake. "I love you so much…"

Connor pushed through the haze of the painkillers, blinking his eyes. If he focused hard enough he could see her—tell her.

I'll never stop proving to her I deserve her. More, we deserve each other.

Yeah, he thought it. He deserved Ellie Richards and her love. For the first time since his parent's accident, Connor Winslow deserved love. He wanted love at any cost. Even if he had to lose her just to feel heartache again. Losing his parents was unimaginable, but if he had to go through their accident all over again he would gladly do it just to have experienced the life he had with them before the dreadful day.

Connor opened his eyes and focused on the blurry form nearby. He could see it really was Ellie still beside him. Her bobbing head went back and forth, loosening the hair from the top of her head. She was out cold. She let out a gentle purr, but he had never seen such a beautiful woman. The need to touch her was an unbearable pain he would endure. With all his will and the strength he had left, he lifted his hand over her wavy hair. It was soft and satiny against his fingers. Her skin was so supple. He tapped her lightly freckled nose. He watched her, for how long, he didn't know.

His throat burned, and he could barely swallow, but he whispered. "Marry me."

The back of his hand mapped the silhouette of her jawline. God, he loved her so.

He cleared his throat again. "Marry me, Ellie Richards. Please. I'm miserable without you."

Ellie's eyes jolted open. "What? Did you just say something?"

"Hey, sleepy head, you're awake."

Her eyes widened as the words resonated in her head. "No. You can't ask me first. I wanted to ask you." She straightened and smoothed her hair away. "Connor, marry me?"

"I almost died and you're arguing with me, already?" He shifted up a little higher. "Can we just agree to disagree on who's asking who and get your lips over here?"

Ellie put her palm over her mouth and stalled. "Uh... not yet... I got some janky morning breath, and I've waited a long time for a kiss." She shot up, darted across the room, and dug through the bag of supplies Jeffrey brought for everyone.

"Don't you think we will have to get used to it someday? Why not leap in and get it over with? Morning breath and all."

Ellie turned, Oh, heck no. I'm not risking anything until you put a ring on it, mister." She pulled a travel toothbrush and toothpaste out and readied it.

Connor held out his hand for Ellie to come to him. She looked around for water and something to spit into. "Come here now." He ordered with lust in his eyes. "Hand me the damn thing."

She hesitated. I give up all my will to you, forever."

She inched forward one slow step at a time. "You are going to get my cooties," she teased, handing it over. He didn't take an eye off of her and slowly placed it in his mouth, brushing it slowly into his own.

"Do you think I'm afraid of your germs?" He continued to snap and bite down on the yellow toothbrush. "We've already exchanged bodily fluids, haven't we?"

S carlet blotched Elle's skin. She tugged at the neck of her sweater. Her eyes darted around the room, trying to rid the minty paste clinging to her mouth.

Connor threw the toothbrush across the room and grabbed a swig of water on the bedside table. He swished it around and spit it out in the plastic container nearby.

Ellie turned around and spit into the trash can, then wiped her mouth on her sleeve.

"Woman, get over here. I'm superman after what I've been through. Your cooties can't hurt me, nor can a little toothpaste." He patted the bed, smiled, and lifted his hand to hers. "What you said earlier about wanting a chance to make it right? I'll hold you to it, but you actually never had a chance of getting away from me. I wasn't about to stop, until…" He winced to pull back the sheet.

He grabbed his ribs. "You're mine. Got it?"

Connor thought the warehouse blaze was blistering hot, but it was nothing compared to the heat he was feeling right now, and no amount of pain was going to keep him away from his woman, now he had her in his sight forever.

"Get in here." Connor patted the bed again.

Ellie eased into the bed gently beside the man who was her happily ever after and the rest of her life.

Connor held Ellie close, and he was home with her in his embrace.

"I wanted to do this right, on bended knee with a ring and all that mushy crap."

"It's overrated if you ask me." She snuggled close. "I don't need formalities. I have you." She looked deeply into his steel gray eyes.

"I want to give you everything that is mine." He shifted his hand under her loose sweater. "I need to feel you."

"Connor what do you think about getting married as soon as we can?" Ellie's ran her nose softly across Connor's face. "I don't want to wait."

"What day is it today?" he asked.

"The twelfth."

"You're moving in with me as soon as they bust me out of here. We're never going to be apart again." Connor pulled Ellie's worn orange cable knit sweater over her head, leaving only a simple white tank beneath.

"You're the boss," Ellie said.

"We're a team," he countered.

"Okay." She shivered with his touch on her skin. "What

about Cade? Do you think he would be up with staying at my house with Jeffrey?"

"Let's worry about that later. And Janet can plan the wedding, if that's okay. She loves that kind of thing. I hope she can plan one in a hurry." He lifted her white tank top, running his fingertips along her skin as she quivered.

"Only if it's small—just family and close friends." Connor, I can't concentrate and I don't think we should be doing this." He could see she was having trouble catching her breath.

"Breath, Ellie. No more talking, chatty-girl. We have a lifetime for talk. I have another agenda entirely right now. Where there's no talking involved." He wiggled his brows.

She laughed. "Are you sure?"

Fingers pulled at her navy-blue sweats. Her breathing became erratic.

"Without a doubt."

"I love you, Connor. I don't want another moment without you." She helped him and pulled at the material, wiggling it to her feet. The hard length of his virility pressed against her, proving he was very much alive.

"I love you, but there's no way we are doing anything that will risk your health. Not here, not now. Mr. Winslow."

"Thank god. I don't think I can." His mouth opened over hers, then bit and tugged at her bottom lip. "Can I... just hold you?"

She nodded and nestled deeper into his grasp.

His slow deep kiss lasted and lasted until he said. "I love you and I promise, I will always tell you so."

CHAPTER 29

*E*llie looked into the mirror of the settee near the window of the mountain house in the room that had once been Thomas and Beth Winslow's. Three weeks had passed since she had moved into Connor's place, and he'd recovered pretty fast, but he was still on leave until after their honeymoon was over. They didn't want to wait any longer to get married. Ellie hung up the phone from the call she received and jumped when Jeffrey rapped at the door and asked to come in.

"Yes, come in."

"You look beautiful sis."

"Thank you."

"Why the long face?" he approached and squeezed her shoulders. "Your pale, are you having second thoughts?"

"No. Never." She walked to large picture window. "Could you please tell Connor I need to see him."

"Can it wait? The ceremony is about to start."

She turned. "No, it can't. I need tell him something in private."

"You're starting to scare me. Are you sure everything is

okay?" Jeffrey hugged his sister close. "If you are getting cold feet just give me the signal and I'll have the getaway car out front."

"Stop. Silly. Yes, I promise everything is fine. Just please ask Connor to come here"

Jeffrey turned and exited the room "On it."

Ellie paced the room until she heard another knock and slid an elongated gift box out of her bag. Her stomach leaped.

"Babe, you okay? Jeffrey said you needed to see me." Connor asked." He closed the door behind and covered his eyes. " It's bad luck for the groom to see the bride before the ceremony."

"Come in. Husband to be. We've had enough bad luck for a lifetime and today is our wedding and nothing will change that for me. It's the happiest day of my life."

He removed his hand and erased the distance. "You're breathtaking." She was the most beautiful bride—*his bride. Mine.* Her golden-brown hair was loosely swept off to the side as soft curls escaped. Her mother's pearls dangled from her ears. The high neckline of her ivory dress was Victorian. When she twirled around, Connor could see the open back of the dress and the hundreds of buttons securing it into a perfect fit. He wondered how long it would take him to get her out of the dress later. She had her own style of sophistication and sultry, and the dress she'd found at a second-hand store looked as if it was made for her.

E llie gasped and a tear escaped. He moved forward and ran his thumb along her cheek. "Why are you crying?"

"You take my breath away. You are the most beautiful thing I have ever seen."

"Come on, I'm supposed to say that."

"come sit." She walked to the bed and patted it."

"You're not going to leave me, are you?"

"Never—ever." Not unless you don't want me anymore."

"Will never happen." Now he was getting worried. "Why the long face, Talk to me. He cradled her hands in his and kissed them. "Ellie."

Connor wore a charcoal grey tuxedo jacket with crisp white shirt and paisley grey silk ascot. And a cream-colored buttoner with greenery. His matching pants fit him in all the right places. His tumbled hair gave him the edge bad boy, fierce dimpled chin and full, lush lips. His furrowed brow slashed over stormy eyes and strong nose. His looks were striking, but it was his depth of heart and soul she couldn't live without. Every moment she had to pinch herself that he was her happily ever after. She fondled the box in her hand and worried about if he would like the contents. "I have something for you. I wanted to give it to you last night, but I had to be sure it was the right thing to do."

"For me."

"For us" she handed it to him as held him tight. "I love you, Mr. Winslow."

"I love, too, Mrs. Winslow to be."

She put her hand over his hand and the box. "it's important you know."

He glanced down at the box and to her again. As she gripped it. "Nothing can change the way I feel about you, Ellie." You're shaking.

"I hope so." She released the gift.

Connor untied the ribbon on the box and eased the lid off. He froze.

Ellie held her breath waiting for some signal—anything.

Connor looked up and back down at the contents in the box. He bowed his head and rubbed his eyes.

Ellie was sick to her stomach and laid a hand on Connors shoulder. He lifted his head and his eyes were red and full of tears. His lip quivered.

"Connor?"

He leaped over her and pressed her down on the bed. And kissed her. He pulled back and stuttered." I can't believe it." He looked into his hand and shook his head. Kissing her again. "We're pregnant?"

She nodded.

"Really? You're shitting me." He ran his hand into his hair.

"Really. I'm around nine weeks or so. I suspected, but so much has happened. I thought it was stress why I hadn't gotten my period. Connor looked a million miles away.

"Ellie, that would be around the time... She placed her finger upon his lips and nodded.

"If you thought you were why didn't you tell me? I was worried about the timing and what happened. I'm sorry."

"Don't you ever be sorry. I was the idiot fool, not you. I was a complete Jack ass."

"We're going to have a baby"

"Yeah, about that... I got a call from the doctor and..."

Connor's coloring changed to ash. "Everything's okay isn't it?"

"Yes, but the tests came back that we might be having multiples." She grimaced and then smiled. The more she thought about it the happier she became. They were already a family.

"More than one baby?" Connor jumped up and paced the room. "more than one baby? You have got to be kidding me?" He went over and knelt before Ellie who was still sitting on the bed. "we did this." He wrapped his arms around her waist and kissed her belly. "Hey you in there. Your mother and I love you already, we don't care if there is one of you or more. We just want you to stay in there as long as you need to be healthy."

"Connor, are you sure you are okay with this? Because I am and I will have these babies no matter what."

"I am more than okay and trust me you will never have to deal with anything ever alone. We're in this together and no matter what life gives us together we're stronger. Forever."

"I was hoping you would say that and I'm sorry I ever doubted that for one second. I just had to tell you in private, so you had a chance if this was too much."

""You're not getting away from me that easy. When I said I loved you I meant forever?"

Ellie knew better, but she just had to be sure. Everything happened so fast.

"Come on woman, let's do this. Be my wife so thee kiddos won't be living in sin." He got up and raised her up.

"Yay!" she tapped his nose and then her stomach. "To the Winslow's." and they both did the happy dance. Until they were startled by a rap on the door.

"Hey sis, is everything okay? Lina is here to help you finish getting your pretty on? And Connor. Cade and Jax are asking where the groom is."

"We couldn't be better. Just a few more minutes and you can send Lina in and Connor will be right out."

Connor nibbled at Ellie's neck and whispered. "Let's makes this official."

Ellie giggled and nodded. "I love you so very much."

Connor turned away and stepped back for final embrace. "Not possible. I love you, more."

"Yeah, well soon enough there will be a lot more of me to love, Dad."

"O.M.G! Ellie." Lina embraced her best friend. Lina wore a magenta shade, capped sleeve stunner. Her dress hugged all her assets perfectly. Her long, black, ebony hair was pulled back in halo braids cascading down her back. "Turn around let me get the full view. I'm glad you picked the tea length dress. Ivory is the 'to die for' color with your skin tone hair color. He's going to be dragging his tongue when he sees you, but you need more blush first."

"He already got a sneak peek."

"What was that about?" Lina brushed the rosy shade over Ellie's cheeks. "There... Much better."

"We needed a private moment." Ellie sad with a wide smile.

Walking across the room, Lina lifted a pair of shoes out of a box. "Ta da! I told you I had the shoes under control, so here are the perfect off-white gold bedazzled Jimmy Choo's for something borrowed."

"Seriously, I can't wear those things. I'll break something for sure." She gasped. "I wanted to wear my high tops with the rhinestones I ordered online. And besides, your shoes probably cost as much as my annual salary."

"Shush, girl, no arguments. No best friend of mine will walk down the aisle with discounted shoes. These Jimmy's are lucky." She crossed her heart. "Let me get your veil on, slip these on now, and you can change into your high tops later."

"Sis, one-minute ETA," Jeffrey rumbled through the closed door.

Lina hugged her best friend and pulled her to the door. "Come on, your *hottie* firefighter is waiting."

CHAPTER 30

*C*onnor stood at the frilly arch of fall greenery and sunflowers overlooking the water and surrounded by the foothills of the Rocky Mountains at his parents' property.His mind was spinning with the news. *I'm getting married and I'm a father.* The cap fidgeted and paced, going over his notes, wearing a path on the grass near the podium. He was marrying them today. Cade and Jax walked toward Connor and the captain, both looking dapper in their matching tuxedos after seating the last of the guests.

"How do you like our monkey suits?" Cade asked. "We clean up well, don't you think?"

"Hey dude, you sure about this? It's not too late to back out." Jax attempted a fake punch at Connor's gut with a Sugar Ray boxing move. "Oh, I forgot this was delivered earlier." Jax handed the letter to the groom.

Connor opened up the special delivery letter and read it. "This is from Parker." He looked at his friends and wondered what the guy had to say. He hoped he wouldn't pull anything to ruin today.

"The nerve, doesn't he ever give up?" Jax asked. "Whatever

happened with the investigation, anyway?" He turned to Cade and said, "What are you not telling me?"

"The captain said he was cleared of any suspicion when it came up for review, and the county didn't press charges. I guess I was a little stressed out and jumped the gun. I feel bad that I scared the crap out of him. The stuff I'd found out about him afterward would make the faint of heart weak-kneed. The guy had a brutal start in his youth, but that's for another day, bro. There're a few other things I'm looking into that aren't meshing. No concern of yours, and we have nuptials." Cade snaked his neck around, dodged his gaze, and whispered. "We've gotta get our boy married off today, right?"

Cade picked up his phone as it vibrated in his pocket and walked around one of the trees. He started pacing back and forth.

Connor guessed Cade was hiding something and it was big, but he opened the envelope from Evan anyway. "Do I really want to do this, today? Maybe, I should wait." He looked up to Jax and slowly unfolded the white stationary.

His brother looked at him straight on. He knew that look and something serious was happening. His gaze darted and he pulled at his hair and began his back and forth thing. Connor read Cades lips as He hung up the phone and trotted back but his eyes were diverted. Son of a b... Fuck!"

"Everything okay?" Connor asked.

"Uh, sure, Bro." He looked down and wiped his nose. "Just business, nothing for you to worry about." He gave a half laugh. He looked around and found his partner Detective Trinity Edwards and waved him over. He leaned in and whispered something and they both looked around. Going all secret ops.

Yeah, Cade's hiding something, for sure and it was serious shit.

Connor opened the letter.

. . .

Connor,

I'm sorry we got off on the wrong foot, and I'm sorry about all the work stuff. I do respect you, and I'm proud to work with you, and believe it or not, it took a lot more time than you can imagine. I have a lot to learn from you, and I'd trust you with my own life. We're not so different, you and me. We have several things in our past that will bind us together. You were not the only one who lost someone the day your parents passed away. I lost my brother that day, and he wasn't just some drunk driver. The events are not as they appeared.

Maybe someday we could talk over a brewski, and I'll even buy.

And, about Ellie, the future Mrs. Winslow... I didn't mean to get in the middle of you two. I didn't handle anything that involved you the way I should have. I had to blame someone for what happened. It was as plain as a five-alarm fire you had it bad for her. You were boots over bunker gear for the woman. I thought you needed a healthy shove for your own damn good. I'm proud to say it was a success.

Congratulations and best wishes.

Evan Parker

P.S. Tell your brother... payback is a bitch.

Connor's stomach sank, but he pushed Evan's words and whatever was going on with Cade away as he folded the letter back into the envelope and handed it to his cousin, Jax. "You keep this. Nothing Parker has to say will get in between Ellie and me." He smiled and gazed at his wife to be. "You two, sit your asses down so we can get this party started." Connor eyed the four white roses placed into the crystal vase, prominently residing near him on the pillar. Each of the roses symbolized Connor and Ellie's parents, Karl and Sylvia Richards, and Thomas and Beth Winslow. He could feel their love as if they were here this very moment.

Connor observed Ellie's bestie Lina half way run to her seat, not looking pleased having to sit in the only open chair next to Cade. He winced and crossed his arms tightly over his chest. Both sat there uncomfortably, trying to ignore the other. Lina sat upright and rigid at the edge of the linen covered chair. Flipping her braid in Cade's direction, she swatted him with the tail across his shoulder. Connor could foresee the signs between the two, and they were about to start their own chapter. Women never got under Cade's skin but somehow, she did and those two were definitely in trouble. They were either going to fall for each other or slaughter one another. He couldn't wait to see the show. But that wasn't the only thing Cade eyeballed, scanning everything, looking for something—someone.

The sun was high in the sky, and the crisp air of autumn cooled the midday sun. The trees were bright amber, golds, and merlot fall colors, and winter was just around the corner.

Music played softly in the background with old and new mixes of every sappy song known to man. Connor and Ellie asked Bill to arrange the music since he was on medical leave and his wife wanted him out of her hair.

Trinity stood situated in the back of the crowd surveying Ellie—his Ellie. Connor was awe-struck catching the silhouette of the woman he was about to marry moving from the shadows behind another frou-frou arch, thirty feet away, under the deck lit with twinkling white lights. She was utterly show-stopping, and he could feel his heart rev up, pounding behind his sternum. She looked his way and blew him a kiss.

Jeffrey whispered something to Ellie and held her by her shoulders, kissing her lightly on the cheek and lowering the small ivory veil over her face.

She is my everything.

Ellie stood arm and arm with her brother who towered over

her tiny frame. Each uneasy step drew her closer to him. Everyone stood and turned as Bill increased the volume of an old eighties Bryan Adams song, *Everything I Do*—one of two songs Connor had requested that were his parents' favorites.

Her ruby cheeks were evident under the sheer veil. Each step she took made his breath hitch, and he swore his heart was going to leap out of his chest at any minute. No one else mattered but *her*, and this was the day she would become his wife. Jeffrey and Ellie arrived within reach as the song ended. He wanted to touch her. Hold her.

"Who gives this woman to this man?" Dan asked.

Jeffrey teetered back and forth from heel to toe and cleared his throat. "I do." He gave Connor an *I'm still watching you*, overprotective look with a little *she's all yours now, sucker.*

Jeffrey lifted Ellie's veil and nodded. He placed Ellie's hand in Connor's and held both for a moment before stepping away with a tearful eye. Ellie's hand trembled under his touch. He understood, with every ounce of his being, she was a gift from God.

Her cheeks were flushed, but her skin was china white and lightly peppered with sweat, not the normal glow he was used to. He ran his touch along her petal soft skin.

Ellie and Connor had decided to keep everything short and sweet, a few traditional elements with their own vows.

"Are you ready for this?" Connor whispered. "I can't wait to share the news."

"Without one single doubt." She paused. "I love you so much." She ran her fingers along his jawline.

For as long as I live, I will never hear that enough.

. . .

He stepped back and went to one knee. She deserved this done properly. He hadn't had the chance when he was in the hospital.

"Ellie Richards, from the moment I saw you I knew my life would change. I'm not sure how I survived before you came into my life, turning it upside down." Ellie giggled along with the laughter of their guests.

She whispered, "I get that a lot."

Connor continued. "I've seen so many ugly things in this world. I was doomed by my own self-destruction." He looked into his future's eyes. "I had it all figured out and thought I was fine just keeping my emotions on lockdown. I believed I was actually living, but I was slowly dying a little each day." He shook his head from side to side and then paused, validating his own admission.

He took a deep breath and blew it out. "You challenge me. You surprise me. I ask myself what I would do if you hadn't come into my life. You gave my darkness light. You silenced the demons." He smiled though his lip trembled.

She stroked him along his cheek again. "Get up, Connor. Please." She pulled him up off his knees. She ran her hand along the fabric of his black tuxedo. "What are you trying to do to me?" Her arms went around his waist, and she pressed her head against his chest. "I'm about to blubber like an idiot. I mean a real ugly kind of cry."

Her eyes pooled and spilled with tears as she bit her lower lip. "We don't want to unleash this on such a beautiful day. Not —the—ugly—cry. We have pictures to look back on the rest of our lives, and I don't want to be a look-a-like of Edward Scissorhands." She snorted.

God, he loved her so.

He cleared his throat. "I'm not finished." He pressed his forefinger to her lips. "You are so beautiful." He continued. "I want to grow old with you and have a dozen kids. You made me believe in life again, Ellie."

Connor shuddered to get the last bit out. He blinked the tears away. His throat was dry as he swallowed. "I don't deserve you, Ellie Richards. But, I will try until my dying breath to prove to you that I will love you forever. If you're lost, I will find you. If you fall, I will catch you. I will never hurt you, and I'll always be there for you."

"**P**lease get up. We're beyond that." She tugged at his hand. "Come on. Yes, you do deserve me, Connor Winslow. It is I who doesn't deserve you. You have taken a woman who didn't have trust or have faith anymore in love," she whispered as she wrapped her arms around his waist. "You had me before I opened my eyes in the hospital. My heart knew you, and I was in love with not what I saw on the surface, though I'm not complaining one bit." She covered her mouth and snickered. "You are so charismatic. You make me feel safe. You ground me and somehow make all my imperfections perfect. You make me feel graceful and elegant.

"You smooth out all my rough edges." She shrugged. "I'm literally a disaster waiting to happen." She snorted, then turned to her brother. "Don't you dare say a word, brother of mine."

Jeffrey put his hands up in defense. "Not a word." He crossed his heart and raised his head up and down in jest.

"I've waited my entire life for you... or a promise of you." She melted further into his body as he wrapped his arms around her.

"I will love you forever, my love. I can't wait to be your wife and the mother of your children."

Her lips brushed against the plane of his jaw and then to his ear. "Will you marry us?"

Connor grinned and pulled back slightly to capture anyone catching what she said.

Ellie looked to the crowd who were all edging closer to hear them, but most were wiping their own tears away. She swayed as she placed her hands on both sides of Connor's face, raised up upon her stilettos, and kissed his forehead.

She could feel crimson color her skin and her heart beat a staccato against her chest.

There were gasps from the intimate group who gathered.

"Ellie and Connor nodded and both screamed, "We're pregnant."

They stood before the crowd half with their mouths wide open. He picked up Ellie and swung her around in elation. He set her back down, then steadied her from toppling off her stilettos. "Oh, I shouldn't have done that." He rested his hand on Ellie's stomach.

Her color faded as quickly as it had risen before. "I'm fine. I think so anyway." Her hand pressed over her mouth.

"Sorry, cap we got a little carried away." Connor laughed.

"Rings." Connor turned to Cade in the front row. Lina and Cade lept from their seats and moved forward.

Connor placed a single princess cut diamond on Ellie's finger with two thin eternity bands of small diamonds on each side of the one karat square cut bauble.

Ellie raised her hand as the diamonds sparkled in the sun. "It's beautiful."

"This was my mother's ring," he said and pointed to the center diamond.

Ellie kissed the ring and placed it over her heart." I don't know what to say. I'm honored. Crap... Here comes the water-works." She fanned herself.

Lina moved closer and handed Ellie Connor's ring, along with a tissue.

Ellie blotted her tears. "It's inscribed," she said.

Connor looked inside the ring and read one word which said it all. *Forever.*

She slipped the simple tungsten steel band onto his left ring finger.

He turned. "Cap, pronounce us," Connor insisted.

"I thought you'd never ask," Captain Dan McClain said. "Ellie and Connor, I pronounce you husband and wife." His graveled voice faded. His blue eyes misted, and he nodded his approval. "Congratulations son, your parents are watching over us today and they would be so proud."

Connor's tough exterior melted in front of Ellie's eyes. She'd recognized what was in his heart. He just had to believe it himself. He took a deep breath and had the biggest face splitting smile. His dark and stormy eyes warmed a brighter blue gray. "We're going to be parents."

Connor squinted to fend away the moisture threatening. "I love you, Mrs. Winslow. We're going to be a family."

The ground shifted underneath him, and he felt light headed. He had to sit down before he blacked out and saw stars. His heart swelled as only the Grinch's could. His internal conflict from years of guilt and inadequacy faded. The nightmares stopped when he'd admitted to himself he loved Ellie and blamed himself no more.

Jax shouted, "We need the med bag, stat!" Laughter erupted. "Just kidding, false alarm, folks. The tough guy's going to be just fine."

He gazed at his wife, the face of the woman who'd believed enough for the both of them. He usually did the saving, but it turned out she actually saved him from himself.

"I'm going to be a father." He looked up into the heavens and yelled. "Do you hear that?"

The music elevated through the speakers on cue with a Bon Jovi song *Thank You for Loving Me.* Another teenage favorite Connor had selected.

"Can I kiss my wife already?" Connor shifted to his right to ask the Captain.

"You may kiss your bride, Connor."

So, he dipped his wife and melted the past away.

The captain cleared his throat. "Ladies and Gentlemen, may I proudly and finally introduce Mr. and Mrs. Winslow's."

Whistles, hoots, and applause came from the onlookers.

Connor Winslow not only got the girl… He got the future he never thought he deserved.

Fire Fighter saves accident victim, but who really saves who?
To the happily ever after…

IF YOU ENJOYED CONNOR AND
ELLIE AND WANT TO READ MORE
ABOUT THE BROTHERS OF SOLEMN
CREED, CADE'S STORY WILL
RELEASE IN 2019.

TO THE CORE

Cade Winslow is deep undercover with a crime ring infiltrating his hometown of Solemn Creed, Colorado and reaching to the outskirts of Denver.

Until... a woman gets into the mix, now she's in danger of ruining the operation he's so close to solving and risks her safety.

Analina "Lina" Ortez loves her new job as the county truancy officer. One of her students has been missing school and word is... he's getting into trouble with his older brother's gang. She won't walk away from her oath or Jamal.

Cade and Lina are thrust together, and this isn't the first time they've met. He has to get the annoying prima-donna out of the way before she blows everything, but Lina and Cade pique the interest of the head of the crime wave.

Cade's spent twenty-three years trying to erase his early childhood, but someone he never wanted to see again threatens all he vows to protect.

And that's not all... Someone from his new sister-in-law Ellie Winslow's past is right in the middle of it and it's not her best friend Lina. Her life, his brothers life, and their unborn twins could be in danger. Nothing will stop him from protecting his family.

ACKNOWLEDGMENTS

Foremost, I'd like to thank, my will and determination to keep going against all odds. Many times, I wanted to quit, so, so many, but couldn't. This book has been a labor of love and so much harder than I ever thought it would be. Years of hard work and persistence made my goals come into fruition. Don't ever give up on your dreams and let no one ever tell you that you can't do something.

My parents, for your guidance and always believing in me when I didn't. Mom, I'm making my heart sing, thank you for being my person. I hope I have made you proud. To my family, for your love and support, you are the wind beneath my wings and ultimately my biggest fans. My friends and clients at James Hair Venture, thank you for putting up with me and my constant yapping about my other career, plotting and scheming. I am forever grateful for your loyalty over the years.

To my husband Tim, the love of my life, you are the heart of all my stories. How did I get so lucky to spend my life with you? To my fur baby, Romeo, thank you for being my writing buddy and teaching me to live in the moment.

Thank you to all my mentors over the years, so many to list, but thank you for telling me to "sit my butt down and get my fingers on the keyboard and you can only write your book." I have learned so much from you. To Lisa Fender, for taking time with me in the beginning when I didn't know what I didn't know. To Helen Hardt, for raising the bar and pushing me to be better, and for showing me you don't have to fear success. To Aidy Award and Lyz Kelly, for holding my hand in the world of self-publishing and giving me a safe place to land. Thank you for all the time you gave willingly. I promise to pay it forward.

To the members of Romance Writers of America, Heart of Denver Romance Writers, Colorado Romance Writers, Contemporary Romance Writers and my peeps in Living the Dream Masterminds, thank you for teaching me the value of a community. My Dream Team, Kathy, Sue, and Sandra, I'm glad we are on this crazy ride together. I couldn't do this without you.

Kelly Johnson my virtual assistant who designed my website and helps me look tech savvy. I'm clearly not. You are stuck with me. My PA-Nikki Brackett for proofreading, edits, and helping me with my social media. My PA extraordinaire Theresa Finn for helping me with my social media groups, and marketing, To my *Hottie's* in *Jodi's Hot Zone*, you rock. I would never be here without each and every one of you. When I say it takes a village for me it takes many. I am truly blessed beyond measure.

To all editors over the years, Julie Cameron at Landon Literary, Cassie Mae Cook and Jolene Perry at Cookie Lynn Publishing, thank you for making my work shine.

Megan at Em Cat Designs for my cover, thank you for making my vision come to life and formatting my print book.

A special thank you to my *go-to guy* at South Metro Fire Authority, in Colorado, Mr Bill Frieling. Thank you for suggesting a shift ride with station 31 when my husband pleaded that his wife was writing a trashy romance novel about firefighters (his words not mine). Also, for enrolling me in a six-week citizen fire academy, this was one of the best experiences of my life. I'm honored for a rare glimpse into your world, your knowledge, a passion for your career and your friendship.

Fire Chief Garcia at Aurora Fire Department and your first responders at station 8, It was truly an honor.

ABOUT THE AUTHOR

Born in California, raised in the heartland of Iowa, and currently residing in the Rocky Mountains of Colorado. Blessed with a successful career in the hair and beauty industry spanning three decades. Married to her best friend, he is the heart of her stories.

Jodi's fulfilling a lifelong passion for writing. Her journey has transcended and evolved from reading to being inspired by the authors that wrote the words. In the Heat of it All is her first Contemporary Romance novel and the first in the Brothers of Solemn Creed series.

She believes in the happily-ever-after. Writing makes her heart sing.

Follow Jodi

https://authorjodijames.com/

Made in the USA
Lexington, KY
12 May 2019